Who was she?

And why didn't she wake up? Shamus asked himself. Doc had said that the head wound was no more than a scratch and that the other bullet had passed through her arm with little damage.

Sure, he was thankful that she'd swooped out of the sky and rescued him. But a lassie wasn't supposed to get mixed up in such things . . . bootleggers and shoot-outs and all. Especially not a lassie who looked like a freckle-faced angel.

Shamus flushed, remembering the curves he'd found under her tattered blouse. He reddened even more, remembering her lacy underthings. Not even the girls at Lady Lucy's wore such provocative unmentionables.

And what the devil was she doing flying an airplane? Most people still thought that if God had meant man to fly he would have given him wings. And as for a woman flying . . . well, it was almost unheard of.

Just then she shifted, and her eyes fluttered open. She focused on him, and in the instant before her eyes closed again, they seemed to light with a spark of recognition. . . .

ABOUT THE AUTHOR

"I owe my inspiration for writing *Wings of Time* to my father," says Carol Duncan Perry. "He was born in 1903, the year the Wright brothers flew the first airplane, and he lived to see man reach the moon. He was amazed at how fast and how far mankind had learned to fly—and all within a single life span. His fascination with planes was just one of the many, many gifts he passed on to me."

Carol and her husband make their home in the Pacific Northwest. They have three children, a calico cat and "the ugliest mongrel canine in the world."

Wings
of Time

CAROL
DUNCAN
PERRY

Harlequin Books

TORONTO • NEW YORK • LONDON
AMSTERDAM • PARIS • SYDNEY • HAMBURG
STOCKHOLM • ATHENS • TOKYO • MILAN
MADRID • WARSAW • BUDAPEST • AUCKLAND

Published February 1993

ISBN 0-373-70537-9

WINGS OF TIME

For Hubert
Resident Hero and Aeroplane Expert

With Special Thanks to The Group:
Betty, Darcea, Ethel, Gayla, Joe & Pat

CHAPTER ONE

THERE IT WAS! Dead ahead. The O-word. A word not to be spoken unless experienced. Oshkosh!

Elizabeth Carmichael gently banked her antique biplane into a wide left turn, her eyes sparkling behind the aviation goggles that protected her from the wind whipping through the open cockpit.

Although still several miles downwind of the Oshkosh airport, she could already see dozens of planes in the air buzzing around like so many bees. For the next week this small Wisconsin town, two hours north of Chicago, would be Mecca to the world of aviation, and she would be a part of it, one of fifteen thousand flyers participating in the pilgrimage to the country's Super Bowl of Air Shows.

Tomorrow she would fly her restored Curtiss JN-4 biplane through a carefully choreographed aerobatic demonstration. With each spin and every loop she performed, she would be reliving the experiences of the first aviators, those daring young men who challenged the sky in fragile wood and cloth flying machines over half a century ago.

As Libby waited for landing instructions she listened to the song of rushing wind whistling through the vibrating wing wires. Her portable radio suddenly let out a static squawk, issuing an order to break from the holding pattern. She acknowledged, and minutes later was on the ground.

She taxied her JN-4, commonly nicknamed a Jenny, into position behind the follow-me truck, then paraded after it down long lines of tethered planes to the parking area reserved for antique aircraft. The driver in the guide truck pointed to a space at the end of the line before pulling quickly out of the way, obviously familiar with the problems of parking a plane with no brakes. Waving her thanks to the guide, she threw the wheel blocks over the side, then carefully climbed onto the lower wing.

It was then she saw it—a deHavilland DH-4, another pre-1920 relic, parked on the next aisle of tied-down planes. Even as her eyes registered the image of the World War I bomber, she felt a familiar fluttering skip in the cadence of her pulse.

She recognized the trembling sensation. It happened every time she saw a DH-4. Libby shook off the feeling, reminding herself she didn't see such planes very often. The antique bomber was as rare as her Jenny. But even after two years she could still vividly remember the sepia-tone photograph she'd once seen of a young couple posed in front of a similar biplane.

She'd paid little attention to the woman in the old picture. It was the man she remembered. From the photograph, she'd been able to tell he was tall, even by today's standards. His mouth was twisted upward in a slight smile, almost as if he was amused by some private joke, and his eyes held a devil-may-care twinkle. Instead of a typical leather pilot's jacket, he'd worn a heavy Irish fisherman's sweater, its distinctive pattern clearly visible. The long fingers of the left hand had cradled a pipe.

Libby knew her reaction, both then and now, was ridiculous. But reason didn't seem to have much to do with it. She'd developed an immediate and unrelenting schoolgirl crush. Never mind that she was well past schoolgirl age. Never mind that the man had probably lived and died long before she was born. She could no more control her response to that photo or to a sighting of that particular model of aircraft than she could stop breathing.

She'd assumed the couple were friends of Howard Winters, the old-time pilot who ran the airfield museum in Chicago, but when she'd handed it to him, he hadn't said a word. Instead, he'd looked at the photo, then stared at her, his eyes widening and the blood draining from his face as if he were looking at a ghost.

"Where'd you find this?" he finally asked in an unfamiliar, subdued sort of voice.

"It was stuck behind the desk drawer in the office. You can't see much of the woman's face, but the man is clear. I thought they might be old flying buddies."

"I didn't know every pilot flying before 1930," Howard told her gruffly, once again looking and sounding like his old self. "Nice old bird, though. Designed as a bomber for the Great War. First plane used to carry the mails, too. Wouldn't mind having a DH-4 for the museum. If I can locate one, you can give me a hand putting it back together."

"Then you don't know who he is?" Libby persisted.

Howard shrugged his shoulders. "I once knew a lot of pilots. Most of them didn't make old bones. Why?"

"I don't know," Libby told him. "He looks...interesting."

"Humph. Probably been dead sixty years. You're spending too much time with old men and old airplanes."

Libby laughed. "You're probably right. But they don't seem to make them as good anymore."

She laid the photograph on the edge of the desk, then, taking him by the arm, pulled him in the direction of the workbench. "I want you to check the layout of the wing spar before I start gluing . . ."

She'd never seen the photograph again. When she looked the next day, it had disappeared. For some reason she'd been reluctant to ask Howard if he knew what had happened to it, but she hadn't been able to forget it, either. Every detail of that faded photograph was clearly etched in her mind. And every time she saw a deHavilland DH-4, she experienced that same strange skipping pulse beat. It was something she'd learned to live with.

"Hey, Libby! Elizabeth Carmichael!"

At the sound of her name, Libby jerked her eyes from the deHavilland and shook off her feelings of déjà vu. Her mouth widened into a welcoming smile when she recognized the woman walking toward her. She'd met Helen Armitage, a World War II WASP pilot, at several air shows during the past two years and didn't try to hide her delight at seeing her again.

"Hi, Helen. How'd you know it was me? Boy, am I glad to see a familiar face."

"Saw your red-and-white Jenny come in. Told myself, 'That's got to be Libby Carmichael.'" Helen laughed. "This is your first time at Oshkosh, isn't it? What do you think? Some party, huh?"

Libby nodded, her smile so wide she could feel the skin on her face stretching. "Some party," she agreed, unable to put her excitement into words.

Her friend chuckled softly, as if she knew exactly what Libby was feeling. "Well, get your bird tied down and I'll treat you to a drink at the refreshment tent. Introduce you to some of the other antiquers, too. Since we're outnumbered by the Buck Rogers pilots around here, we tend to stick together."

"Thanks," Libby told her. "I thought I knew what to expect, but this is unbelievable. I'll never find my way around. It's so...so big...so many planes...and people. I need to get registered and check in with the air show coordinator, but I don't know where to start. Is it always this crowded?"

Helen laughed again. "You think today's crowded? Wait until tomorrow when the show really starts. They're expecting over eight hundred thousand spectators this year. Now that's a crowd. But don't worry. Before you know it, you'll be walking around like an Oshkosh veteran. When are you scheduled to fly?"

"Tomorrow." Libby bent to secure the hold-down lines to the Jenny, then willingly followed her friend through the parking lot toward a cluster of tents set up along the edge of the field.

"Howard didn't come with you?"

"No, he wasn't feeling up to the trip." Libby blinked against the sudden moistness in her eyes. She and Howard had planned both the trip and her flight demonstration together. The crusty old pilot had drilled her over and over in the flying dogfight maneuvers she'd be performing tomorrow. She'd thought he'd be on the ground watching, but it wasn't to be.

"Well, you can tell him all about it when you get back," Helen said crisply. "He's done more of these shows than you, me and any other three pilots combined. To hear him tell it, he invented the event. Missing one occasionally is charity—good for his soul to let us lesser lights shine every once in a while."

Libby realized that Helen knew how much she missed Howard. She laughed as her friend had intended, then followed her to a table on the other side of the refreshment tent. Along the way she acknowledged a dozen introductions and soon felt as if she was among old friends. They were a mixed collection of old and young with a special interest in the oldest antiques, the dual wing, fabric and wire machines that started it all.

It wasn't long until the conversation turned to reminiscing, and when the group learned Libby was a protégée of Howard Winters, several had a favorite Howard story to share. Libby leaned forward, listening, enthralled. Some of the stories were familiar. Others she'd never heard before.

"He still carting around that shamrock?" asked one old-timer.

"He has a shamrock," Libby confirmed.

The elderly pilot nodded. "That'll be the same one. He babied that plant like an infant. Took it everywhere. Never could understand it. He isn't even Irish."

"Howard's one of the last of the original barnstormers," interjected another old-timer. "'Course he went on to bigger things. He ever tell you he owed his success to Charlie Lindbergh?"

Libby shook her head. "He's mentioned Lindbergh occasionally, but I didn't know they were friends."

The man laughed. "Oh, he never claimed friendship." His voice lowered to a conspiratorial level. "Told me once that Howard Winters wasn't his real name, either."

"Not his real name? I don't understand," Libby began.

"Well," the old pilot confided, "he told me he made a bet with a bunch of Chicago hoods that Lindbergh would be the first man to fly solo across the Atlantic. Guess that was some time in 1926. Leastways, that's what he said. 'Course the bookies were glad to take his bet. That twenty-five-thousand-dollar prize for the first solo from New York to Paris had been on the books since 1919, but nobody'd ever claimed it. 'Course in 1925 nobody but a bunch of barnstormers or mail service pilots had ever heard of Charles A. Lindbergh, either.

"Anyway," the man continued before Libby could interrupt, "when Lindbergh landed in Paris in '27, Howard collected his bets. He said the bookies weren't real happy but they had to pay up 'cause it wouldn't have been good for business if word got around they'd welshed. But Howard said he figured the climate might be a mite healthier elsewhere. So he took his money, moved to California and changed his name. Told me it was twenty years before he dared come back to Chicago."

"Is that a true story?" Libby couldn't help asking.

"Hell, I don't know," the old-timer said. "That's the way he told it to me. 'Course, Howard always could tell a story about as good as he could fly."

Libby joined in the general laughter around the table. It had made a good story. But was it true? She made a mental note to ask Howard as soon as she got home.

Helen showed Libby the way to the airfield offices before saying goodbye. By the time Libby completed registration procedures, picked up her rental car and checked into her motel, it was dark. She grabbed a quick supper at a restaurant near the motel, then, unable to resist, drove out to the airfield for one last look at her Jenny.

She couldn't help smiling at the sight of the bright white-and-red biplane tethered in the moonlight. She'd made a promise to herself a long time ago that one day she'd fly her own plane here. Now that time had finally come.

Her mother had never approved, never really understood her daughter's interest in flying airplanes. But Mom always approved working for goals, Libby reminded herself. It was her most often preached lesson. Yes, Libby decided, if Mom was still alive, she'd be proud of me.

Libby wished Howard could be here with her. It had taken her eight long years to get this close to her dream, and Howard had played a big part in her quest. He was her only family now, the grandfather she'd never had, the father she could barely remember. When Howard's heart had started acting up, she'd almost postponed her plans. Howard hadn't wanted her to wait.

If she was honest with herself, she'd admit she hadn't wanted to wait, either. Yes, she missed him, but, she reminded herself, she would see him again soon. Then she would share her triumph with him. Together they could relive every loop, roll and spin.

Besides, whether Howard was in Chicago or here at Oshkosh, Jenny would still be alone when she was up in the air. Hers was a solo-flight dream. Tomorrow that dream would come true. She'd fly her own plane at Oshkosh!

FRIDAY MORNING DAWNED cool and gray. Clouds hung low overhead, and a breeze blowing from the northeast off nearby Lake Winnebago was brisk enough to ruffle whitecaps on the surface. It was not, Libby decided as she surveyed the sky, an auspicious day for flying.

She realized that in the hours before flight time, the cloud cover could drop even lower, or the wind could blow the sky completely clear. Just like the old days, she thought. In spite of today's advanced aviation equipment, flying a small plane still waited on the weather.

She took one more look at the threatening sky, then headed toward the coffee tent.

Libby spotted Helen at the back of the tent even as she selected a cup of coffee at the counter.

"You going to fly?" her friend asked abruptly as Libby approached.

"If I can get off the ground. But unless the ceiling lifts, you can expect an abbreviated program."

Helen seemed to relax. "Good. I was afraid you'd insist the show must go on."

Libby laughed. "I know I'm stubborn, but I'm not stupid. I'd like to live to fly another day."

"Right attitude. We'd have a few more old-timers around here if they'd followed that adage."

"All I can do is wait on the weather," Libby told her. "Just like the original barnstormers."

"You certainly look the part," Helen said, obviously recognizing the roaring twenties vintage of Libby's dark riding breeches, knee-high boots and masculine tailored broadcloth shirt with its narrow knitted tie.

Libby smiled her thanks, draping her brown leather flight jacket and barnstormer's neck scarf across the back of her chair before sitting down. It was an idiosyncrasy on her part, but she always dressed in period, even down to the 1924 twenty-dollar gold piece tucked into her breeches pocket.

"Are you completely authentic?"

"Not down to the skin," she admitted, "just everything that shows."

"But I thought barnstormer scarfs were always white silk. Yours is blue."

Libby caressed the blue silk with her fingers. "Isn't it beautiful? It was a good luck gift from Howard. I thought it was supposed to be white, too, but Howard assured me that the first woman pilot he ever knew wore a scarf like this one. It's supposed to match my eyes."

"Well, if Howard says it can be blue, then it can be blue," Helen replied lightly. "Nobody disputes his version of the barnstorming era. I mean, after all, in history books versus a living relic, there's no contest. The relic wins. Right?"

"Right," Libby agreed, adopting Helen's joking manner. "Right from the horse's mouth."

As performance time neared, they walked toward the flight line parking area. The clouds, pushed southwest by the winds, now hung suspended, dark and churning downwind from the airfield. Libby fingered the lucky gold piece in her pocket and cast a nervous glance at the rolling thunderheads. Anvils of the gods, pilots called them. The turbulence of those rolling clouds could spell disaster, even to modern aircraft. If caught in the storm, her wood and wire Jenny wouldn't stand a chance.

"What do you think?" she asked Helen, who'd volunteered as prop spinner to start the Jenny's engine.

"It looks okay," her friend said, "but keep your eyes open. I don't like those clouds to the south. If the wind shifts..."

"I know," Libby said, trying to shake off a sense of foreboding.

"We can check the latest reconnaissance photos if you want."

"I did," Libby said. "Official reports say conditions are unsettled. That's all the photos show, too."

Skies over the airfield remained clear as takeoff time approached. She would be okay, Libby told herself, if she stayed in her designated airspace and kept a wary watch on cloud movement. Just in case, she studied an aerial map, locating several clear fields as emergency landing spots. If she got into trouble, she wanted a bolt hole.

She took one last look at the clouds, shivered and once again rubbed her lucky gold piece before slipping into her brown leather jacket and wrapping the blue silk scarf around her neck. As she pulled the close-fitting leather helmet over her short curls, she kept her eyes carefully focused on her destination above her. Then, using the lower wing as a step stool, she climbed into the cockpit.

She deliberately refused to look again at the distant clouds as she fastened her seat harness, adjusted her

goggles and smoothed soft pigskin gloves over her
hands. Only then did she signal Helen to spin the propeller.

Helen gave a thumbs-up sign as the engine caught.
The Jenny began taxiing to the end of the runway.
Libby turned and watched for the signal from the
tower clearing her for takeoff. For this flight she'd left
her portable radio behind. There was no place in the
open cockpit for anything that wasn't securely
strapped or bolted down, not when the Jenny would
soon be turning cartwheels in the air.

At the green light, Libby opened throttle. The Jenny
lumbered down the runway, moving awkwardly over
the ground. To keep the wings level in the crosswinds,
her hands worked the control stick as her feet tap-
danced on the rudder pedals. The Jenny gathered
speed.

The old biplane had no speed gauge, forcing Libby
to rely on the sight of the scenery slipping past her and
the feel of the controls to know when she reached lift-
off momentum. Seat-of-the-pants flying, they called
it in the old days. It was just as accurate a description
now as then.

The little biplane strained into the wind, like a
puppy pulling at a leash. Libby pulled back on the
stick, lifting the nose. Suddenly, magically, the Jenny
was airborne. Once in the air, the tiny aircraft lost its
look of awkwardness. Libby and her Jenny became
one with the wind, as graceful as a dragonfly cavort-
ing in the breeze.

"The secret of a successful flying show," Howard
always told her, "is to fly your tricks where your au-
dience can see you." Libby followed his advice, keeping her plane inside the block of sky that could be seen

from the airfield. As she crisscrossed the length of the field, gaining altitude with every pass, she kept the crowd entertained with a series of loops and slow rolls. Finally she was soaring at five thousand feet, as high as she could go and still expect to be seen from the ground.

A laugh of pure joy escaped her lips as she threw the Jenny into a series of aerobatic maneuvers that duplicated the dogfighting tactics of the World War I pilots who'd invented them. Jennys like this one had been the trainers for those early air warriors, and to Libby's mind, no plane could have done it better.

Nearing the end of her planned program, she put the biplane into a steep climb, deliberately destroying the lift that kept the plane in the air.

As the Jenny stalled, the nose fell forward. Libby kicked the right rudder, sending the biplane spinning nose down toward the earth. She kept her eyes focused on the ground below and, despite the disorientation of her plane's corkscrewing spiral, allowed the Jenny to continue plummeting earthward.

When she'd dropped to fifteen hundred feet, she could almost hear the crowd's gasp of anticipation. She kicked the left rudder to halt the spinning motion, shoved the stick all the way forward, then hauled back on it again. The plane leveled off, and once again the Jenny began to fly.

With a cry of jubilation, Libby reached again for high sky. She looped the small plane once, twice, three times. As she completed the last loop she threw the Jenny into another steep climb, then began her final stunt, a tight U-turn maneuver called a chandelle.

Concentrating on the air in front of her and orienting herself to the ground during her series of loops,

Libby didn't notice the shifting winds that sent the clouds in the southwest chasing after her. As she completed the chandelle, flying back the way she'd just come, she was suddenly face-to-face with the menacing tower of the storm.

She dropped one wing, a desperate effort to escape, as a shiver of fear vibrated up her spine. But it was already too late. Still fighting against the pull of the swirling updraft, Libby and her fragile biplane disappeared into the seething caldron of the storm.

It was cold. So cold. The dark, icy turbulence completely enveloped Libby and her small plane. The penetrating cold numbed her fingers and her senses. Howling wind muffled all other sound. Only the regular vibration of the airframe and the feel of the stick under her hand told her that her engine was still running. She was flying blind, at the mercy of the storm.

She lost all sense of time as hail slashed at her exposed skin and attacked the fabric covering of the trembling biplane. The frigid cold burned her lungs. Wind whipped the ends of the blue scarf around her face. Frantically she juggled control stick and rudder pedals, trying to gain some semblance of control.

The altimeter spun wildly, leaving her with no concept of altitude. She knew an updraft could toss her high enough to smother her engine. A sudden downdraft would smash her into the unseen ground somewhere below. The freezing wind pulled the scarf from her neck. She had no time to think, to even admit to fear. Her arms ached with the effort of fighting the controls against the wind.

She had no idea why she looked to the left of the cockpit. Nor did she take time to analyze her actions. When she saw what appeared to be a pool of quiet gray in the midst of a rolling caldron, she acted instinctively. She kicked the rudder—hard—and sideslipped into the hole.

Libby was suddenly trapped in a tunnel of eerie gray and ominous silence. She could see the propeller still spinning, but no noticeable disturbance of the air. She had no concept of direction or dimension. She could no longer feel the cold, but shivered anyway. The sense of nothingness surrounding her was as terrifying as the raging storm she'd temporarily escaped.

The propeller suddenly sliced through a curtain of mist, and she flew out of the gray cloud into bright sunlight. Only when she realized that the droning noise in her head was not the wind, but the sound of the engine beating against her eardrums, did her mind begin adjusting to the idea that, against all odds, she was alive. She twisted in the cockpit, searching in all directions to locate the storm, and experienced a moment of panic when she found nothing around her but a calm blue sky.

Necessity forced unanswered questions to the back of her mind as Libby put the Jenny into a gentle climb, listening intently for sounds of damage.

By all rules of nature and aviation, neither she or her fragile biplane should have survived. She could see tatters of wing fabric fluttering in the breeze, but the little engine purred quietly and the propeller continued to turn smoothly. She blinked against the fog in her goggles. If the singing of the wind in the wing wires sounded a little flat, that was understandable. It was, in fact, a miracle the wood, wire and fabric biplane was still in the air. A few tears in the wing covering and a little slack in the tension wires wasn't much, almost no damage at all.

Satisfied the Jenny would stay in the air, Libby turned her attention to the ground and felt another jolt of disorientation. A patchwork of green, yellow and brown fields stretched almost endlessly beneath her, broken only by the occasional dusty ribbon of a country road.

She shook her head to clear her sight, but the terrain remained unfamiliar, alien. She didn't recognize a single landmark.

Where were the white concrete strips of Highway 41 and Interstate 94? Mentally, she reconstructed the aerial map she'd studied before takeoff, but nothing looked familiar. The ground below her was too desolate, too undeveloped, too rural—a checkerboard of waving grasses and cultivated fields in which nothing moved. Was that twisting ribbon of blue in the distance the Wisconsin River... or the Mississippi? Had she been blown that far?

Swallowing against the panic rising in her throat, she spotted a small plume of curling smoke rising from a dark spot in the center of a field to the south and banked the Jenny in that direction.

She was almost over the field before she was able to distinguish the distinctive outline of another antique biplane fallen victim to the storm. It was crumpled, nose down, in the middle of the field. A plume of smoke rising from the wreckage grew larger every moment. Circling overhead, she searched anxiously for signs of the pilot.

When she saw a lone figure on the far side of the wreckage, arms waving enthusiastically in the air, she released the breath she hadn't realized she was holding.

Using the plume of smoke to determine wind direction, she made a low pass over the field while her eyes searched the terrain. Satisfied she'd encounter no hidden ditches or other traps, she circled around the edge of the field, then, heading directly into the wind, gently set the Jenny on the ground. After a moment of hesitation she left the engine running, not yet ready to turn off that reassuring sound.

Did she know this pilot?

The impression that she should flickered through her mind as she watched him approach carrying a battered-looking suitcase. Although he seemed familiar, both his identity and the circumstances of any former meeting eluded her. She was only sure he hadn't been one of the antiquers she'd met the day before.

He seemed to hesitate a moment as he examined the tattered Jenny. Then he jumped lightly onto the edge of the wing by her cockpit and leaned forward.

"It's pleased I am to see you, laddie," the man yelled to make himself heard above the sound of the engine. "Do you think you could be giving me a lift?"

CHAPTER TWO

THE SOUND of the man's rich, rumbling baritone with its lilting Irish brogue dispelled Libby's sense of recognition. The only place she'd heard a brogue like his was the last time she'd watched *The Quiet Man* on the late-night movie channel. Of course, his own mother would have trouble recognizing the man now. He still wore helmet and goggles, and the rest of his features were hidden under a layer of grease and grime. He did have a nice smile, though, his teeth showing white and strong against the dirt on his face.

"Are you all right?" she hollered back, surprised at the husky sound of her voice. Evidently fear and tension still had control of her vocal cords.

"Better since I saw you circling around up there," he answered. "Did Zeke send you?"

"Zeke?"

"Not out of concern for my carcass, I know, but I thought he might be worried about his plane and his cargo."

"I don't know Zeke." Libby yelled. "I don't know where—"

"Hey, you don't sound old enough to fly," the man interrupted, his voice accusing, his eyes searching her face.

Libby straightened in the cockpit. *As if he could tell how old I am,* she thought. "I got here, didn't I?" she yelled.

"Yeah, kid, you sure did," he answered, grinning again. "I just thought—" His head snapped up, his attention suddenly focused on the other side of the field.

Looking over her shoulder to see what had distracted him, Libby's eyes widened at the sight of the great black car careening across the field. Good heavens! Had she stumbled into the middle of a movie set? She'd never be able to put a name to the car, but she'd bet they hadn't built one like it in over half a century.

"Ah, hell! They followed me. Look, kid, we've got to get out of here."

Even though he was yelling to be heard above the sound of the Jenny's engine, Libby could hear the urgency in the man's voice. She looked first to him, then back to the black car barreling toward them. It was closer now, close enough for her to see something being extended out the window.

Libby blinked. *No, it couldn't be!* She blinked again, but it didn't change the scene. The car was still racing toward them, and unless she was completely crazy, those were guns hanging out the windows.

The drone of her plane's engine muted other sounds, but the tiny puffs of dust rising from the ground between her and the car seemed to reinforce her impressions. "But what... Are they shooting at us?" Her voice was a husky shriek.

"They're not tossing shamrocks," the man yelled.

Still hanging on to the suitcase, he began threading his way between the struts and wires on the wing, scrambling toward the front cockpit. "Don't worry," he called over his shoulder, "I can fly."

"You can hitch a ride, buster. My plane. I fly."

Libby didn't wait to see his reaction or even if he'd heard her words. Those puffs of dust were closer now. Unless she was caught in the midst of some weird nightmare, someone was shooting real bullets! As she pushed the throttle forward, the Jenny began bumping across the pasture. She saw the man throw the suitcase into the front cockpit, then dive, head first, after it.

"Damn cocky kid," Shamus Fitzgerald yelled as he struggled to right himself in the cockpit. He turned to look at the car, still racing toward them, gaining ground every second. But the Jenny was also moving, bouncing across the rough field. He straightened himself in the seat, then cussed again. The crazy kid was heading straight for the fence!

His grab for the stick was automatic, but his rescuer seemed to know the instant he touched the controls. The stick vibrated under his hand, a slight, almost imperceptible movement, the message as clear as if he'd heard it shouted in his ear. *"Keep your hands off my stick."* Shamus raised his hands in the air in a gesture of surrender and to let the kid see he wouldn't interfere.

He had only time to grab a breath as the little biplane shuddered and spun, one wing tip almost brushing the fence as the pilot wheeled into sharp turn, leaving the Jenny facing full field. The car was still racing toward them. The now obvious takeoff route would cut across the pursuers' path, but at an angle and going away.

Shamus experienced a reluctant surge of admiration. The kid's voice might not yet have changed, but he seemed to know what he was doing . . . if he could handle the tricky crosswind takeoff. Shamus grabbed for the harness straps as the Jenny began picking up speed.

As the tiny plane crossed in front of the Packard, Shamus flinched. He couldn't hear the whine of bullets but he could see the results as they flew past him to rip through the fabric on the opposite side of the cockpit.

"Get this baby off the ground," he yelled, knowing even as he did that the kid couldn't hear him. But the nose of the Jenny lifted, just as if his rescuer had taken note of his unheard command, and they were suddenly in the air. As the biplane strained toward the sky Shamus again experienced that surge of admiration for the pilot's obvious flying skills. He was controlling the little plane as competently as a marionette master, holding the wings level and true in the face of capricious winds that seemed determined to upend the tiny craft.

As the Jenny climbed higher Shamus kept his eyes riveted on the ground and the pursuing black car. Zeke's plane was burning furiously now but Shamus had accepted its loss when he first crashed.

His rescuer continued to point the tiny biplane toward high sky. They were flying at five thousand feet when the pilot finally leveled off. In the distance, the big black car didn't look nearly so menacing. Neither did the small figures of men he saw standing near it.

The Jenny gave a tiny wobble, jerking Shamus's attention from the ground. Why was that crazy kid flying in circles? Didn't he know which direction to go?

Shamus raised an arm and gestured to the south, then smiled when the plane turned in that direction.

A quick visual inspection of the wings assured Shamus the tattered little aeroplane would stay in the air. More than once he'd seen RAF planes as battered as this one make it safely across the Channel to home field after tangling with the Kaiser's flying circus. It had all depended on the pilot, and although Shamus was sure the kid in the rear cockpit wasn't old enough to have flown in the Great War, he was equally confident of the young flier's skills. Takeoffs and landings were, after all, the most dangerous parts of flying. This kid, whoever he was, had proved he could handle both, and in a damaged plane, at that.

For the first time since his aborted landing attempt at the rendezvous point earlier this morning, Shamus felt his tension ease. He didn't know where the Jenny had come from, but he'd never seen a prettier sight than those flashing red wings circling overhead.

He'd have to thank the kid properly once they were safely on the ground. He'd offer to help with repairs on the Jenny, too. It was the least he could do, considering the timely rescue. And when he got his hands on Zeke Vincent, he'd take it out of his hide. Zeke should have known better than to involve Eddie in one of his smuggling schemes.

And Eddie should never have agreed, Shamus reminded himself. Hadn't he warned the kid to steer clear of Chicago's bootleggers? But the orphaned boy he'd unofficially adopted had seen only easy money when Zeke hired him to make the flight.

Eddie claimed he hadn't known Zeke was involved in smuggling when he accepted the job. Maybe he hadn't, Shamus admitted. But he should have had enough sense to question the big money Zeke was offering for what was supposed to be a routine flying job.

Thank the saints he'd discovered what Eddie was up to and had decided to fly the cargo of bootleg whiskey himself. Otherwise, it would have been Eddie who would have been caught in the hijack attempt.

The boy was too gullible, too trusting. It came, he supposed, from Shamus trying to be both father and big brother, which was a laugh anyway, since he couldn't remember having either. But Eddie's big brother had been Shamus's closest friend, and because of that he'd tried to do his best for the boy.

He'd keep on trying, but Eddie was going to have to grow up now, and fast. The suitcase under Shamus's feet guaranteed it. If the two cases of Scotch, left behind in the burning plane, had been all the cargo, he would have been able to tell Zeke to write them off and forget it. The suitcase prevented that. It had taken Shamus only one quick look to know there was a fortune in the neatly bound bundles of greenbacks stacked in that case, money he had no doubt was completely illegal. This suitcase must have been the reason for the attempted hijacking.

The money wouldn't be Zeke's, either. Zeke Vincent was a hustler, but too small-time to have collected a bankroll that large. And that meant whoever owned it would be looking for Zeke.

Who was Zeke's boss? Probably Al Capone, Shamus reasoned. Or maybe Bugs Moran. Of all the Chicago gang leaders, those two were the biggest, and fierce rivals, as well. Most underworld gang leaders observed territorial boundaries, but not Capone or Moran. Neither would hesitate to ignore the unwritten truce between the various criminal elements to strike a blow at a hated rival. Stealing the fortune in the suitcase would be a major coup for either organization.

He should have let it burn with the plane, Shamus decided. But he hadn't, and now it was too late. He'd have to hang onto it until he could get it back to Zeke or to whoever owned it. He could only hope Zeke would retrieve it before he and Eddie were dragged into the middle of the bootleggers' war.

Shamus's thoughts were yanked to the present when the Jenny suddenly shuddered and tipped forward into a shallow dive. Instinctively he grabbed the stick, easing the nose of the plane upward into level flight again.

Something was wrong! It took a split second for his mind to register the fact that he'd felt no resistance on the controls. He almost stood in the seat, twisting to look over his shoulder at the rear cockpit, then spit out a curse and slammed himself into the seat. The kid was slumped over, head resting against the side of the cockpit, a trickle of red rolling slowly down the side of his face. Another darkening patch was evident high on the arm of his brown leather jacket.

Shamus felt his stomach churn and the taste of fear rise in his throat as he grabbed again for the controls and pushed the throttle to full power.

In what seemed like a lifetime, but was actually closer to ten minutes, he was circling above home field, the bright green Shamrock Flying Service painted on the side of the hangar welcoming him. He made one quick circle of the field then took the Jenny to ground.

As the wheels touched earth, Shamus cut the throttle, guiding the little plane toward the front of the hangar. The Jenny had barely stopped rolling when he jerked off his seat belt and began crawling over the fuselage toward the rear cockpit.

"Hey, who are— Is that you, Shamus?" Eddie yelled as he came running from the hangar.

Shamus didn't turn to answer. He yanked the release from the pilot's harness straps and lifted the slight form from the cockpit, his mind busy cataloging impressions. Still breathing, praise the saints. And the hole in the center of the dark jacket stain was high on the arm. Shouldn't have hit anything vital. He forced himself to look at the boy's head and let the breath gush from his lungs in a single rush. No hole. Just a long, gashing slash in the leather helmet. A graze!

Balancing the pilot's slender form in his arms, Shamus stood up carefully on the edge of the wing, then jumped to the ground and headed toward the hangar office.

"Who's that? What happened? Where'd you get the Jenny?" Eddie's questions tumbled over each other as he trotted to keep up with Shamus's long strides.

"We didn't have time to introduce ourselves," Shamus growled, fear and exhaustion making his voice fierce. "He plucked me out of a pasture minutes before some of Zeke's associates arrived to finish their shooting practice. Got me away clean, but he wasn't so lucky."

"Oh, God, I didn't think—"

"You should have," Shamus snapped as he yanked open the door to the office and laid his burden on a dingy cot. "Get me a bowl of warm water and a rag," he told the hovering boy without bothering to look at him. "And make sure everything's clean."

He carefully lifted the kid's head to remove the goggles, barely taking note of long dark lashes or the chalk white skin that lay underneath. "You should have left me there," he growled to the small limp form in a guilt-ridden voice as his fingers worked to unfasten the helmet. "I'm sorry, kid. You didn't deserve this." Gently he eased the damaged helmet away and froze as his fingers tangled in a snarl of soft curls.

"Ah, no, it can't be..." The anguished whisper tore from his throat. He rocked back on his heels, staring at the wee lad who'd risked life and plane to rescue him, not realizing he was holding his breath, not even realizing Eddie had entered the room.

"He's going to be all right, isn't he, Shamus?" Eddie's anxious voice broke the silence in the room as he tiptoed to the side of the cot, carefully balancing the basin of water in his hands.

Seconds later the basin clattered unheeded to the floor. "Holy saints!" the boy exclaimed. "But he's... That's a girl!"

WHO WAS SHE? Where had she come from, appearing out of the sky like some angel of mercy at just the right moment to pluck him out of that field? Shamus raked his fingers through his hair, an unconscious gesture of frustration. His eyes continued to rest on the woman in the middle of his bed. She looked so fragile, like delicately painted porcelain, her cheeks softly brushed with pink. But there was no hussy's paint on her face. He should know. Hadn't he washed it himself?

Why didn't she wake up? Doc Baker had promised she'd be fine. He'd never doubted the old man's word before. This time he was almost afraid to let himself believe.

"She's going to be all right, isn't she, Shamus?" Eddie asked in a voice that almost, but not quite, managed to disguise a tremor. "Doc said she would..."

"Yeah," Shamus assured him, straining to keep his voice matter-of-fact. He could hear the guilt and concern in the boy's voice and regretted his earlier harsh words. Maybe, if nothing else, this would make Eddie more cautious.

"She'll be all right," he repeated, "but it might be a while before she wakes up. Why don't you go on to bed?"

"No. I'll stay, too. It's all my fault."

"Part yours," Shamus agreed. "And part mine, but mostly Zeke Vincent's. Trying to lay blame doesn't change a thing, Eddie. Right now we need to take care of her. Get some rest. You'll have to play nurse tomorrow. We don't want anyone else to know she's here."

"You'll wake me if—"

"I'll wake you if I need you," Shamus promised. "She'll be herself tomorrow, just like Doc said. When we find out who she is, we'll know what to do."

He waited until he heard Eddie pull the door closed behind him, then turned his attention back to the bed. Short tousled curls spilled over the top of the bandage Doc had tied around the graze high on the girl's forehead. One hand grasped the coverlet, clutching the folds so tightly her knuckles looked even whiter than the sheet under her fingers.

Shamus stepped closer. Her dark eyelashes lay in half moons against her cheeks—a rich mahogany

brown that exactly matched the soft curls framing her
face. Shadowed hollows under high cheekbones and
a smattering of freckles across the bridge of her small
straight nose emphasized her look of frailty. Her
mouth, now tight-lipped in pain, would be soft and
sultry when relaxed.

Why didn't she wake up? Doc had said the head
wound was no more than a scratch, and the other
bullet had passed through her upper arm with little
damage. She'd probably fainted from shock and loss
of blood. All in all, Doc told him, she was lucky.

That had been Shamus's reaction, too, when he first
pulled her from the cockpit, but that was before he'd
realized she was a lassie, not a lad. A lassie wasn't
supposed to be shot, especially not one who looked
like a freckle-faced angel. She might have fooled him
into thinking she was a lad at first, but he'd have to be
dead to have ignored the soft skin, lithe limbs and en-
ticing curves he'd discovered underneath her bloody
blouse.

Shamus frowned as he recalled the strange-looking
garments he'd found under that blouse. They were
similar in design to a two-piece union suit, but with no
buttons or openings, and made of a silvery looking
material that had molded her body like a second skin.
Under that— Shamus felt the heat flood through his
body as he remembered his first glimpse of those skin-
colored provocative wisps of lace. Even the girls at
Lady Lucy's wouldn't be brazen enough to wear such
scanty unmentionables.

Who in the devil was she, anyway, and what was she
doing flying an aeroplane? Shamus asked himself
again. He'd heard of a few women pilots, had actually met one once, but women in flying machines were

oddities, almost freaks. Even pilots like himself were considered a bit tetched. Most people still believed that if God meant for man to fly, He'd have given him wings. Besides, Shamus knew all the pilots in this part of the country, both the men and the planes they flew. He'd never seen, never even heard of a woman flyer or a bright red-and-white Jenny.

The woman shifted again. One hand fluttered upward, as if reaching for something, then fell back to the bed. Her lips moved. She made a small mewling sound, then a moan. Her hand trembled.

Shamus stared down at the bed, remorse welling in his eyes. He felt so helpless. "Everything's going to be all right, lassie," he promised quietly. "I'll take good care of you." He reached out to lightly touch her.

Her hand became still. Dark eyelashes fluttered against her cheeks, then opened.

By all the saints, he'd never seen such eyes—large, violet-blue, like the hyacinths his mum used to plant around the front stoop. They were focused on him, a look of bewilderment and confusion in their depths.

Her gaze moved from his face to his hand resting on hers, then returned once again to his face. She pushed herself back against the pillows, her eyes wide with shock. Then a tiny light of recognition sparked deep in her eyes. "Who...who are you?" she finally stammered.

He made a slight formal bow. "Shamus Fitzgerald, at your service. It's sorry I am we didn't have time to introduce ourselves earlier. And I'm sorry for... I'm sorry you were hurt. But I promise, everything's going to be fine. You're safe. I'll keep you safe." The last sentence was spoken like a vow.

Libby gave a little gasp and squeezed her eyes shut. She remembered now . . . the car coming toward her, little puffs of dust surrounding the Jenny, the man diving into the front cockpit as she raced her plane across the pasture and all but threw it into the air. Then . . . nothing. She couldn't remember what happened next. The man . . . Was this the man in the field?

She opened her eyes again. He was still there, the man who said his name was Shamus. As her eyes found his face, she gave another gasp, a sound between confusion and fear. She did know him! She hadn't known his hair would be almost raven black or his eyes a deep midnight blue, but she'd seen his face before, and now she couldn't seem to look away. She felt that familiar, disquieting skip in her pulse. But it couldn't be. *He* couldn't be.

He seemed to realize he was the cause of her agitation. "Don't let this ugly Irish mug frighten you, colleen. You're safe. I wouldn't hurt a hair on your head. No more than I already have, anyway." His voice was a soft deep rumble of regret.

He was the same, but he couldn't be. Libby shook her head, ignoring the sudden throb of pain. "But . . . But you can't . . . You're not . . ." The words were only a whisper of sound. She struggled to raise her head, then collapsed against the pillow.

Shamus leaned closer, caught by the look in her eyes.

"But you should be dead," she finally blurted out, then covered her mouth with her uninjured hand, like a guilty schoolgirl appalled at what she'd just said.

His laugh rumbled from deep in his chest. "Sure an' I should . . . and probably would be if you hadn't showed up. But as you can see, I'm very much alive and completely unharmed, all thanks to you. Can you tell me your name? Where you're from?" he asked gently, watching the bewilderment cloud her expressive eyes.

"From the storm," she finally said. "I got caught in the storm. When I flew out, I didn't know where I was. Then I saw you. I . . . I thought the storm had caught you, too."

Shamus frowned. He didn't remember storm clouds in the area today. Of course, he'd been otherwise occupied most of the time, and isolated thunderheads weren't unusual this time of the year. It didn't matter now anyway. "What's your name?" he asked softly.

"Libby," she said, almost by rote, then her eyes widened again, the curtain of fog in her mind swirling into confused patterns.

He couldn't be the man in the old photograph, regardless of how much they looked alike. She rolled her head against the pillows in a futile effort to clear her confused thoughts, and was repaid by another stab of pain.

Shamus reached out to touch her cheek. "Lie still now, colleen. Thrashing about will only hurt your head. It's only a graze. You'll feel better tomorrow."

Her movements ceased, as if compelled by the soft warm pressure of his hand against her cheek. She tried again to clear her thoughts, to make sense of what apparently was, yet couldn't be. Her mind grasped at an image. "My plane . . ."

"The Jenny's fine. Well, at least in better shape than you are at the moment. Won't take much to get her looking good as new. I've got her locked up right and tight in the barn. We'll take good care of her . . . and of you."

"Is it still Friday?" she asked, trying for a sense of the familiar.

"No," he told her, a slight frown marring his forehead. "It's Thursday."

Libby gasped. "It can't be Thursday. Thursday was yesterday."

"You're just a mite bit confused," he assured her. "You've a nasty gash on the head, and it's a mighty sore arm you'll be having. You're entitled to be a little mixed up. Don't let it worry you now. Can you tell me your last name, Libby? Do you remember?"

"It can't be Thursday," Libby repeated in a bewildered voice, not even hearing his last question. How could it be Thursday? Her demonstration flight at Oshkosh was on Friday. She was sure. Hadn't she and Howard been planning it for months? "No, it has to be Friday, July twenty-third," she insisted, not even realizing she'd spoken aloud.

"Aye, it's the twenty-third," Shamus agreed, a note of relief evident in his voice. "You've got the dates right, just confused the days. It's Thursday, July twenty-third, 1925, just like the calendar says." He gestured toward a spot on the wall on the other side of the bed. "Now, can you tell me the rest of your name?"

It took a moment for her to understand what he'd said, but even then Libby's mind rejected the information. She jerked her eyes toward the wall, seeking the calendar he'd pointed to, ignoring another burst of pain in her head. She didn't bother trying to distinguish the days of the week. Her eyes fastened on the large black letters at the top of the calendar, the ones reading "Curruther's Feed and Seed, 1925."

"Can you remember the rest of your name, Libby? What's your last name?"

"Carmichael," she said, her voice a thin thread of sound in the sudden pandemonium of her thoughts. It wasn't possible. It couldn't be....

She felt a black curtain flutter at the edge of her mind. This was a dream. A nightmare. It had to be. The curtain began to close.

Frantically she reached out for something solid, something real. Her fingers closed around the reassuring warmth of a strong hand. The panic receded. Slowly, she relaxed, giving in to exhaustion. *What a crazy dream... Will I remember it when I wake up?*

As her eyelids fluttered closed, Shamus bent over her. Her fingers clutched his hand for another moment, then gradually relaxed their hold. As her chest rose and fell in a soft rhythm, he released an anxious breath. She was asleep, apparently a deep relaxed sleep. Just what she needed.

Her small hand, still resting in his, felt dainty and fragile. Who would have believed such a small, soft hand had the strength to control an aeroplane the way she did? He certainly wouldn't have, not if he hadn't been there.

"Just who are you, Libby Carmichael?" he softly asked the sleeping woman, then gave a weary sigh. It didn't really matter. Not who she was or where she'd come from. She'd saved him. She was hurt. She was his responsibility now. Somehow he'd have to keep her safe until he got this mess straightened out.

He released her hand and carefully tucked it under the coverlet. His eyes were still on her face as he straightened, but he turned abruptly when he heard the door creaking open behind him. When Eddie poked his head inside, Shamus gave a quick shake of his head, and gestured with his hand for quiet. Eddie retreated from sight. With one last look at the sleeping woman, Shamus followed him out of the room.

"I . . . I know you told me to catch some sleep," Eddie stammered. "But I couldn't. Not until I found out . . . Is she all right?"

"She's fine," Shamus assured him. "She woke up for a few minutes. Her name's Libby Carmichael. She's weak and a little confused. Seems to think this is Friday instead of Thursday. But she knew the date was July twenty-third. She's sleeping now, and that's the best thing for her."

Shamus watched Eddie's mouth break into a grin as the anxiety drained from his eyes and knew the boy's relief mirrored his own.

"Zeke show up down at the airfield?" he asked. As the boy shook his head, Shamus sighed. "Maybe it's just as well you're still up, then. Think I'll go into town and ask a few discreet questions. The sooner we find him, the better for us. You sit with Libby until I get back, just in case she wakes up again. But I don't think she will. More than likely she'll sleep like a baby until morning."

"I could go looking for Zeke," Eddie said.

But Shamus shook his head. "Have to be careful who I ask. You might not know who was safe and who wasn't. I'm sure we're not the only ones looking for him. Whoever owns that suitcase will be wanting it back. So will the hijackers. Likely no one knows Zeke hired you as a substitute pilot. So unless they find Zeke first and he talks, I don't think anyone can make a connection between him and us. I'd just as soon keep it that way.

"She'll be safer this way, too," Shamus added, gesturing toward Libby's room. "The hijackers are going to be looking for a red-and-white aeroplane, but nobody will believe that lass was the pilot."

Eddie shuffled his feet. "All right, Shamus. If you really think... I made a mess of it, didn't I?"

"It was a mistake, all right, but not the end of the world," Shamus answered slowly. "And I think you learned something. Zeke offered you too much money for a routine job. That usually means something's wrong. We'll get out of this if we're careful," he promised. "Whoever owns that suitcase ought to be happy just to get it back."

Eddie didn't look completely convinced, but at least he looked a little less tense. Shamus gave him an affectionate cuff to the shoulder. "You sit with the lassie. I'll be back in a while. And Eddie, don't worry. It's sure and a fact the saints were with me today... sending the colleen and all. I don't see as why they'd be deserting us now."

CHAPTER THREE

LIBBY SHIFTED RESTLESSLY in the bed as a bright light struck her full in the face. Grumbling incoherently, she roused herself enough to identify the source of annoyance, a shaft of sunlight poking its way through a rip in an old-fashioned roll shade. Even then, it took a moment or two for her to begin to wake up.

When she shifted her weight onto her elbows, a stab of pain radiating from high on her right arm brought her quickly to consciousness. With the memory of last night's strange dream tugging at the edge of her awareness, she let her gaze roam the room as her mind skittered through a confused mass of impressions.

Her bed was a scratched and scarred antique iron bedstead. Large faded pink roses intertwined with gray-green leaves and scrolling ribbons decorated the papered walls. A single naked light bulb hung from a cord in the center of the ceiling. Bare springs squeaked as she shifted her weight, the sound failing to interrupt her inspection of the sparsely furnished room. Her gaze moved lightly over the small chestlike piece of furniture sitting in the corner, her mind absently registering a chipped crockery bowl and large pitcher sitting next to a folded towel on the otherwise unadorned top.

Suddenly more alert, she jerked her eyes back, her gaze dropping to the front of the chest. There were no drawers, only two doors that opened outward, like a cabinet. With a low groan she let her head fall back to the pillow, not understanding how she knew, but knowing, nonetheless, that behind those doors would be the third piece of the commode set—the chamber pot.

Libby's breath escaped in a little gasp. Where in the world was she? The room reminded her of a stage set or an old, old movie...almost as if she'd stepped back in time.

She shook her head in bewilderment as the details of her strange dream struggled to the forefront of her mind. Slowly, afraid to look, but unable to stop herself, she twisted around to face the wall on the other side of the bed. It was there, just as it had been there in her dream, that impossible calendar with its impossible date of 1925.

It wasn't a dream! Unless...unless she was still dreaming. She deliberately pinched herself on the arm, wincing at the sharp pain but convincing herself she wasn't still asleep. Her eyes darted to the calendar. If she wasn't dreaming, was she crazy?

No, she told herself firmly. She wasn't crazy. There had to be an explanation. She was Elizabeth Marie Carmichael, born in Chicago, Illinois, on March 19, 1966. Yesterday, on Friday, July 23, 1993, she was at Oshkosh, Wisconsin, flying a demonstration in her antique Jenny. She and the little biplane had been flying a perfect performance until she'd been pulled into a thunderhead.

But she'd survived. She distinctly remembered battling the wind and hail. Even in the worst of nightmares she couldn't have imagined the details of that! She remembered breaking out of the storm into clear blue skies, too, both she and the Jenny miraculously undamaged.

The rest came rushing back now, a jumble of memories and images. First came the man in the field, then the car racing toward them, guns protruding from the windows.

"Aye, it's the twenty-third," the man who said his name was Shamus had told her. "You've got the dates right, just confused the days. It's Thursday, July twenty-third, 1925, just like the calendar says."

Libby let a low groan escape. Her hand moved automatically to brush back the hair on her forehead. When her fingers encountered the gauze bandage tied around her head, she hesitated, frowning, struggling to remember more. Slowly she extended an arm, wincing at the pain near her right shoulder, but her eyes were riveted on the long sleeve of her unfamiliar clothing. She was still trying to accept the fact that she was dressed in nothing but a man's old-fashioned nightshirt when a slight creaking sound warned her the door to her room was being opened.

Her eyes jerked toward the door as she automatically clutched the sheet to her throat. It was him! The man from the photograph. The man from the dream. The man from last night who said his name was Shamus Fitzgerald.

No, that couldn't be right. He couldn't be the man in the photograph and be here now! There had to be an explanation. There had to be.

She watched warily as the man eased the door open. His lips curved upward into a smile that made her catch her breath.

"Top of the morning to you, Libby Carmichael," he said, speaking softly. "It's good to see you awake.

Aye, it's a sunshine day for sure.'' He stopped just inside the door.

When had she told him her name? Libby frowned, trying to remember. She knew he was waiting for her to say something. But what? She had so many questions. Where to begin? And how? Her voice was caught in her throat. Instead of speaking, she stared, knowing her confusion must be apparent in her expression.

He took a step closer to the bed. ''My name's Shamus Fitzgerald. We met last night. Well, no, yesterday afternoon, but we didn't get around to introducing ourselves until last night.''

''I remember . . .'' she said, then hesitated when she heard the quiver in her voice. She cleared her throat. ''I remember some of it, anyway. And I told you my name was Libby Carmichael?''

''Aye, that you did. A kindness it was, considering . . .''

Libby watched a small grimace flicker cross his face. He shifted his weight from one foot to the other and seemed to hesitate as if not sure of what to say.

''Sure and it's a fact you'd have been better off never meeting up with the likes of me,'' he added, the words rolling off his tongue in an exaggerated Irish brogue. ''Not that I'm ungrateful, mind you. That little red-and-white Jenny of yours was about the most welcome sight I've ever seen.''

He smiled again, a slow, lazy smile that crinkled the laugh lines around his startling midnight blue eyes and exposed a peekaboo dimple in his left cheek. In other circumstances, Libby knew she'd have responded to his warm smile like a contented cat being offered a bowl of cream. As that thought flickered through her mind, it added to her confusion and her fear.

Who was he really? And why had he told her that outrageous story? She knew her apprehension must show on her face when his smile faded into an expression of gentle reassurance.

"I'll not be harming you, Libby Carmichael," he said quietly, his voice a gruff rumble that sent tingles along her spine. "I owe you my life. You'll be safe here."

Safe? The word jolted her memory. She shook her head, flinching with the movement, and raised a hand to the gauze tied around her forehead. "I was shot, wasn't I? I thought I was dreaming, having a nightmare or something. But it was real...."

She shook her head again, this time more vigorously, making her tousled curls dance around her face. "I remember the black car, the men with the guns... everything."

Even though she uttered the words, the sequence of events was only a hazy, half-believed memory. Libby searched Shamus's face, hoping that his expression would tell her it wasn't really true, that it was all a bad dream after all. But there was no look of shock on his face, only resignation and regret. As her gaze held his, she accepted that part of her crazy dream as reality.

"Who were they?" she demanded, with a sudden flash of indignation. She sat up abruptly, forgetting in her agitation to keep a firm hold on the coverlet clutched to her throat. "Why were they shooting at us... at you? What did you do?"

Shamus's eyes followed the falling coverlet, his gaze skimming the feminine contours barely concealed by Eddie's worn nightshirt until he suddenly realized what he was doing. He jerked his eyes to her face, chastising himself, then frowned, puzzled as well as intrigued by the woman's seeming acceptance of his presence in her bedchamber as well as her abrupt change in demeanor.

The sight of her in his bed, injured and helpless, prompted his protective instincts and increased his sense of guilt. But the challenging tilt of her stubborn little chin and the matching mutinous expression in her eyes warned him she was not as gentle and helpless as she looked. At least she didn't think so. And her question caught him by surprise. She made it sound as if it was all his fault.

Sure he was responsible. If she hadn't come to his rescue, she wouldn't have been shot. But why should she assume he'd done anything to provoke the attack? Unless she knew more than she was saying....

"Well," she demanded. "Are you going to tell me who was shooting at you and why?"

Shamus bit back a quick retort. He supposed she was entitled to a bit of temper. It was his fault she'd been hurt. But what kind of brazen hussy was she anyway, sitting in his bed, talking about being shot? She wasn't exactly calm, but she wasn't crying, either. She did seem wary, maybe even a little disbelieving, more angry than afraid. By all the saints, any other woman would be hysterical by now. Of course no other women he knew would spend her time flying around the countryside in an aeroplane, either.

Shamus ignored her question as he tried to sort through his list of facts and conflicting impressions. Most confusing was her total lack of self-consciousness at entertaining him in a bedroom while clad only in borrowed nightclothes. Even in these enlightened days of 1925, he reasoned, a good girl would be horrified to find herself in such circumstances. But surely a real Sheba would be more suggestive, more teasing. Libby Carmichael seemed to be both and neither. She was provocative, yet at the same time blithely unaware of her impropriety.

Shamus carefully masked his thoughts. What did he know about the woman, after all? Nothing except that she claimed her name was Libby Carmichael and that she'd suddenly appeared to rescue him. He'd found no identification in her plane, not even a change of clothes. So where had she come from? And more important, why?

Aye, she was a puzzle, all right. He owed her his protection, but not necessarily his trust. Not until he knew more about her. Besides, if she wasn't involved, she was better off not knowing anyway.

"There's nothing to tell," he finally answered. "It's none of your worry."

Libby wasn't sure she'd heard him correctly, not until she saw the set of his square jaw and the look of determination in his eyes. "Not my worry," she gasped. "Someone shoots me, and it's not my worry?"

"It was a mistake," he said abruptly, "a misunderstanding. Like I said, none of your concern."

To Libby, his voice sounded like a parent chastising a petulant child.

"I'll take care of it. You're safe here," he continued, apparently unaware or unconcerned about her escalating temper. "No one will even have to know you were involved."

"I wasn't involved. I was shot!" Libby told him angrily. She clenched her teeth, but kept her eyes glued to his face as she mentally counted backward from ten to one. "If that's the way you deal with misunderstandings, I sure don't want to be around if you ever have a real disagreement. Why in the blazes should I care if anyone knows I was involved? I'm the victim here, the one who got shot, not the one doing the shooting. What did the police say?"

Shamus's sudden boom of laughter confused her. She didn't understand what was so funny. He finally took pity on her look of puzzlement to explain.

"Police? You think I should have called the police? Lady, you sure haven't been around Chicago long, have you? The last thing we need to do is call the police." His voice turned sober. "I'm not really involved in all this, either. I'm a pilot. That's all. I got caught in the middle, just like you."

His last few words barely registered on Libby's consciousness, her attention caught by a single word. "Chicago? I'm in Chicago?" she asked in an unbelieving voice.

"At the moment you're actually in Curruther's Corners," Shamus told her, suddenly alert to the alarm in her voice. "Close enough to Chicago to make little difference, but far enough away not to be found. I hope."

Curruther's Corners? She'd never heard of it. Of course she only had his word she was anywhere near Chicago. It was a long way from Oshkosh...at least a long way to be blown by a storm. Almost as impossible to believe as his ridiculous claim that it was 1925.

Her eyes flicked uneasily to the calendar on the wall. Chicago in 1925? She'd never been interested in history, except in connection with aviation, but even she knew about Chicago in the Roaring Twenties. If it was true, it would explain a lot.

It couldn't be true. It was impossible. It couldn't really be 1925. Could it?

She gave the calendar another anxious glance. The year 1925 would explain the old-fashioned look of the room and the vintage car, maybe even the men with the tommy guns, if what she'd read about the era's gangsters and their choice of weapons was true.

No, her thinking was crazy. She couldn't be in 1925. Time travel was the stuff of make-believe. It didn't exist. So why the calendar? And last night, why had he insisted it was July 23, 1925? Maybe he was the crazy one. Or was it some cruel kind of joke?

"Where did you think you were, anyway?"

Libby blinked as his voice broke into her confusion. What had he said? She looked up, trying to mask her growing apprehension. "What?"

"If you don't know you're in Chicago, where do you think you are?" he repeated.

"I don't know," she said finally, dropping her head against the pillows. "I told you...I told you last night. I got caught in a storm. I was lost."

She moved restlessly as his eyes searched her face. "Well, don't worry about it now," he finally said. "We'll get you fixed up in a few days, then you can go on your way, or back where you came from. Where're you from, anyway?"

Libby hesitated. She was in big trouble if she was really in Chicago in 1925. No, it was impossible! On the other hand, if he was crazy, she was still in big trouble. *Careful, Libby,* she told herself. *Don't let him know anything's wrong.* But if she really was in 1925

Chicago, she had to get out of this bed. It shouldn't be hard to confirm... or disprove. "Maybe a long time away from here," she muttered wearily, wondering if she really could go back where she came from.

"What did you say?"

"I said...I mean..." Libby thought frantically. Had he heard her? Delaware. That sounded something like her mutterings. "I said, I'm from Delaware."

"A storm blew you all the way from Delaware?"

She didn't have to look at his face to recognize his disbelief. She could hear the distrust in his voice. She was going to have to be very careful, she realized. If he wasn't crazy and she told him where she was really from, he'd certainly think she was. He'd probably call the little men in the white coats... if they had men in white coats in 1925.

"Of course not," she stammered. "I'm originally from Delaware but I don't live there anymore. I've been flying across country the last few weeks." She turned her head toward him and failed to suppress a shiver when she met the intense look in his eyes.

"You're tired," he said abruptly. "I shouldn't have kept you talking so long. Probably hungry, too. You missed supper last night." He turned and walked toward the door.

"Wait," Libby called, trying to deny the emotion she felt rising in her throat. She didn't want him to leave. She didn't want to be alone. He was the only real thing she knew in this crazy unknown world.

"Don't worry," he said, apparently recognizing her unspoken plea. "I'll not be leaving you alone, but I can't stay here. I've got a flying service to run." He stuck his head out the door and called a name. In seconds, a tall, gangly boy slipped into the room.

"This is Eddie," Shamus said, propelling the teen-ager toward the bed with an encouraging pat on the back.

Libby drew a breath as Shamus gave the boy a quick affectionate grin, softening his chiseled features and lighting a spark deep in his dark blue eyes. "He'll bring you some breakfast in a minute. And he'll be staying with you. You stay in bed until—"

"Now wait a minute . . ." Libby started to protest.

"—until Doc Baker sees you on his rounds this afternoon," Shamus continued, completely ignoring her protest. "Then you can do whatever Doc says is okay."

Eddie shuffled his feet. "I'll take good care of you, ma'am. I'm real sorry you were hurt. I didn't—"

"Of course you're sorry, Eddie. She knows that," Shamus interrupted. "Run along and get her breakfast now. You've got all day to talk."

He turned to her, pinning her to the pillow with another enigmatic look from his midnight blue eyes. Libby felt the air escape from her lungs in a sudden rush.

"I probably ought to warn you," he said, his bland voice a contrast to the humorous twinkle in his eyes. "Eddie will talk your ears off, if you let him. He fell in love with that pretty little red-and-white Jenny of yours."

"My Jenny?" Libby suddenly gasped. "Where is it? What happened—"

"Your aeroplane's fine," Shamus assured her. "I told you last night, but I guess you forgot. It's safe and sound in the barn out back. Needs a little fabric work, but otherwise should be good as new."

"You're sure?" Libby asked, suddenly realizing how important her plane might be. If she'd really landed in 1925, she'd come in the Jenny. It might be her only way of getting back to where she belonged.

"I'm sure. You can see for yourself as soon as Doc lets you up. Eddie can do the dope and fabric work for you, if you like. He's a good hand. I taught him myself."

"I can make my own repairs." She saw his eyebrows rise at her statement and was surprised when he refrained from challenging her.

"Maybe Eddie can help you, then," he said mildly. "It will give him something to do. But that's for later. Today, you stay in bed and do as you're told."

Libby drew another deep breath, ready to protest.

"Look, Libby," Shamus said, apparently recognizing the look of rebellion on her face. "Give the kid a break and behave yourself. Eddie's worried about you. He heard the doc tell me to keep you in bed until he checked you again. If you don't follow Doc's orders, the boy will blame himself."

"A doctor is really coming here . . . to check me?"

"Well, of course he is. He's a doctor. He goes to see sick people. What'd you expect, for sick people to go see him?"

"No, I guess not." Libby tried to restrain her grin but knew she'd failed when she saw the strange look he threw her. She couldn't help it. A doctor who made house calls, for heaven's sake. Maybe it really was 1925.

"All right, Shamus," she told him, suddenly capitulating. "You can stop worrying about Eddie. I won't give him any trouble. I'll rest until the doctor gets here."

Shamus gave her another suspicious look, but must have finally decided she was sincere, or that he wasn't going to be able to do anything about it if she wasn't. He nodded abruptly. "Good. I'll have a quick word with Eddie, then shove off. And don't worry. I'll take care of everything."

Libby let her eyes follow him across the room. So he'd take care of everything, would he? Great.

All right, she'd admit she'd trusted him last night. She remembered grabbing his hand to make her nightmare go away. It hadn't, of course. And maybe it hadn't been a nightmare. But for some reason, clutching his hand, she'd decided everything was going to be all right.

She'd trusted him this morning, too, when he'd told her she was safe. Even if he was arrogant, bossy and infuriating. "Not your worry," she mimicked, then gave an unfeminine snort. If it wasn't her worry, she didn't know whose it was. She was, after all, the one who'd been shot. Obviously Shamus Fitzgerald thought she was too helpless to be told what was going on. He'd handle it, he said. And he probably would, too. He looked capable of handling most things.

But he wouldn't be able to handle her biggest worry, Libby realized with a sudden depressing insight. If he wasn't crazy, if she really was in 1925, she'd bet Shamus Fitzgerald wouldn't have a single idea about how to get her back to 1993.

The problem was, neither did she.

CHAPTER FOUR

TO LIBBY'S DELIGHT, as well as her chagrin, the doctor arrived, as promised, shortly after lunch. Despite her assurances to Shamus, she'd cajoled Eddie into letting her out of bed to rest in an overstuffed chair by the window in the front room.

On her abbreviated tour of the house from the bedroom to the parlor she'd found nothing to dispute her host's claim that she was truly in the 1920s, and her first sight of the old doctor was almost enough to finally convince her.

He pulled up in front of the farmhouse in a dusty Model-T Ford, its cloth top showing evidence of fraying across the ribs. He was carrying a bulging, scratched leather doctor's bag and was dressed in a baggy suit that fit the movie set image of the 1920s. A brisk summer breeze flapped the wide-cut trousers against his legs and lifted the edge of his coat to expose wide striped suspenders. His polka-dot tie was attached, slightly askew, under a startling white celluloid collar, and a well-bitten pipe stem protruded from one coat pocket.

Doc Baker, she decided, was certainly a far cry from the dress-for-success medical specialists she was used to seeing.

''Thought I left orders for you to stay in bed,'' the doctor growled when he caught sight of her huddled

in the parlor chair, clutching the blanket she was using as a shawl over the thin nightshirt.

"I felt like getting up."

"Well, then, I guess you'll do," he drawled in a de-
cidedly mid-Western twang, "but I'd like to check my
handiwork, just the same. Don't get much practice
treating bullet wounds these days. Like to keep my
hand in." His eyes twinkled.

Libby liked him immediately. "Why?" she asked,
grinning in spite of herself.

"Why what?" Doc Baker teased as he unwound the
gauze from around her head and discarded it on the
floor. "Why don't I get much practice or why do I
need to keep my hand in?"

He bent closer to peer through the glasses perched
on the end of his nose at the wound on her forehead,
then sat back, seemingly satisfied. "That'll do. Keep
it clean and leave it open to the air. Once the scab
drops, it'll barely even leave a scar."

"Both," Libby said answering his earlier question.

"Well, now, I tell you, folks in Curruther's Corners are mostly peaceful. They got no call to go
around shooting people. Come to think of it, the last
gunshot wound I treated, before you, that is, was two
winters ago. The widow Weizer shot at a fox coming
out of her chicken house. The fox turned out to be an
old hobo trying for a free dinner. Took me nigh onto
an hour to dig all the buckshot out of his backside,
and him yelling the whole time."

Libby winced. "It must have been painful," she said
sympathetically.

"Not so much." The old doctor laughed. "His biggest complaint was that I was wasting good Scotch on
his backside. With this prohibition business the good

stuff costs the farm. That old hobo was a wary sort. Knew to avoid the poison passing for cheap whiskey these days. Said he wasn't a drunk, but he did appreciate a good drink now and then.

"I tell you," Doc continued, warming up to the subject, "rotgut's killing more people than bullets these days. Over two thousand dead from bad liquor this year alone. Damn shame a decent drink costs the earth. Heard the other day that decent Scotch was going for nearly fifty dollars a case. If this keeps up, I'm gonna be forced to start making my own. For medicinal purposes, of course. But at least that way I'll know it's not poisoned.

"Let me get a look at that arm now. We don't want it festering."

Libby dropped the blanket and eased the night-shirt from her shoulder. "But if you don't have any patients with gunshot wounds, why do you need to keep in practice?" she asked.

"Call it professional pride." The old doctor grunted as he gently pulled the bandage from her arm. "Besides, never can tell when I'll need the skills. Who would've guessed, for example, that Shamus's cousin would come visiting and accidently get too close to some bootlegger's hideout."

Cousin? His statement caught Libby by surprise. She stared at him mutely.

"That is what happened, isn't it?" he asked, eyeing her intently.

"Yes, I mean, I guess so," Libby stammered. "It all happened so fast. But it makes sense."

Doc nodded, a look of relief passing over his face. "That's what Shamus said. Thought I had the right of it. Known Shamus for a lot of years. Didn't think he'd be involved in anything shady. Not that kind of man. Why, he took that boy in to raise when the mother died, just because he'd known the older brother during the war. Still, I had to make sure. Even if you are his cousin.''

Libby swallowed in surprise. "He told you I was his cousin?''

"Yep. Explained all about the estrangement with his mother's side of the family, too, when I said I didn't know he had any family. Good thing, you being his cousin and all.''

He grinned at her, his eyes still twinkling. "I'll pass the word that Shamus has family visiting. It'll help keep down the talk about a pretty little thing like you staying in his house. But if I were you, I wouldn't say anything about getting shot. Not a tale for simple country folk, if you know what I mean. If anybody asks, tell them you fell or something. Most of them wouldn't know the difference between a gunshot wound and a dog bite if they saw it. Shamus says you got clean away, so whoever shot you shouldn't have a clue about where to look, especially if they don't hear tales of gunshot wounds. It was a good thing Shamus was able to fly you out of there, wasn't it?''

Libby swallowed. "Yes, I guess it was," she agreed, not knowing what else to say.

"Well, now, looks like that arm's going to do fine, too. Be sore for a while. You keep a close eye on it. Keep it dry and change the bandage once a day. And tell Shamus to get hold of me if it starts looking red or puffy.''

"But I can get out of bed?''

The doctor chuckled. "You're out now, aren't you? Sure, you can do just about anything you feel up to doing, but you'll do better staying quiet for the next few days. Give your body time to rebuild the blood you lost. Unless you need me earlier, tell Shamus I'll be back to check you in a week. You'll be staying that long, won't you?''

Libby's head was whirling. Everything about Doc Baker, the way he looked, his conversation, added evidence to Shamus's claim that this was 1925. Surely this sweet old man wouldn't be fooling her, which meant that somehow, for some reason, she might really be in 1925.

"I don't know how long I'll be here," she told him, "but I guess it will be that long anyway."

"Good. Good," the old doctor said, patting her lightly on the shoulder. "Shamus needs a family and he and the boy could both use a woman's touch around here. Not that the good women of Curruther's Corners, and that includes my daughter, haven't tried. She's going to be pea green when she finds out you're staying here, even if you are a cousin. Just how close is the kinship, anyway?"

"I . . . I'm not sure," Libby stammered. Drat Shamus Fitzgerald. If he was going to make up a story he could at least have clued her into her part.

"Well, I don't reckon it matters. Just the word cousin will keep the old tabbies quiet. And I promise you, my dear, I'm no gossip, but just between you and me, I hope it's a very distant kinship. My old bones tell me that you're exactly what the doctor ordered for that boy. Never did hold with all that buzzing around in the sky. He needs something to keep his head out of the clouds and his feet on the ground. No, don't bother getting up. I know my way out. That scamp Eddie used to collect scraps, scratches and broken

bones like a dog collects fleas. You just sit there, rest
and think about what I said.''

Libby couldn't have moved if she tried. She watched
through the window as Doc's Model-T chugged down
the driveway. In the distance she could see rooster tails
of dust chasing another car winding its way along the
road at the bottom of the hill. Eddie had told her
Shamus's airfield was on a flat just beyond the brow
of an adjacent hill, and although she could see nothing of the airfield from the window, two planes in the
air above the field both belonged in the oldest antique category, at least in her world.

She wasn't sure exactly what finally convinced her
she was really in 1925. Maybe it was the doctor's matter-of-fact comments about prohibition or the sight of
the new-looking old-fashioned radio sitting in the
place of honor against the parlor wall. She only knew
that at this moment, she believed.

Dear Lord, help her. How had she managed to land
in this mess? And if being seventy years out of time
wasn't enough of a problem, or being shot at by what
reason told her had to be a gang of real live bootleggers, it now seemed she was going to have to deal with
the intentions of a kindly old matchmaker.

That disturbed her most of all, the doctor's intentions and the object of those intentions. Yes, one six-
foot-tall male pilot named Shamus Fitzgerald was going to be a major problem. He was even more attrac-
tive in person than he'd been in that picture, and even
though she'd tried to deny it, she was sure now that he
and the man in the photograph were one and the same.

He'd attracted and intrigued her even before she met
him face to face. Fantasy, she was discovering, was
easier to deal with than reality. That she'd actually met

him had to be a fluke, some cosmic event gone wrong. She had to believe that, just as she had to believe the time warp would eventually correct itself and she'd go back where she belonged.

ALTHOUGH LIBBY was anxious to investigate her new world, she realized the soundness of Doc's advice to rest when she woke the next morning with a lethargy that was completely uncharacteristic. But one day spent mostly in bed and in a borrowed nightshirt was enough. Besides, she was tired of dragging a blanket around with her every time she crawled out from under the covers.

"Where are my clothes, Eddie?" she asked when the boy brought in a breakfast tray.

"They're…they're hanging in the water closet," he said, "but Shamus won't like—"

"Shamus doesn't have to wear them," she said sweetly. "Can you… Oh, never mind, I'll get them. Then you can tell him you had nothing to do with it."

"No. I'll get them," Eddie said quickly. He was back in a couple of minutes, handing her the freshly washed pile of folded clothes, her underwear carefully tucked inside the folds of her riding breeches.

"Where's my blouse?" she asked as, without thinking, she casually separated the lacy bra and bikini panties from the pile and laid the thermal body suit to one side, grimacing at the tear in one sleeve. She looked up in time to catch a bright red blush creep up Eddie's face.

"It…it was ruined," the boy stammered. "Maybe one of my shirts will fit."

He bolted from the room before Libby could answer, and it took her a moment to realize what had caused his discomfort. She chuckled to herself and carefully tucked her underwear out of sight. "Get used to it," she muttered to herself, "or you'll find yourself labeled a scarlet woman."

Eddie returned moments later with a collarless white shirt—probably his best, Libby decided as she rolled the sleeves to elbow length. She laid the heavy socks and high leather boots aside. Bare feet would be fine in the house. It was, after all, summertime.

Once dressed, she wandered into the parlor and, surprised to see Shamus still home reading the paper, started to retreat. As she stepped backward he looked up to see her in the doorway. He rose quickly to his feet, his gaze locking with hers. She felt the heat rise in her face as his eyes traveled over her, resting briefly on the stretched front of Eddie's shirt before traveling slowly down the well-fitted breeches to her brightly polished bare toenails.

"That won't do," he said gruffly. "You can't go out of the house like that, not wearing trousers."

"As it happens, I don't feel like going out of the house," Libby said, "but at least it's better than Eddie's nightshirt. Besides, it's your fault my blouse got trashed."

"Trashed?"

"Ruined. At least Eddie said it was ruined. And that was your fault. Getting mixed up with a bunch of bootleggers."

Libby took a deep breath. She'd fully intended to confront him about his associates, for Eddie's sake, but maybe not this soon. On second thought, it was probably better to get it over with. He was here. She was here. There might not be a better opportunity.

"You ought to be ashamed, you know," she began, "getting mixed up with a bunch of gangsters. Think about the kind of example you're setting for the boy."

Shamus took a step toward her, but Libby refused to retreat. "Good thing Doc doesn't know what you're involved in," she added. "He likes you. Thinks you're great, looking after Eddie, taking care of me. He said it was lucky you were there to rescue me. And that reminds me, whatever made you tell him I was your cousin?"

"I had to give him some reason to have you here," Shamus said, the expression in his eyes testifying to his discomfort. "Nice girls don't... I mean... Well, saints help me... Ladies don't stay in gentlemen's homes. They don't go around flying aeroplanes or getting shot, either," he added in what seemed to Libby to be an afterthought.

"Humph," Libby snorted. "Since I am here, and I do fly airplanes, and I was shot, I guess that means I'm not a lady, right?"

"I didn't say that and I didn't mean... Oh, hell, I mean heck. Look, Libby, you know this isn't exactly a usual situation."

"Oh, never mind," Libby told him. She hadn't meant to get sidetracked onto that subject anyway. "So," she said returning to her original subject, "did you get your misunderstanding cleared up?"

She didn't miss the sudden suspicion mingling with the bright flicker of anger in his eyes.

"Not yet," he said, his voice almost a growl. "But I will."

"Think they'll replace your plane?"

Shamus gave a bitter laugh. "Not likely. But it wasn't my plane, anyway."

"Then it must have belonged to—what was his name? Zeke? And what does he have to say about losing his airplane? Does he know you have a bunch of bootleggers after you?"

The surprise on Shamus's face would have been comical if the look in his eyes hadn't been so fierce.

"How did you know about Zeke? Did Eddie let it slip? Or maybe you already knew? Maybe you were working with him. Is that how you turned up at that field so conveniently?" He took a step toward her.

This time Libby unconsciously retreated a step. Dear heaven, what had she said to make him so mad?

"Oh, no, you don't. No running away."

He covered the space between them and had a restraining hold on her arm almost before Libby realized he was moving.

"I want to know how you knew about Zeke?"

Libby rarely lost her temper. At the moment she knew she was very close to doing so. She stiffened under his hold, letting her eyes drop to his hand on her arm for a moment before looking angrily into his face.

"You told me, you big oaf," she snapped. "Almost the first thing you asked when you jumped onto my wing was, 'Did Zeke send you?' Then you babbled something about his cargo. Now let me go."

The anger in his midnight blue eyes dimmed to confusion for a moment before Shamus dropped his hand and stepped away. Libby absently rubbed the place he'd touched.

"I'm sorry, Libby. I forgot I'd said that." His gaze dropped to her hand, still rubbing at the spot on her arm, and his face blanched. "I didn't hurt you, did I?"

Libby quickly dropped her hand and stepped back. "No. No, you didn't hurt me. Just startled me."

His gaze raked over her again, this time lingering on the vee produced by the two buttons she'd been forced to leave open on Eddie's shirt. For a moment Libby imagined the look in his eyes had softened. Then his gaze became flint hard again.

"I'd better see about getting you something to wear, too," he added, before Libby could protest. "Doc Baker's daughter is about your size. Maybe she'll lend you something..." His voice trailed off as he turned toward the door.

Dismissing her, was he? Libby stiffened her spine. He'd avoided her all yesterday, then accused her of God knew what. He'd tried to placate her like some simpleminded child, given her a look that made her knees weak, then leered at her like a satyr. Now he was trying to relegate her to the category of a doll that needed to be dressed. Well, he wasn't going to get away with it. Not this time! She followed him across the room.

"Just one minute, Shamus Fitzgerald," she demanded in her most imperious tone of voice. "I want some answers. Just what kind of mess am I in, anyway? Are those...those gunmen still looking for you? Are they looking for me because I had the bad judgment to help you? Who's this Zeke character and what's he got to do with it? Is he a bootlegger, too?"

Shamus stopped in mid-stride and spun around to face her. "You're safe here, Libby. I told you that. As long as you do what I tell you, you don't have to worry."

"And if I decide I don't want to do what you're telling me, am I safe then?"

If the subject hadn't been so serious Libby would have laughed at the perplexed look on Shamus's face.

"But why would you do something like that? You don't know what's involved."

"Exactly my point," she said. "I'm not used to someone else taking care of me. I don't know how it works here, but where I come from, I take care of myself. I need to know what's going on."

Shamus shook his head. His bewilderment seemed genuine. "But you're a woman," he protested. "Don't you have a family? Anyone to help you?"

Dear heavens, now he was feeling sorry for her. "It doesn't matter whether I do or not," she persisted. "I'm still responsible for myself. Now, tell me. What kind of mess did I land myself in when I dropped into that field to pick you up? You owe me that much."

"You're not going to like it," he said after a moment or two of apparent contemplation, "but if you insist, I guess I do owe you that much."

"Yes, I think you do," Libby returned wryly. "So what kind of bootlegging scheme are you involved in? None of that poisoned stuff, I hope. That would shatter Doc Baker's illusions."

"I'm not a bootlegger," Shamus protested. "I told you, I got mixed up in it by accident. Shamrock, my flying service, was hired for a routine flying job, something we do every day. That's one way we make our living. Only this time the cargo turned out to be slightly illegal, and apparently the shipper wasn't the only one who wanted it. It was probably the competition chasing us."

"Probably? Don't you even know? Who hired you? Who owned the cargo? And what was it? Bootleg whiskey?"

"Bottled and bonded Scotch I brought over the border from Canada. But when I got to the landing field, those gentleman with the black car and the tommy guns were waiting for me. They should have waited a little longer...until I turned off the prop and got out of the plane. Instead, they barrelled across the field to meet me, guns blazing. So I took off. Unfortunately, they'd put so many holes in my wings that I didn't make it very far. I crashed just a few miles away."

"And that's when I showed up?" Libby asked.

"Right. As to who owned the whiskey, I'm not sure. Probably Capone, but it may have been Bugs Moran."

"Capone? You mean Al Capone?" Libby gasped.

Shamus nodded. "I said you wouldn't like it."

"Just what kind of a fool do you think I am, Shamus Fitzgerald?" Libby demanded. "First you tell me you got mixed up in this by accident. Then you admit you took a job from Al Capone. Even if I'm not from around here, I know that name. No way could you have accepted a job from Capone and believed it was just a routine flying job. That man's the number-one black hat in the country."

"Black hat?"

"Bad guy, gangster, criminal. Surely you don't consider him an upstanding member of society?"

"No, of course not," Shamus said. "You use some strange words sometimes. Just where in Delaware are you from, anyway?"

For a moment Libby panicked, but she forced herself to hide it. Where? She couldn't think of the name of a single town or city in the state. "Delaware's so small it doesn't matter," she said quickly, "and it's not home anymore anyway. Don't try to change the subject. Explain about Capone."

"I didn't say Capone owned the shipment. I only said he might have. Shamrock was hired by Zeke Vincent. I don't know who he was working for. I didn't know he was working for anyone. But after what happened, I think he was and I think it was either Capone or Moran. Working for one, and betrayed his boss to the other gang. Capone and Moran are the only two bosses who'd break the territory laws to attack each other."

"So you don't know who's after us, but you *think* it must be either Capone or Moran? Well, great. That sounds just great. Nothing like a dull life, I always say." Libby collapsed into a nearby chair.

"Libby, are you all right?"

"Just peachy keen," she said, sitting up straight. "A-one okay."

"Oh. I was afraid you were going to cry."

"I do sometimes cry, Shamus. But only as a release for emotion. To cry in the face of disaster is futile. It accomplishes nothing. And there's no question about it. This is a certified disaster."

"It's not that bad. I told you I'd take care of it. Besides, neither Capone nor Moran are looking for us. They're looking for Zeke. They don't know anything about me flying the plane or you playing rescuing angel. Even if they do find out about me, they'll never suspect you. After all . . ."

"Yeah, I know. I'm a woman, and women don't go around flying planes or getting shot. I've heard it before."

Shamus ignored her comment. "So you see, it's like I told you before all this talking. There's nothing to worry about. Soon as I find Zeke, I'll get this cleared up."

"If one of those two gangsters don't find him first."

Shamus shook his head. "Word on the street is both men are looking for him. He'll be laying real low and staying far away from that crowd. I'll find him, or he'll find me."

"How can you be so sure? Shamus Fitzgerald, are you hiding something?"

"Good Lord, you're suspicious, aren't you? I told you how I got messed up in this. What else do you want? And why shouldn't Zeke get in touch with me? I was flying his plane. I'm probably his only ticket out of here. With the mess he's gotten himself into, I think he'll be planning to leave."

Libby wasn't sure whether to believe him or not. What he'd told her sounded like the truth, or at least part of it. She gave a little sigh. She couldn't help being relieved. She hadn't really wanted to believe he was a true villain.

"I sent Eddie down to the airfield. He'll be back by noon. You going to be all right alone until then?" Shamus asked.

"Of course I will. If you'll leave me the newspaper I'll just sit here and catch up on the world until Eddie gets back. Which paper is it?"

"The *Trib*, of course," Shamus said, frowning. "You really like reading the newspaper?"

"Of course I do. The *Chicago Tribune's* been my favorite for years. Do you know it's still going strong six—I mean, I'll bet it's still around sixty or seventy years from now. Good strong paper with an enlight-

ened editorial policy, don't you think?'' She managed
to swallow her near gaff and gave him a bright smile.

Shamus returned her smile with a look of bewilderment. ''I didn't think women read newspapers, nothing but the advertising and gossip, anyway,'' he said,
still shaking his head, but thankfully, handed her the
paper anyway.

You, Shamus Fitzgerald, have got a lot to learn, she
thought as her eyes followed him out of the room.

Libby devoured the paper for information that
might help her in this unfamiliar world. Reading the
news she'd always considered history on fresh news-
print, with the ink still damp enough to smear, was
disorienting, but served as a forceful reminder of the
mess she was in.

The editorial page was filled with discussions of the
recent Dayton, Tennessee, Monkey Trial and the one-
hundred-dollar fine given schoolteacher J.T. Scopes
for teaching evolution. Coal mines in West Virginia
were on strike. The French had bombed Damascus.

''Ready-roll'' cigarettes, she was both amused and
dismayed to read, were advertised as ''good for the
digestion,'' and were selling for twenty cents a pack.
Hip flasks, high Russian boots and hollow canes were
fashion accessories.

IN THE NEXT couple of days she learned from Eddie
that the farmhouse and barn, now doubling as a hangar for her Jenny, belonged to Shamus, but that he
leased most of the acreage to neighboring farmers.

''Shamus ain't much of a farmer,'' Eddie confided. ''He'd rather fly. Shamus says that someday
soon aeroplanes will fly all the way across the country, and maybe even the oceans. He says aviation is

going to change the world. And we're going to be part of it, him and me.''

It was at times like those Libby found it difficult to keep from blurting out confirmation of Shamus's view of the future. What would they think, she wondered, if she told them that such cross-country flights, even trans-ocean flights, would one day be made in a matter of hours, or that half a century from now man would be walking on the moon?

Curruther's Corners, she also learned, was located about ten miles west of Chicago, and had, thus far at least, escaped the lawless, promiscuous wickedness of the big city. The prosperity of the jazz age was invading the small community, however. She saw it rolling by the farmhouse on the spoke wheels of Model-T Fords that daily traveled the dusty roadway at the bottom of the hill.

At her request Eddie brought home a map of the area from the airfield, and after careful study, Libby decided that in her time, Curruther's Corners had become the Bellwood-Hillside area. The dusty road at the bottom of the hill might even be part of the Eisenhower Expressway. One thing for sure, the slightly rolling terrain of Shamus's farm and airfield would one day be covered in concrete and asphalt, and the waving grain fields would be replaced by shopping centers and convenience markets.

Shamus had been as good as his word. He returned one night, a package containing "a proper dress" tucked under his arm. Doc Baker's daughter had picked it out, he told her.

Libby smiled, remembering Doc's comments about his daughter's interest in Shamus as she unfolded the brown butcher paper.

Why, the little witch! Cousin or no cousin, Doc's daughter wasn't taking any chances. She must have shopped all over town to have found such an unattractive outfit. Libby knew she'd look like a refugee from a girl's convent school in the dull gray middy blouse and matching pleated skirt, but nevertheless she managed to give Shamus a smile. "Tell her I appreciate it," she said. "I'll try to return the favor some day."

Libby immediately tucked the unattractive clothing in the back of the closet, and despite Shamus's obvious disapproval, continued to wear her breeches and one of Eddie's shirts around the farmhouse.

As her strength returned, so did her restlessness. She saw less of Shamus now. He left the house each morning before daylight for the airfield. It was often long after dark when she heard the chugging sound of the Model-T that meant he was home.

In the evenings she found herself torn between hoping he'd be home early and hoping he'd be late. He was often arrogant and bad-tempered and always seemed to be issuing orders, but she sometimes caught him looking at her with a wary, speculative interest in his midnight blue eyes.

His strange moods never seemed to bother Eddie. Libby found herself intrigued by the close relationship between the gregarious, almost grown boy and the taciturn man, who was so obviously the boy's hero.

It took her over a week to gather the strength or the nerve to inspect her airplane. When she pulled open the creaky barn doors, she had to blink back her tears. There it was, her only link with home, looking desolate and abandoned, parked in the center of the unused barn. Dust motes floating in the slices of sunlight shining between the cracks in the walls made the entire scene seem even more depressing.

"It's not as bad as it looks, you know," came Shamus's familiar voice from over her left shoulder.

Libby gasped in surprise and pivoted on her toes. "I didn't hear you," she said shakily.

"I was heading for the house when I saw you coming this way. Thought you might want company. I was afraid your first look might be something of a shock," he added, nodding toward the plane. "I know she looks pretty forlorn right now, but there's no structural damage. I checked her over carefully. Be stupid to fly her before doing the fabric repair, but a few supplies and some elbow grease should have her looking like a lady again in no time."

"Thanks," Libby said huskily. "You're right. My first look was something of a shock."

Libby shifted uneasily. She'd silently accused Shamus of avoiding her, but now told herself it was better he had kept his distance. His closeness was infinitely disturbing—disturbing in a way she didn't want to acknowledge or analyze. Uneasily, she turned her back to him and stepped closer to her plane.

He followed silently.

Libby stopped in front of the wings, looking up to inspect the ricochet scratches along the metal cowling of the engine compartment.

"Red-and-white's a strange color combination for a Jenny," he said, abruptly stretching his arm over her shoulder to trace the furrows left by the bullets with his finger. "Who did the color conversion?"

Libby caught her breath as his arm briefly brushed against her shoulder. "I did. Most of it, anyway. A friend of mine helped," she said, looking up, her voice strained.

"A beau?"

"No. Just a friend. A pilot who used—who knows Jennys."

Shamus's eyes seemed to bore into hers, but when she declined to say anything else, he looked away.

"She's a pretty lady," he said. "Bright, bold, a little different. I've never seen another red-and-white aeroplane, but somehow the color seems to fit. You and your... your friend did a good job. She reminds me of you. You make a good team, you and your Jenny." He removed his hand from the side of the plane and rested it on her shoulder.

Libby found herself trying to decipher the strange look in his eyes. She gave a little shiver and ducked away, pretending to inspect the tattered wing fabric. "Yeah, well, we're both a little worse for wear right now," she said with bravado.

"A little battered," he agreed, "but nothing time and care can't cure."

Libby took another quick breath. "And money," she said quickly. "You're familiar with prices around here. Can you give me an estimate of how much supplies are going to run? Most of the tears look like they can be patched, but I'm going to have to replace the fabric along the right wing tip."

"Not much. When you feel like working on her, I'll have your supplies here. Or if you'd like, I'll even get started on it now. I would have already, but you said you wanted to do it yourself."

"I do," Libby said, nodding. "I put her together by myself. Built her a piece at a time from several old junkers. It wouldn't feel right if I didn't do my own repairs. But I need to know how much the supplies are going to cost me. I . . . I'm not familiar with Chicago prices."

"Why'd you build her from old wrecks?" he asked. "There are so many surplus Jennys around, the government's selling them new, still in the crates, for fifty dollars. Even if you'd wanted to change the color, it would have been easier to start with a new one. Unless you got the crashers free. But even then, with the cost of moving them, your dope and fabric, it doesn't make sense."

Libby ducked her head, hoping he hadn't caught her expression. Surplus Jennys, still in their crates, for fifty dollars? She supposed she'd read that somewhere, but those days were long gone, or had been long gone when she put her Jenny together. Good Lord, a single original bolt had often cost her that much! She couldn't explain that to Shamus, but she would like to have seen the look on his face if she could.

"We didn't have that kind of supply in . . . in Delaware," she said hastily. "And that doesn't matter now. How much, Shamus? Can you at least give me an estimate?"

"If you insist on doing the work yourself, only about forty or fifty dollars for supplies," he said reluctantly. "And don't worry about that. I'll take care of it. It's the least I can do."

Libby shook her head. "No, I'll do it myself."

She saw his jaw clamp tight. He swung on his heels and in long loping strides moved toward the door, but not before she heard some of the words he was muttering under his breath. "Stubborn...hard-headed...exasperating...female...."

Even as she fingered the twenty-dollar gold piece in her pocket and blinked against the mist in front of her eyes, she couldn't help smiling.

CHAPTER FIVE

IT WAS TIME. Certainly this was the best opportunity Libby had found to go to the city without enduring another argument with Shamus. He'd left at dawn for a flight to St. Louis, and Eddie was at the airfield for the day. With a little luck she might even be back before either of them knew she was gone. Although, to be fair, she would leave a note pinned to her pillow.

With a look of disgust on her face, Libby pulled the ugly gray skirt and middy blouse from the back of the closet. She'd worn it only once, the day Shamus insisted she dress "properly" when he took her into Curruther's Corners to buy a pair of shoes. The general store had provided only a limited selection. Indeed, the only pair she'd found to fit was a lace-up oxford with a squat, ugly heel. Granny shoes, she called them, and although she was certainly no expert on twenties' styles, she would bet they were as unstylish as the hated dress.

It was now early September. The scar on her arm still showed red, but she'd regained the strength in her arm working on her airplane.

She'd carefully scrubbed the oil, dirt and grime from the surface of the plane in readiness for patching the torn fabric. The wing tip fabric, too heavily damaged for patching, had been cut away, exposing the wooden wing ribs. New linen would have to be stitched to the frame then covered with numerous coatings of the volatile dope mixture needed to strengthen the material into a slick hard finish.

Libby held her lucky gold piece between her fingers. Not enough, she knew, but there was another way. She had finally stopped going to bed at night hoping when she awoke she'd be back where she belonged. No, the cosmic clock was not going to adjust itself automatically. She was going to have to help herself, and the way to do that, she'd decided, was with her plane.

She'd planned carefully, spent hours studying the daily newspaper. This was, she read, the era of prosperity. Average wages were up to thirteen hundred dollars a year. All she had to do was find a job and earn the rest of the money she needed.

Libby knew she'd never find a job that paid anywhere close to that amount. In fact she suspected the quoted amount was an all-male average, anyway, but as a female she might expect to land a job for about half of that. Six hundred and fifty dollars a year, maybe two dollars a day. Impossible!

Look on the bright side, she reminded herself. She only needed about fifty dollars. If she was careful with spending money, she might have all she needed in a couple of months. She wouldn't need it in a lump sum, either. Once she had the cost of the linen, she could buy her other supplies in small quantities.

Shamus was still insisting he provide the repair supplies, but something in Libby prevented her from accepting. Was she afraid his help would be a pull to keep her here? Might even prevent her return? Maybe. All she knew was she had to do this herself.

She'd need new clothes, too, of course. She'd be lucky to land a job as a cleaning woman, dressed as she was, but that's where her twenty-dollar gold piece came in. The department stores were advertising ready-made dresses for as low as a dollar and forty-five cents. With careful selection, she should be able to outfit herself with a basic working girl's wardrobe and have enough left for train and trolley fare until payday.

Libby took a last look in the small shaving mirror above the sink, then carefully tied her gold piece into the corner of one of Shamus's handkerchiefs and tucked it securely into her waistband. She was ready.

As she walked down the dusty drive to the even dustier road, Libby couldn't help feeling exhilarated. It was a mile from the farmhouse into Curruther's Corners where she'd catch the ten-twenty train into the city. Although she knew it wouldn't look the same as it did in her time, Union Station had been at the same location since before World War I. From there she could catch a trolley downtown, or at least to an El transfer point. As she remembered, the elevated train that circled the downtown Loop had been in operation since before the war.

Once downtown, she was confident she could find her way around the twenties version of the shopping district. Many of the larger stores were, in her time, located along Michigan Avenue's Magnificent Mile, but the original shopping center had been several blocks south of Wacker Avenue along State Street. Carson Pirie Scott, Chicago's second most famous store, survived in the late twentieth century in its original building, designed at the turn of the century

by Louis Sullivan, one of the first builders of sky-
scrapers.

And Marshall Field's, the granddaddy of Chicago's department stores, with its Tiffany dome and its
giant brass over-the-sidewalk corner clocks, would be
standing where it had always stood, in the one hundred block of North State Street at the very heart of
the old shopping district.

Libby had worked at the giant store one summer in
high school. She couldn't help smiling at the thought
of what would happen if she dared to list that employment period on an application. But, she told herself, more seriously, if, as a green teenager, she'd been
able to convince the store to hire her, surely she could
do so again.

Several hours later Libby found herself on the lower
level of Marshall Field's, next to a bright red sign
reading "Coffee—5 cents." She had no intention of
wasting her small horde of money on lunch, but surely
she could afford a cup of coffee. Besides, she couldn't
pass up the experience of actually buying a cup of
coffee for a nickel. It would be like living a legend.

As she scooted onto the high counter seat, an over-
weight burly man plopped down on the next seat to
her, his large hand slapping a dollar bill against the
countertop as he called, "Coffee and apple pie."
Libby stared at the bill, similar to, yet completely different from any dollar bill she'd ever seen. When she'd
paid the ticket seller at the train station with her
twenty-dollar gold piece this morning, he'd muttered
something about "hard change" and handed her a
ticket and a fistful of coins. It had taken her a moment to realize the tiny yellow coins, mixed in with
silver and copper, were actually five-dollar gold pieces.

So petite in size, they seemed almost insignificant among the more familiar looking coins, and especially small in relation to the cartwheel silver dollars used in her world only in the gambling casinos of Nevada and Atlantic City.

She ordered a cup of coffee, smiling in return at the cheerful greeting of the counter girl. Then she carefully retrieved Shamus's handkerchief from her waistband and untied the knot that contained her money.

"The peach pie's real good today," the waitress told her. "It's only a dime."

Libby shook her head. "Coffee's fine."

"Well, if you change your mind, let me know. Coffee refills are free."

As Libby sipped her coffee, she watched the other customers at the counter. Women outnumbered men, the majority obviously shopping housewives. The more affluent shoppers would be lunching at one of the store's other, more elegant eating places. This luncheon counter was strictly for the budget-minded.

A small number of the counter customers were probably store clerks or office girls who worked nearby. But, Libby realized with a sense of disappointment, none were Marshall Field's employees. She placed her cup in the saucer with a sigh.

Employees probably weren't allowed to eat in public. Her walking tour of the store had given her an idea which departments employed women as clerks but no suggestion as to which ones might be hiring. She'd hoped to meet one of the clerks she'd seen and maybe discover which departments might be hiring before she invested in new clothes. Dress that was right for a position in first-floor lingerie would be wrong for the notions department or second-floor ladies' dresses. She didn't have enough money to make a mistake.

Caught in her own thoughts, Libby hardly noticed when the counter girl appeared in front of her. "Want a refill?" she asked.

"Yes, please," Libby told her. "And I think..."

"Hey, girlie, what're you trying to pull?" the man on the stool next to her suddenly bellowed. "You gave me change for a dollar. I gave you a fiver."

The counter girl stepped back. "No, sir, I'm sure it was a dollar."

"It was a five, I tell you. If you think you can cheat Gus Chambers, think again. You owe me four dollars."

Libby's gaze moved from the blustering man to the counter girl, who was nervously twisting her hands in front of her.

"What is going on here, Miss Riley?" a somber voice suddenly demanded from somewhere over Libby's shoulder.

He'd moved so quickly and so quietly Libby hadn't seen or heard him approach, but one look at his stern features and the conservative black suit with its white carnation pinned to his lapel had told her he was a floorwalker, the twenties version of store management and security guard.

It was not the first time in the past few weeks that Libby had had occasion to thank her penchant for television's late night movies. Who would ever have believed she'd need the apparently trivial information she'd retained from such shows?

"I'll tell you what's going on," the customer growled. "Your girl's trying to cheat me. Gave her a fiver, and she only gave me change for a dollar."

"I never did, Mr. Simmons. Honest. He ordered coffee and apple pie and put a dollar bill on the counter."

"Give the customer his change, Miss Riley, and I'll see you in the office."

The girl's face blanched and her eyes grew wide. "It was a dollar, Mr. Simmons, honest. I wouldn't..."

Libby knew she was going to have to get involved. If she read the expression on the floorwalker's face correctly, the girl was about to lose her job.

"Excuse me, sir," she said, speaking directly to the man in the black suit, "but if the gentleman would examine his wallet, I think he'll discover he was mistaken and that he still has his five-dollar bill. He paid his bill with a dollar. I saw it lying on the counter."

"You saw a five," the man argued.

Libby shook her head. "It was a one dollar bill. I particularly noticed George Washington's picture because it was so...so clear. So was the blue ink. It must have been a new bill."

"Would you like to check your wallet, sir, in the event Miss is correct?" the floorwalker asked in an emotionless voice.

Libby let out a carefully concealed breath of relief. She'd almost said that she'd noticed the bill because it was so large. And how would she have explained that comment?

Under the watchful eye of the floorwalker, the man retrieved a battered-looking wallet from his pocket, and with only a cursory look at its contents, grudgingly agreed that he might have made a mistake.

"Perfectly understandable, sir," the floorwalker said formally. "Mistakes do happen." Then with a curt nod to Libby and a quiet, "Be more careful, Miss Riley," he walked away.

Libby sat stoically, staring straight ahead as the customer hastily scooped his change from the top of the counter, then with a scowl in her direction, climbed off the stool and disappeared into a crowd of shoppers.

"Oh, miss, thank you. If you hadn't said something, Mr. Simmons would have fired me for sure," the girl told her.

Libby smiled and shook her head. "I didn't do anything special. I did see the dollar." Her face grew pensive. "Would he really have fired you? I mean, it was your word against that man's."

"Not with you sticking up for me that way. Oh, he wanted to, all right. I'm not one of his favorites, not proper enough, if you know what I mean. He's an old-fashioned stick. Tried to get me fired when I bobbed my hair, but he couldn't because there wasn't no rule against it. He can't this time, either, thanks to you. I want to thank you for that. My name's Maisie... Maisie Riley. If ever there's anything I can do for you, well, we Rileys don't forget a kindness done."

"You're welcome, Maisie. As I said, I'm glad I was able to help," Libby told her. "My name's Libby Carmichael."

Libby started to extend her hand, but stopped herself with an awkward gesture as she remembered handshakes between women were a thing of the future. She smiled instead, suddenly noting the girl's pinked cheeks as well as the twenties style bobbed hair half hidden under the waitress cap. She'd bet the below-the-knee skirt and large wraparound apron weren't the girl's usual dressing style, either. In fact, she'd bet she was talking to her first honest-to-goodness flapper.

"Look," Maisie said suddenly, "I noticed you didn't order anything to eat, and, well, I wondered... I mean, soon as the lunch crowd thins out, I'll be off work and eating my own lunch. I've got plenty, if you'd like to share. Really. I mean, I know how it is when—" She broke off.

"Thanks," Libby said quickly, trying to cover the awkwardness. "I'm really not very hungry, but I would like to talk with you. You see, I'm new in town. I could use a friendly ear and maybe some advice. I need a job. Do you know if the store's hiring?"

"You'll never get one, not here, I mean, not in those clothes," Maisie said bluntly, then, as if she'd suddenly realized what she'd said, her face flooded with color that almost but not quite concealed the spots of rouge on her cheeks. "Oh, my gosh, I'm sorry. I didn't mean... I mean I didn't..." Maisie's voice trailed off.

Libby liked Maisie's candor and could sympathize with her obvious embarrassment. She, too, often suffered from the speak-before-you-think syndrome. "How right you are," she told Maisie and gave the girl a grin. "This dress is impossible. A friend of a friend picked it out for me. I hated it on sight, but, well, I... I lost my luggage in an accident, so it's all I have to wear. That's why I need some advice. The styles are a little different here than where I come from. I'd really appreciate you giving me some tips and maybe the name of a shop or two. It's obvious I need to look like I shop here if I want to work here, but I doubt if I can afford that. I certainly can't afford to waste my money buying the wrong things."

Maisie nodded, her color receding to normal as Libby's explanation relieved her embarrassment. "I could do that," she said with obvious enthusiasm. "In fact, I think there's an opening in cosmetics. I heard this morning that Stella had to quit on account of her husband." Maisie shook her head in disgust and wrinkled her nose. "Said he didn't want a wife who worked. Didn't want a wife with any money she could call her own, I'll bet.

"Anyway," Maisie continued, "Stella's job is probably still open. You talk real educated. Mr. Gibbons in employment will like that. But you'll need an outfit to wear to employment as well as working clothes. Maybe we can... Uh-oh." She broke off quickly. "Mr. Simmons is heading this way," she whispered under her breath. "Meet me under the clock at the Washington entrance in an hour, okay?"

As Libby nodded in acknowledgement, Maisie moved to the other end of the luncheon counter. Libby slipped from the counter stool, hesitated for a moment, then deliberately turned away from the frowning floorwalker. She didn't like Mr. Simmons. Besides, she didn't want to give him another good look at her. She'd rather he didn't recognize Marshall Field's new cosmetics girl as the woman at the luncheon counter.

Counting your chickens before they hatch, she reminded herself, but somehow even the truth of that old saw didn't dampen her spirits. Surely a little late twentieth century knowledge of makeup art would be a plus. With Maisie's help maybe she could pull it off. She had to. Everything depended on her getting a job.

LIBBY CARMICHAEL was driving him crazy!

It was the only explanation, the only reason Shamus could give himself for being caught in the crush of cars that always clogged Michigan Avenue on Friday afternoons. Traffic jams in downtown Chicago got worse every week. He knew it. Everyone knew it. But he hadn't given the traffic a thought when he discovered Libby missing from the house.

He'd panicked in that first moment of discovery, afraid that Zeke had finally shown up, afraid that somehow Libby's part in rescuing him two months ago had been discovered, that she'd been taken hostage for the return of the suitcase.

Then he'd found her note. At first, relief replaced his fear. Frustration had followed. Now, he was just plain mad.

No doubt about it. She was driving him crazy. Why else would he be trying to find one lone woman in this crowd? He didn't even know where to look. "Gone shopping downtown," she'd said in her note. Shopping for what? Hadn't he told her he'd get anything she needed?

Shamus swore under his breath as the ugha-ugha sound of a car horn blasted somewhere behind him. Chicago's population now numbered nearly a million, and he'd bet every blasted one of them had picked this Friday afternoon to come downtown. He watched the people scurrying along the sidewalk, then looked again at the unbroken sea of cars in front, behind and on both sides of him. Too many cars. Someone should tell Mr. Ford to slow down production, give the road builders a chance to catch up.

But that wasn't his concern now. Libby was. How would he ever find her? He didn't even know where to look. Crazy, he repeated to himself. Absolutely bonkers.

He should go home. Wait for her there. Eventually she'd turn up.

But what if she didn't?

She wasn't used to Chicago, had probably never even been in a city as large as this one. And she was alone. She didn't have the slightest idea of what could happen, especially to unescorted ladies on a Friday night. Shoppers and shop girls would be heading home by now, would have caught the five-ten train. She hadn't. Union Station was the first place he'd looked.

One more time around the block. If he hadn't found a parking place by then, he'd head back to Union Station. Maybe she'd show up for the six-ten train. If she didn't . . . If she didn't, he'd decide what to do then.

Shamus turned onto State Street, still searching for a parking space when he saw a car pull out from the curb several feet in front of him. Ignoring the squeal of brakes and the sound of angry horns around him, he nosed into the just-vacated spot.

Although most of the stores had closed a short time ago, a few last-minute shoppers still lingered along State Street's sidewalks, inspecting merchandise in the windows, or stood bunched on the corners, waiting for the trolley. He walked slowly down the street, examining each group of people he passed. He reminded himself that this was a big city. He knew Libby could be anywhere, but surely this, the heart of the shopping district, was his best hope.

A group of young women on the other side of the street caught his attention. Shop girls, probably discussing plans for the weekend.

His eyes moved on, sweeping both sides of the street, stopping to examine a group under the Marshal Field's clock. Now there was a lady. A shaft of late afternoon sunlight slipped between the tall buildings, burnishing the dark curls peaking from beneath her smart cloche hat with auburn fire. She wore white gloves on her hands, and the dainty heels on her feet emphasized the smooth curving length of leg exposed by her knee-length dark pleated skirt.

He wasn't sure he approved this new look in fashion that made it hard at times to distinguish the ladies from the Ladies, but he certainly appreciated some of the benefits.

He moved closer, his gaze shifting to the woman's companion. One encompassing glance labeled her as flapper, a name originally bestowed on the young, trendsetting college girls who, defying fashion and common sense, let their rain galoshes flap unfastened around their ankles. The term was now used to describe any young girl who defied the censure of her elders by bobbing her hair, raising her hemline and rushing to meet the future.

This girl, in her bright pink dress, with her blond hair bobbed into a sleek cap that hugged her head and her hemline daringly short, certainly fit the description.

As he walked closer to the two women, his gaze moved on down the sidewalk, seeking Libby in each and every cluster of people along the way. He passed the clock, moving to the street edge of the sidewalk and let his gaze wander back for a last appreciative glimpse of the woman with auburn curls.

The glimpse of a flashing white glove and a particular movement of the woman's head brought him to a sudden frozen stop. Impervious to the jostling of other pedestrians pushing past him, Shamus, not quite ready to accept what he'd seen, turned for a closer look at the lady.

Logic told him the woman wasn't, couldn't be Libby, but that gesture, the way the woman had unconsciously tilted her chin was so familiar, so exactly like Libby's.

"Libby," he breathed, a sound so soft it was all but inaudible. "Libby?" This time his voice was stronger, the question in it more precise, but still not loud enough to travel from where he stood to the two women.

He was positive she couldn't have heard him, not above the clatter of automobiles along the crowded street or the chatter of pedestrians moving by. Perhaps it was a nudge of the subconscious that told her she was under observation. But for whatever reason, the woman turned her head toward him. Puzzled blue eyes met his, widening in surprise. Then she smiled.

Shamus almost gasped, so potent, so lethal was her smile. Even as the muscles across his lower torso tightened, he accepted the blow to his senses like a fighter receiving a well-placed punch to the solar plexus.

She danced toward him, radiating an unsuppressed excitement, and in a gesture as natural as sunlight grabbed his arm. "Shamus! Whatever are you doing here?"

With his senses still reeling from the effect of her smile, her touch on his arm threw his earlier fears and exasperation into turmoil. He almost bit his tongue in his effort not to tell her *exactly* what he was doing here. Disgusted with himself for his confusion and with Libby as the cause, Shamus shook his head, a dazed fighter trying to clear his senses from an unexpected blow.

If Libby realized his state of mind, she gave no indication of it. A determined effort allowed him to clench his hands into fists instead of following his inclination to grab her.

He took a deep steadying breath as Libby, still holding his arm, widened her smile.

"Oh, Shamus, guess what? I've got a job!"

Shamus blinked, her words destroying the rest of his control. Desperately he tried to hang on to the remnants of his temper, but it was too late.

"No," he roared, knowing even as the word escaped his lips that he was making a mistake.

Libby dropped his arm, stepping away from him as if his presence was poisonous.

"You, Shamus Fitzgerald," she told him fiercely, "can go straight to Hades."

One look at the determined tilt of her chin and the fury blazing from her eyes warned him he might have already arrived at that particular destination.

CHAPTER SIX

LIBBY HADN'T SAID A WORD, not one, during the entire drive from town to the farmhouse.

Neither had Shamus.

He'd decided to give her a chance to calm down before mentioning the job again, but as he turned the car onto the dusty driveway, a quick glance in her direction told him his strategy hadn't worked.

Sweet saints, she was in a huff, although for some reason, she seemed to be trying to hide it. At first glance she looked relaxed, her white-gloved hands resting casually in her lap. But that straight rigid back and the way she'd planted her feet firmly against the floorboard to prevent herself from swaying across the seat toward him every time the motorcar hit another rut told a different story. For sure it wasn't the scenery outside the windshield that kept her staring so straight ahead. If she'd chanced to glance in his direction since he'd bundled her into the front seat, he'd been unable to catch her at it. Besides, her chin was tipped forward at that obstinate angle he had learned to recognize.

Nope. No question about it. She was still mad, all right.

His fingers tightened around the steering wheel. Women! He'd never understand them, especially not this woman, not even if he lived a hundred years. Why was she so determined to refuse his help? Saints knew he'd do as much for any woman needing help, but in Libby's case, he owed her.

Mentally Shamus began to collect his arguments as he let the car roll to a stop at the side of the house. "Libby," he began quietly.

"I will not quit my job," she interrupted, each quiet word clipped and determined. "I'm sorry you disapprove, but this is something I have to do." Without waiting for him to answer she grabbed her packages from the floor, twisted the door handle and jumped down from the running board.

Muttering under his breath, Shamus slammed the door on the driver's side and hurried after her. Fire and damnation, wouldn't she even let him help her out of the motorcar or carry her packages? He caught up with her at the porch and took hold of her elbow, offering to assist her up the steps.

"But why?" he persisted. "Why do you want a job? I told you I'd take care of you. If you want anything, all you have to do is tell me."

When Libby stumbled on the step Shamus tightened his grasp on her elbow. She stepped quickly onto the porch, regaining her balance, and whirled to face him, effectively shaking loose his hold on her arm. Her eyes were wide and rounded in surprise, almost shock, as if she hadn't expected him to be there.

Bewildered, Shamus met her gaze. He'd seen that look once before, that first night when she'd opened her eyes to find him by her side. He'd felt the same shock, the same gut blow to his senses then as he did now. It was similar to the sensation of being caught in an accidental tailspin. All his senses screamed for action, but his mind urged caution, knowing if he made one wrong move he'd crash and burn.

"You don't understand," she said with visible effort. "I need the money to fix my Jenny."

"Dammit, Libby. I told you I'd repair your aeroplane. I owe you that much."

Libby hesitated. How could she explain? His casual touch on her arm had just confirmed what she'd already known. His touch pulsed and burned like a brand, stealing her breath and shaking her reason. She couldn't ignore the strange attraction that seemed to flow between them. When he'd taken her arm, she'd felt the shock right down to her toenails. But she didn't belong here. Not in this time. Not with Shamus. The longer she stayed the stronger the pull between them became.

She knew Shamus also recognized the attraction. She saw it in the way he looked at her, felt it even as she forced herself to keep her distance.

It wasn't right. It couldn't be. She was here by mistake. She didn't belong. He did. She had to get away, go home before she became hopelessly entangled in this time, before the pull between them became even stronger, before something irrevocable happened.

Her airplane was her way home. She didn't know how she knew or why it was, only that she had to get the Jenny airworthy...by herself. She couldn't expect Shamus's help. The ties between them were already too strong.

She shook her head. "No. It's something I have to do myself."

"Of all the ornery, pigheaded..."

Libby forced herself to take a deep calming breath. "Look, Shamus," she said, hoping she was succeeding in her effort to keep her voice calm and patient. "I'm not deliberately trying to make you mad or embarrass you, either, but what's the big deal? It's perfectly respectable for a woman to have a job. And this is a respectable job. I mean, I haven't hired out as a pilot or any of those other no-nos for ladies. Why, even the good people of Curruther's Corners will approve of your cousin working at Marshall Field's. Or at least none of them will criticize you because of it. And you know it. You can't give me one good logical reason not to keep my job."

Neither waiting for nor expecting an answer, Libby pulled open the screen door and stepped into the hallway, dumping her packages, her gloves and her hat on the hall seat before entering the parlor.

Once again Shamus followed.

"Can't you, just once, do as I ask?"

Libby studied his face. Shamus rarely asked, only ordered. Admittedly most of his orders were couched in the guise of polite requests, but orders just the same. So what was different this time? Why did she feel so uneasy? Although he was often dictatorial in his manner, she'd learned he usually had good reason for his actions, even if he declined to reveal them.

"I'm sorry, Shamus," Libby told him, "but I must do what I think best. You've given me no reason not to."

"Dammit, Libby," he began, then broke off abruptly. He shifted his weight.

"You'll have to give me a better reason than that."

"It's just... Well, it would be better if you stayed closer to home. Why take a chance..." His voice trailed off.

She was right, Libby thought. He was hiding something, something he didn't want her to know, something he'd decided she was better off not knowing.
Libby sighed. She had believed they'd already fought
this battle.

"A chance of what?" she asked softly.

"Nothing. I . . . I was thinking of something else."

"I don't believe you," she told him, "and you
might as well tell me what you meant, because I'll find
out in the end."

"All right. All right. Why take a chance of being
seen or recognized?" he said, unable to keep exasperation out of his voice.

"Recognized? But why should—" Libby began,
then broke off as she realized not only what he'd said,
but what he'd meant.

"A chance of being seen or recognized? It's the
bootleggers again, isn't it? Blast it, Shamus, I thought
you'd cleaned up that mess long ago. You said not to
worry, that all you had to do was talk to that Zeke
character. It's been over eight weeks. Haven't you
talked to him yet?"

"No, I haven't talked to him yet. Saints know, I've
tried. He's dropped from sight. But you don't have to
worry."

Libby groaned. "Oh, brother, does that sound familiar," she muttered.

"I only said it would be better if you stayed out of
sight," Shamus said defensively.

Libby thought for a moment. "If he hasn't been
found yet, he must be well and truly hidden. Right?
And if he talked to anyone before he disappeared and
told them about you or Eddie, then they would have
come looking by now. And they haven't, have they?"

Shamus shook his head. "No, not that I know of," he admitted.

"Then I don't see the problem. It's obvious Zeke doesn't want to be found. Maybe it's not as important as you thought." She shrugged her shoulders. "Maybe he just decided to forget the whole thing. I mean the plane burned, and the cargo in it. Right? Nothing he can do will change that. Maybe no one's even looking for him."

"They're looking," Shamus said. "Ah, hell, maybe you're right. At least you're right about there being no danger unless Zeke surfaces and talks. Otherwise there's no connection between us. No one else knew he'd hired Eddie or someone would have been here before now. So I guess you can keep the job."

"Well, thank you for your permission. I intended to anyway."

"Ah, Libby, don't be like that. I'm only trying to do what's best. I don't want you hurt."

"I know that," Libby said softly, unable to deny his plea. And she did believe he was trying to protect her . . . misguided as that protection might be.

Besides, this mess wasn't all his fault. She knew he blamed himself because she'd been shot. She felt guilty about that. It wasn't his fault she'd been above that pasture at that particular moment. That had been beyond the control of either of them—some trick of cosmic fate. But she couldn't explain that to him. All in all, the meeting had been fortunate for both of them. She'd gotten him safely away and he'd provided her with sanctuary in this time. She might have been in real trouble if she'd had to make her way in this world completely without support.

Libby remembered the relief she felt the first time she saw him, not even knowing who he was and long before she knew she'd crossed some kind of time barrier. Still confused, disoriented and lost, she'd seen him waving his arms to attract her attention, and for the first time since being pulled into the storm, she'd believed, really believed, that she'd survived. Her relief on seeing the other pilot had survived a crash had somehow translated into the belief that everything was going to be all right.

Mentally she replayed the scene in slow motion—Shamus beside the burning plane, Shamus walking toward her as if he hadn't a care in the world, dragging that ridiculous-looking battered suitcase with him....

Libby frowned, knowing something was wrong with that picture. Why had Shamus had a suitcase, especially a monster of that size? He wasn't that far from home, nor was the flight that long. He'd hung onto that suitcase even as he'd jumped onto the wing of her Jenny, hung on to it as he threaded his way through the wing wires to reach the front cockpit as bullets sprayed around them.

Why? And why was he so sure someone was still looking for Zeke?

Shamus must have seen the sudden questions in her eyes. "What's wrong, Libby?" he asked. "All I said was I didn't want you hurt. Surely that's not—"

"The hijackers were after more than a few cases of Scotch, weren't they?" She spoke out loud, even as she managed to put the pieces of the puzzle together. "It wasn't the Scotch they were after at all, was it, Shamus? It was the suitcase. What was in it?"

Shamus's color faded beneath his tan. His eyes shifted from her face to a spot somewhere behind her on the wall. "What suitcase?"

"You know very well which one. The one you dragged from the plane."

Silence stretched like a curtain between them. Shamus stood rigid, hands clenched at his sides, his mouth firmly clamped shut. But Libby was determined he'd answer.

"That's it, isn't it? That's why you're so sure they're still looking for Zeke. They want the suitcase. What's in it? Where did you put it?"

Shamus let out a sound between a growl and a groan. "Forget it, Libby. As you said, Zeke appears to be well and truly hid. Just forget it."

"No," Libby told him, refusing to back down. "What was in it?" she demanded again.

"You don't want to know."

"I most certainly do," she answered. "Shamus..."

Shamus couldn't figure out how she did it, but one way or another, she always managed to wear him down, to frustrate, exasperate and drive him completely around the bend. He wondered if anyone or anything had ever made her back down once she made up her mind. Saints knew he hadn't been able to.

"All right, all right," he told her, his exasperation evident in his voice. "Since you insist on knowing, I'll tell you. The suitcase contains a sizable fortune, all in neatly bundled packages of greenbacks, and all, I'm sure, completely illegal. Now, Miss I-have-to-know, are you satisfied?"

"Money? The suitcase is filled with money? You've still got it?"

"Of course I've got it. What am I supposed to do with it? Why do you think I'm looking for Zeke?"

"Get rid of it. For heaven's sake, Shamus, why did you get mixed up in it? It's dirty money. It's... it's dangerous."

Shamus gave a bitter laugh. "Sure an' I know it's dirty and it's dangerous. What do you think I've been trying to tell you? And how the hell am I supposed to get rid of it if I can't find Zeke? I don't know who it belongs to. What am I supposed to do, walk up to Capone and say, 'Excuse me, Big Al, but did you by any chance lose a suitcase full of money?' Or I could ask Moran instead. Either way, I can imagine the reaction. Neither one of them would wait for explanations. I'd be alive only long enough to hand it over."

Shamus paused for a breath and, seeing the look on Libby's face, forced himself to lower his voice. "So far no one knows I have it or that I was involved with Zeke at all. But if either one of them finds him first, that won't last long. He doesn't have the suitcase, and believe me, it won't take him long to tell them who does."

"Why not let the police—"

Shamus threw up his hands. "Now that's a dandy idea. If, and it's a big if, I managed to find an honest one, what makes you think he'd believe me? But chances are better that whoever I turned it over to would have the word on the street in minutes. Whoever owns that money wouldn't hesitate to kill me out of frustration if not out of revenge for turning it over to the police."

"Okay, okay, I get the picture," Libby said, taking a step backward. Thankfully, she felt the edge of the couch behind her just as her knees gave out.

Shamus moved toward her. "Ah, hell. I had no business telling you. I'm sorry I lost my temper."

Dazed, Libby shook her head. "You should have told me weeks ago. Maybe we could have figured out something."

"No. Dammit, Libby, that's why I didn't tell you. I didn't—I don't want you having anything to do with it."

"Believe me, I don't want to have anything to do with this mess, either," she told him. "But it seems to me that option was lost the minute I landed my plane in a certain field and picked up a certain gentleman carrying a certain suitcase. The question now is what's next?"

"Nothing," Shamus said flatly. "You don't do a thing. I keep on quietly looking for Zeke and trying to find out who he was working for without raising any suspicions."

Libby shivered. She supposed she couldn't really blame Shamus for trying to keep her out of it. He'd kept his secret to protect her, just as she was keeping her secret to protect him. That thought didn't comfort her one bit.

Shamus was in real danger! A couple of cases of booze were one thing, a suitcase full of money quite another. If they found out, if they found him... She shivered again.

"Ah, lass," Shamus said softly, joining her on the couch, "I didn't mean to be scaring you. That's why I didn't want you to know. Come on, now. Stop your trembling."

Libby was only vaguely aware when he gathered her into his arms. She knew he was trying to offer comfort, but it wasn't working.

What, she wondered, would he think if he knew it was her fear for him, not herself, that was making her tremble? She'd be away from here soon, back where she was supposed to be. She was convinced of it. But what about Shamus? They'd never stop looking, not with a suitcase full of money involved.

"Nothing's changed," he told her. "I promised I'd take care of you and I will."

Think, Libby, think, she told herself. *You don't know how or why you came here.* What if it was for some specific reason? To help Shamus and Eddie? Neither of their names appeared in the history books, not that she could remember. But what if they, or one of them, was supposed to? What if being here wasn't an accident, but some cosmic plan? She had foreknowledge, at least in this time, even if it was somewhat sketchy. But what? What did she know that would help? She had to do something. She was as convinced of that as she was that one day she'd go home. One thing for sure, she'd never find out staying hidden here at the farmhouse.

"I'm keeping my job," she said quietly. "Knowing about . . . about . . . Well, it doesn't change that."

"All right," Shamus said reluctantly. "It might not be a bad idea, anyway. If anyone comes looking—in the daytime, anyway—at least you'd be safely away."

"Shamus, if you knew for sure who Zeke was working for, what would you do?"

"I'd turn the suitcase over to him. I don't want it. But first I have to be sure. If I turn it over to Capone when it belongs to Moran, or vice versa, the fat will be in the fire."

"And what are you doing to find out?"

"Mostly keeping my ears open," he admitted. "I don't dare ask too many questions. The wrong person might hear about it."

Oh, Lord, what a mess. It sounded like one of those damned-if-you-do, damned-if-you-don't puzzles to Libby. Shamus had to know, but didn't dare ask to find out. On the other hand, the information wasn't likely to just fall into his lap, either. Maybe if...

"Shamus," she said quickly, "you said no one would suspect me of being a pilot or of having anything to do with rescuing you. What if I tried to find out who Zeke worked for? I mean, I could be an old girlfriend or a cousin or something. I could ask around and—"

"No! No, Libby. Leave it alone," he repeated. "All we need is the wrong question to the wrong person to lead right back to me, and if you were asking questions, they'd never believe you weren't involved. After all, you're supposed to be my cousin. You stay out of it. Then no one will believe you know anything about it. I mean, after all, women don't..."

Libby gritted her teeth and lifted her hands in a gesture of surrender. She'd do what she had to do, but there was no need arguing the point.

"Don't tell me. I know. Women don't involve themselves in such matters."

Shamus nodded, giving a sigh of relief. "That's what I've been trying to tell you," he said. "Praise the saints, you're finally listening."

Libby pulled herself away from him, thankful to find that once again her knees were steady. "If that's all for now, I'm going to change."

She kept her eyes averted as she moved toward the door. One small gesture, one sign of encouragement from her and he'd have her in his arms again. She couldn't afford that. But dear Lord, how she wanted to. She stopped to retrieve her packages, determined to act as if she didn't feel his eyes following her every move.

"Libby," he said, his voice suddenly soft, its tone as startling as that rumble from deep in his chest. It was almost as physical as a touch.

Libby jerked her head up to discover him standing beside her. She swallowed trying to gain control of her chaotic emotions. When he reached out to touch her, she took a hasty step backward.

Shamus frowned and let his hand drop to his side. The look in his eyes was confused, wounded. It took all Libby's determination to stop herself from reaching out to him. But she couldn't do it, couldn't allow herself or him that small comfort. *He belongs here. I belong in my own time. We don't belong together.*

"I...I just wanted to tell you, I like your new dress."

Libby couldn't move.

He hesitated another second, then turned abruptly toward the door. "Guess I'd better go over to the airfield and check in with Eddie." Then he was gone.

Libby leaned weakly against the doorframe, blinking back sudden tears. *He belongs here. We don't belong together.* She couldn't let anything happen between them, no matter what she wanted.

Why, drat it, did he have to be the man who could turn her knees to jelly with a single look? It simply wasn't fair. But there didn't seem to be anything she could do about it. So that was that. Better to stick to her original plans, get her plane repaired and go home. The sooner she was away, the better for both of them.

In the meantime, Shamus had landed himself in a fine pickle, as Howard would say. He needed help, no matter how he tried to deny it. It had been eight weeks and he was no closer to solving his problem with the suitcase then he'd been in the beginning.

Libby sighed. She still thought her idea was a good one. She had a better chance of finding out who owned the suitcase than he did. Shamus obviously didn't think much of her acting abilities. If only he knew...

Libby couldn't help smiling at the thought. She realized part of his refusal of help was fear for her safety. She was neither surprised nor offended by his attitude. After all, in the mid-twenties, women were just beginning to emerge from the kitchen. At least he treated her like an intelligent being—most of the time, anyway—and that was by no means the universal attitude of the times.

She'd do it anyway. Help him whether he approved or not. What Shamus didn't know wouldn't hurt him.

She'd bet Capone was the key. History said he'd survived the gang wars to become kingpin. She'd have to find a way to meet him, some way that wouldn't arouse suspicion or lead back to Shamus if anything went wrong.

She'd heard Capone often visited speakeasies in the city. She'd bet he owned several of them in addition to being the bootleg supplier for more. Which ones? she wondered. Would Maisie know? The girl had said she liked new jazz, and Libby would bet she didn't just listen to it on the radio.

That was it! She'd ask Maisie if there was any way she could meet Capone. If Maisie couldn't help, well, maybe something else would turn up, especially if her idea of being here for a purpose was correct.

In the meantime, she'd get the work started on her Jenny. "God helps those who help themselves," she reminded herself. When the time came for her to go home, she wanted to be ready.

CHAPTER SEVEN

LIBBY PEERED DOWN the dimly lit street. There was no one on the sidewalk, no cars on the street. In fact, with the exception of an occasional light shining through drawn shades, there were no signs of life at all. She didn't know what she'd expected, but this quiet, dead-looking neighborhood definitely wasn't it.

She tried to ignore the shiver of fear running down her spine. When Maisie told her that rumor said Capone was supposed to be at the Lazy Cat tonight, Libby had known this was her chance. The timing couldn't have been better. Shamus wasn't due in from a flight to St. Louis until just before dark. By then Libby would have already left for downtown. He wouldn't know what she was up to until it was too late to stop her. And if she managed to speak to Capone, to find out if Zeke had ever worked for him, Shamus wouldn't be able to stay mad.

Her only miscalculation had been thinking she could get away from the farmhouse without letting Eddie know where she was going. But the boy had proved unbelievably persistent, and had taken the watchdog role Shamus had assigned him seriously. She'd been unable to leave without him shadowing her. Now she had not only herself but Eddie to worry about, and the atmosphere on the dark, deserted street wasn't doing anything to preserve her confidence.

"If your friend gave you the right address, it should be halfway down the block," Eddie said from behind her.

"Are you sure? It seems so quiet."

"They wouldn't want the neighbors complaining," Eddie assured her. "The club'll be in the basement. Holds down the noise. All these old houses have below street entrances. That's where the band and dance floor will be, anyway. Might have a couple of gaming rooms and, uh . . . well, other kinds of entertainment in the upstairs rooms, but they don't make so much noise."

Libby gave him a suspicious look over her shoulder. "Sounds like you've been here before."

"I've been in a few speakeasies," Eddie told her, "not this one, though. I think most of them are pretty much the same."

Libby nodded. She hesitated for a moment, then turned to make one last plea. "I really wish you'd go home now, Eddie. I'm grateful you came this far with me, but Shamus is going to be furious. There's no need for you to get in trouble, too."

Eddie grinned. "Shamus is gonna spit nails. But I'd be in even more trouble if I let you go by yourself." His grin faded. "I sure hope you know what you're doing. I wish you'd wait for Shamus."

Libby shook her head. "I can't wait, Eddie. I explained that. Capone's supposed to be here tonight, not some other time."

"Well, Shamus ain't gonna like it. But if you're going, I'm going. Once you're inside, I'll wait a few minutes before coming in. Don't worry about me."

"Maisie said this was a nice club."

"I hope she's right, but don't forget, if it looks like trouble's coming, get out fast. I'll be right behind you."

Eddie was so solemn in assuming the role of adviser that Libby almost smiled. His acceptance of the idea that something might go wrong with her plan made Libby hesitate again. She knew she was right to attempt this, even if it was risky and even if she knew Shamus would disapprove. Whether he admitted it or not, Shamus needed her help. Eddie at risk, however, was another matter.

"Eddie, if you won't go home, why don't you wait outside. That way..."

Eddie shook his head. "If you go, I go. And if we are going, we'd better get moving. We're going to start attracting attention, standing around on the corner like this. There might be eyes behind some of those shades."

For a moment Libby almost backed out. She weighed the pros and cons one last time.

"Libby?"

"I'm going. I'm going," she said quickly, and before she could change her mind, walked down the sidewalk, resisting the urge to look over her shoulder. One house, two, three. There it was. The drapes on the first floor window facing the street were open only enough to expose a lifelike statue of a sleeping cat.

Libby put her hand on the wrought-iron banister leading from the sidewalk down the partly enclosed stairwell to a solid wood door at the bottom of the steps. She managed to stifle a nervous giggle when she saw that the door, illuminated by a small light above it, was painted green.

A green door, for heaven's sake! Nervously, she looked over her shoulder, then rapped a quick tattoo with her knuckles. When a sliding panel suddenly opened, she jumped backward, managing to swallow a small scream.

"R—Roy sent me," she stammered to the unblinking eyes behind the screen. The peephole panel remained open for a moment, then slammed shut with a decisive click. A moment later, the green door swung slowly inward.

Drawing a breath for courage, Libby stepped over the threshold into a small, dimly lit hallway. Her fingers twisted the chain handle of her beaded bag as she tried to ignore the tickling of the ostrich plume tucked into her hair.

"Club or game rooms?" asked a rough-sounding voice behind her.

"Club," she said, peering into the shadows behind her. All she could see was the dim outline of a man. "I'm . . . I'm meeting friends," she added nervously.

"Straight ahead," the voice told her.

Libby nodded, then walked down the narrow hallway until she came face to face with another door. This one was also painted green, and it had neither peephole nor doorknob—at least, none she could see. She shrugged her shoulders, then with a show of courage she wasn't feeling, knocked.

The door swung open quickly and quietly. Bright light, the chatter of voices and the wailing sounds of a muted trumpet greeted her. Libby breathed a sigh of relief. This was more like it, more what she'd expected.

A large mirrored ball, rotating slowly, hung from the ceiling in the middle of the room, dispersing twinkles of light onto the dancers below. Small round tables and chairs stood in shadows beyond the edge of the brightly illuminated dance floor.

From the bandstand the closing refrains of a tune Libby recognized as "I'll See You in My Dreams" wavered in the air for a moment, then swung into the rhythm of "Yes, Sir, That's My Baby." Couples began moving off the floor, making room for a half dozen ladies spotlighted as they began the lively foot-swinging movements of the Charleston.

Libby peered anxiously into the dimly lit area until, with a rush of relief, she spotted Maisie's familiar face at a table near the bandstand.

"Is he here yet?" she whispered to Maisie as she slid into one of the small wooden seats.

Maisie shook her head. "Not yet. He might not even come. Roy just happened to mention that Capone liked the band's new trumpet player. The band's moving to a new gig in New York tomorrow, so he said Capone might come for their last night."

Libby tried to still the butterflies in her stomach, telling herself she only felt nervous because Maisie looked so worried.

"I don't know why you'd want to meet him, anyway," her friend continued. "He's not a very nice man."

"I know he's not," Libby agreed, "and I only want to talk to him for a minute." She hesitated, then sighed. "It's a long story, Maisie, and better for you if you don't know it."

"Well, I just hope you know what you're doing because—" She broke off abruptly when a man suddenly slid into an empty seat on the other side of the table.

"Hey, Maisie, this the friend you were expecting? Let me buy you two girls a drink."

"I don't—" Libby began, stopping abruptly when she felt a quick kick against her ankle.

"Thanks, Roy," Maisie said quickly. "We'd like that. Libby, this is my friend Roy. Roy, meet Libby."

"Hi, Libby. Maisie said her friend was pretty. She was right. This your first visit to the Lazy Cat?"

Libby nodded. "Thank you for letting me come."

"Any friend of Maisie's is a friend of mine, right, Peanuts?"

Maisie grimaced. "My name's not Peanuts. I'm grown up now," she told the man, then turned to Libby. "Roy's from my old neighborhood," Maisie explained. "He runs the Lazy Cat."

"Just assistant manager, Peanuts," he said grinning at Maisie's scowl. "But what the hay? That's good enough to get a couple of drinks on the house. Advertising, you know. Besides, you two Shebas add a bit of class to the place. So what'll you have?"

Libby, who usually limited her alcoholic beverages to an occasional beer with her pizza or a small glass of white wine before dinner, glanced anxiously at the shot glasses filled with dark, ominous-looking liquids on the adjoining tables. Somehow, she doubted if her usual order would be appropriate. She gave Maisie an anxious glance.

"A cocktail, I guess," Maisie said. "How about a Between the Sheets?"

"Sure," Roy said. "How about you, Libby? Name your giggle water."

"Ah, a Between . . . I guess I'll have the same," she finally managed to stammer.

"You want to try a Bee's Knees, instead?" Roy asked, apparently detecting her inexperience. "It's made with gin instead of brandy."

Libby smiled her gratitude. "That sounds good. Okay, I'll try it."

"One BTS and a Bee's Knees coming up. Don't go away. I'll be right back."

Maisie giggled. "Oh, Libby, if you could have seen your face. Haven't you ever had a Between the Sheets before?"

Libby shook her head. Sexual liberation, at least as expressed in language, had evidently begun earlier than she'd believed. The 1920s just might have been able to tell the 1960s something. "A Between the Sheets? I've never even heard of one. I can't believe they named a drink that."

"Everybody says they're good. I don't really like them that much, but I had to order something. For a minute there I was afraid you were going to say you didn't drink."

"I don't, not much, anyway. Is that why you kicked me under the table?"

"'Course it is. If you don't drink, what kind of reason you got for coming to a drinking club?"

"You're right. I'm sorry, Maisie, I wasn't thinking. But I won't be able to drink too much," Libby warned her.

"Doesn't matter. If you just sip, you can make one drink last a long time. That's what I do. Roy doesn't mind, so long as we dance with some of the customers. He likes you. I could tell. He might even ask you to dance himself. What do you think?"

"About what?"

"About Roy, of course. Do you like him?"

Like him? Libby realized she hadn't even paid him much attention. Now that she thought about it, she guessed one would call him fairly handsome, but compared to Shamus, he'd made little impression. Oh, Lord, what had made her think of that!

"He seems nice enough, I guess," Libby told her, stalling for time. "But I thought he was your boyfriend."

"Roy? No how. I told you, he's from my old neighborhood. Used to tie my pigtails together when I was a kid. He's a good sort, I guess. Roy was my brother's best friend when they were growing up. Now Roy's a bootlegger and Frank's a cop." Maisie sighed. "That's what happened to most of the kids in my old neighborhood, you know. If you grew up on Archer Avenue, you grew up tough. Most of the boys are either bootleggers or cops. The girls married their old school sweethearts and now they sit home taking care of the kids, worrying about their husbands getting shot and wondering which old friend is going to do it. Don't matter which side they're on. One's about as good a target as the other. That's not for me. I don't date anybody from the old neighborhood."

Roy returned with their drinks, then, to Libby's relief, rushed back to the bar. She scanned the crowd, looking for Eddie, finally locating him on the other side of the room and silently giving thanks when she saw the beer mug in front of him. She knew better than to hope the mug would contain sarsaparilla, but at least beer wasn't as potent as most of the bootleg liquor available.

Libby watched the dancers anxiously, remembering Maisie's statement that she would have to dance. After a minute or so, she began to relax. She couldn't help enjoying the sweet jazz and swing music of the band. She knew she wouldn't be a star performer, but decided, if she had to, she should be able to fake most of the steps. She had the opportunity to prove her theory a few minutes later when she gave in to Maisie's silent urging when Roy returned to the table to ask her to dance.

Roy turned out to be an enthusiastic if not polished dancer. When he returned her to the table Libby was laughing and a little breathless from her efforts to follow his lead through the band's lively version of "Keep Your Skirts Down, Mary Ann." She'd found herself enjoying the dance and fully expected him to ask for a second when a sudden disturbance at the door drew his attention.

She heard Maisie's quickly drawn breath when a group of six men entered and then stopped in front of the door. "Torpedoes," Roy muttered under his breath, then hurried toward them.

"What did he say?" Libby asked.

"Torpedoes. You know, hired gunmen," Maisie explained.

Libby drew a quick breath. "Is it him? Capone?" she asked, fear tightening her vocal cords. Now that the moment was almost here, she found herself wishing she'd never thought of this plan. Reading about Al Capone in the history books, even in the newspapers was one thing. Actually confronting him was another.

This was for Shamus, she reminded herself. She could do it. She wouldn't let herself chicken out now.

"It's not Big Al," Maisie whispered. "The man in brown, that's Bugs Moran. He shouldn't be here. This is Capone's territory. There's going to be trouble."

"But what . . ."

"Either Moran heard Capone was going to be here and plans a showdown or Big Al wanted Moran to think he was going to be here and it's a trap."

The room had become hushed, making the band sound even louder. As Roy led the group of men across the room toward a table on the other side of the bandstand, the low hum of conversation began again.

"I don't like this," Maisie said. "Come on, let's get out of here."

Libby quickly searched the crowded room for Eddie and finally saw him standing by the green door. He must have had the same idea as Maisie. A look of relief crossed his face when his eyes locked with hers. When he made a motion toward the door Libby grinned in relief and nodded. Eddie slipped out the door.

Maisie stood up and casually began walking toward the back of the room. Puzzled, Libby followed her. "The door's the other way," she whispered in her friend's ear.

Maisie shook her head. "Not that door. We'll find another way."

Recognizing and accepting the extent of her friend's fear, Libby frantically looked toward the door. Eddie was outside by now. He'd be waiting for her.

"What's going to happen?" she whispered to Maisie, not really wanting to know the answer, but afraid not to hear it.

"Maybe nothing," Maisie whispered back. "But I don't like it. Moran may be waiting for Capone or Capone might have planned a trap for Moran. There's no time to think about it now. Come on. Maybe we can . . ."

The rest of her sentence was drowned out by the sudden ringing of an alarm bell. Libby looked over her shoulder to see one of the waiters place a thick bar across the door she'd entered.

"It's a raid," Maisie shrieked. "Just my luck. And Frank will probably be first through the door. Oh, Lord, Libby, if my brother finds me here, he'll most likely kill me. Or drag me home to Mom, which will be even worse. Come on, this way. Hurry," Maisie urged.

Most of the club's patrons were suddenly moving toward the same corner of the room as she and Maisie. Above the shrieks, yells and other sounds of pandemonium, Libby thought she detected the sound of running footsteps from above. The band broke in the middle of a ballad, then plunged into a lively polka. As noise and a rising hysteria continued among the customers, the band played on, its volume increasing even as the crescendo of noise in the club increased.

"Too late," Maisie hollered to make herself heard above the noise. "They've found the back door, too. Come on, this way." With a quick look over her shoulder to see if Libby was following, she began pushing her way out of the crowd.

Now was not the time to ask questions, Libby decided as she plunged blindly after Maisie. She could only hope the girl knew what she was doing. Dear Lord, she prayed silently, please let Eddie get away.

Even above the roar of the crowd, Libby heard the sound of splintering wood behind her. The barred door hadn't stopped them long.

"Quick, under here," Maisie said as she lifted a piece of the dusty skirting covering the back of the bandstand. Libby ducked under the curtain, her eyes scanning the area supporting the high bandstand. In the dim light she could barely make out the cross timbers bracing the structure above them. She only had time to spot three main support columns before Maisie joined her under the bandstand, dropping the skirting behind her. Now their only illumination was an occasional pinprick of light from tiny holes and tears in the skirting.

Libby stood still for a moment, consciously trying to remember the location of the support columns and letting her eyes adjust to the small amount of available light. "Take hold of my shoulder and keep your head down," Libby whispered to Maisie. "Anybody who lifts the skirting will see us if we just stand here. I think I can remember the direction to one of the larger supports. Maybe it's big enough to hide behind. But be careful. With all the bracing, it's going to be like trying to find our way through a maze blindfolded."

It took them several minutes and one near fall before Libby felt the dimensions of the wooden column beneath her hand. She knew they weren't truly hidden, but perhaps they would escape detection if the area wasn't given a close inspection. At least they were far enough back from the perimeter of the bandstand to not be seen immediately if someone raised the curtain and just glanced in.

The band had finally given up the effort to disguise the sounds of the panic produced by the raid. There was no music from above now, only the sound of hoarse shouts, the tinkling of glass being broken and the gurgling sound of liquid being poured out.

"They must be dumping the kegs," Maisie whispered. "Uck. You can even smell it. Poor Roy. He's going to have a mess to clean up this time."

"This time? You mean this has happened before?"

"Well, of course," Maisie told her. "Every couple of months, anyhow. Roy says its all part of doing business. All the speakeasies get raided, kinda on a schedule, he said. Convinces the drys that the police are doing their duty. Frank says most of the cops are honest, even if they don't like trying to enforce prohibition, but there are enough dishonest ones that someone nearly always tips off the speakeasy before the raid starts. Usually they don't find more than a night's supply of liquor behind the bar. I don't think Roy knew about this one, though, or he'd have told me to leave. He knows Frank'll have a fit if he ever catches me in a raid. He'd be mad at Roy, too."

"What are you doing?" Libby asked when she heard Maisie moving around behind her.

"Fixing to sit down, that's what. You might as well, too. We're going to be here awhile."

Libby wasn't sure how long they waited in the dark. The sounds in the club faded, telling them that most of the Lazy Cat's customers were gone, though whether they had managed to escape or been arrested, Libby had no way of knowing. But there were still several people in the club. She could hear the low rumble of voices and the occasional tinkle of another glass bottle being broken. In the almost silence they heard the sound of footsteps approaching their hiding place several times, and each time held their breath until the sounds moved away.

As footsteps approached once again, Libby felt herself stiffen. She could feel Maisie doing the same beside her. This time, as she waited in the dark, Libby realized the footsteps weren't moving away as quickly as before. Her breath became shallow, then stopped altogether when she heard the rustling of the skirting.

Libby blinked as light from the raised curtain penetrated their hiding place, then swallowed a scream when a flashlight caught her squarely in its beam. The beam wavered for a moment before moving to Maisie.

"Mary Margaret Riley, what are you doing here?" a voice behind the light beam whispered frantically.

Libby felt Maisie flinch. "Go away," her friend whispered resolutely.

The curtain dropped. The sound of footsteps moved on around the bandstand, stopping at a position nearer them. Once more the curtain moved.

"Go away," Maisie ordered again.

This time Libby could see the policeman more clearly. He was young, probably about Libby's age, with red hair, freckles and a mouth that looked as if it was used to smiling. At the moment, however, his expression was worried.

"Hush," he whispered. He looked over his shoulder, then made a show of poking at the skirting. "Just keep quiet. I'll be back to get you after we've got the place padlocked and everyone's gone. You hear me, Mary Margaret? Stay right where you are. Don't try to get out on your own. You'll get caught sure."

Maisie clutched at Libby's hand. In the near darkness Libby saw her friend nod. The light beam flickered across the floor, then disappeared as the opening in the curtaining was dropped, once again plunging them into almost total darkness.

Both girls held their breath as they heard a second set of footsteps approaching.

"All clear back here?" they heard a male voice ask.

"All clear," a second voice replied. "I even checked under the bandstand. Nothing there but some dust and a bunch of mouse droppings."

Libby stifled a shiver of disgust. She suspected Maisie was doing the same.

"Okay," said the voice again. "Let's get this place boarded up and get back to the station."

Libby slowly released her breath as the sound of two sets of footsteps receded into the distance. Moments later, even the small pinpricks of light shining through the bandstand skirting disappeared. Now it was truly dark.

Libby waited for a minute or two, until all sound had disappeared as completely as the light. Maisie hadn't made a sound, had, in fact, hardly moved since her whispered command to the young policeman to go away.

"Who is he? Did he really say he'd be back?" Libby asked in a whisper. She wasn't taking any chances, even if it did seem the club was deserted.

"Joseph Francis McGillicutty," Maisie answered in a whisper that failed to disguise her unhappiness. "And yeah, he'll be back. But it might be awhile."

The sound of depression in Maisie's voice surprised Libby. She didn't think her friend's mood was caused by fear of being caught in the raid. It was obvious the young policeman knew Maisie and he'd promised to help. If anything, Maisie should be feeling more cheerful.

"I'll bet he's from your old neighborhood, too," Libby said in a joking voice. "He seemed nice. You could tell he was worried about you."

"I guess," Maisie said. "We used to be good friends, but he doesn't approve of me now."

"You don't know that," Libby told her. "After all, he could have arrested us. Or if he didn't want to do that, he could have just left us here to find our own way out. Instead, he warned us we'd get caught if we tried and told us to wait until he could help. Sounds to me like he likes you a lot."

"Maybe," Maisie finally agreed. "He asked me to go to the Policemen's Ball with him last year."

"That doesn't sound like he disapproves to me. Did you have fun?"

"I didn't go. I told you, I don't date guys from my old neighborhood."

"Oh." Libby didn't know what else to say. It sounded to her as if Maisie wished she hadn't made that rule.

Libby shifted uneasily, not wanting to knock against any of the cross braces supporting the bandstand. She wasn't sure how well they were anchored. Time seemed to have stopped, aided by the darkness and silence around them.

Had Eddie escaped the raid? She had to believe he had. It had been several minutes after he disappeared out the door that the raid alarm sounded. She knew he'd be frantic when he couldn't find her. She could only hope he'd realize she was hidden safely inside. She knew he wouldn't go home and leave her to find her own way.

"How...how long do you think we'll have to wait?" Libby asked.

"Probably an hour. Maybe more," Maisie told her.

Libby felt her heart sink. Eddie might wait for her awhile, but not that long. He'll go to Shamus for help, she realized with a sudden dread.

She'd known Shamus would be mad when he found out what she'd done, but she'd counted on being home safe and sound before he found out. If Eddie went to him with the story that she was missing... Oh, dear heaven, he was going to be furious!

CHAPTER EIGHT

LOOKING FOR LIBBY Carmichael was getting to be a
habit—a circumstance Shamus found increasingly
frustrating. Sweet saints! The woman was driving him
crazy. In the few short months since she'd appeared
above that pasture she'd managed to turn his life upside down. She was stubborn, exasperating, infuriating and this time—this time she had gone too far.

Hadn't he told her to stay away from Capone?
Hadn't he told her he'd find Zeke Vincent without her
help? Where was she now?

Eddie swore she wasn't among the customers arrested in tonight's raid on the Lazy Cat. The boy had
made it outside only minutes before Chicago's finest
swarmed into the illegal drinking club. He'd hidden in
the shadows, watching the club's customers and employees being loaded into the paddy wagons, until the
premises were emptied and the doors padlocked. After the paddy wagons left, he'd searched the surrounding neighborhood, but he hadn't been able to
find a sign of Libby.

Deliberately Shamus fed his anger in his attempt to
keep his fears at bay as he followed Eddie's directions
through Chicago's dark streets. After hearing Eddie's
story, Shamus was convinced Capone had planted the
rumors he would be at the club tonight to lure Moran
into the open. The raid had been a trap. War between

the two gangland lords was heating up. It wouldn't take Moran long to retaliate, and with Libby missing, she might well be caught in the middle.

Shamus almost wished Libby had been arrested. At least he'd know where she was, and a few hours in jail might have taught her a lesson.

But she wasn't in jail. He'd checked there first. And if Eddie was right, she hadn't escaped the club, either. Could she be trapped inside, waiting, hiding? Was she afraid of the dark? What if she'd been injured, falling unnoticed in the mad scramble of customers to make the exits as the raiding police swept through the front door?

Shamus tried to ignore his fears as he neared his destination. He parked on an adjacent street and moved cautiously down the alley toward the club. The building looked dark, deserted. Boards nailed across the splintered front door told the story of the recent raid.

He circled the building slowly, looking for another entrance. A window tucked into the dark recesses of the back porch seemed to be his best bet, he decided. Once inside he'd be able to find an entrance from the ground floor into the basement.

As he looked around for something to pry up the sash, he heard a slight sound, then saw a flicker of light in the alley. Wondering who else might be prowling around the padlocked club, Shamus flattened himself against the building and waited, all senses alert.

He saw the cop first, the brass buttons on his blue uniform catching the dim light as the man pulled himself through the small alley-level window.

Shamus frowned, trying to make sense of the scene. The raid was over, the club padlocked. So what would one of Chicago's finest be doing crawling out a window of the club?

He had his answer seconds later when a small blond woman came scrambling through the window on her hands and knees. The knowledge that he was witnessing a rescue, not an arrest, registered on his subconscious at the same time he realized the woman looked vaguely familiar. Then a second face appeared in the window.

Libby! It was Libby, her tousled curls looking almost black in the night. Caught in the beam of the policeman's flashlight, her eyes were wide and dark in her white face. There was a smudge of something on her cheek, and a broken ostrich feather dipped forlornly over her left eye, but she was smiling as she began wiggling through the narrow opening.

He'd never seen a sight so welcome or so beautiful, and for a moment he almost forgot his anger. His knees were weak, his senses spinning. He knew it was more than relief making him feel this way, just as he had known it was more than anger and fear that sent him racing into the city after her.

Being mad at Libby was a constant state of mind, as constant as the knowledge that she obeyed his orders only when it suited her purpose. But anger was the only shield he had to prevent her from driving him completely crazy. Only this time it wasn't working.

Shamus didn't realize he'd moved from the shadows until he saw the cop turn toward him, hand moving toward the billy club hanging from his belt loop. The only attention he gave the policeman was raising his hands in a conciliatory gesture as he continued moving toward the trio in the alley. He knew the exact moment Libby recognized his presence. Her body stiffened in shock. He recognized a brief flicker of relief in her eyes only to see it replaced by one of fear.

"Eddie. Is Eddie...?" she pleaded in a broken whisper.

"Eddie's fine," he assured her, almost dizzy with the knowledge that it was her concern for the boy, not the sight of him, provoking that expression of terror. He moved a step closer.

Libby clasped her hands together in front of her, her slender body swaying like a leaf in the wind. Shamus had seen it before, that sudden collapse of control after a battle—exhaustion and the body's demand to stand down once it recognized the danger was over. He recognized it now and with a muttered oath jumped forward to catch her before she tumbled into the dirt of the alley floor.

She swayed into him as his arms enfolded her, his body absorbing the tremors she seemed unable to control. He felt her arms go around his waist, clinging for support.

"I'm sorry," she whispered, the words all but muffled against his chest. "I...I'll be all right in a minute."

"Dammit Libby, I told you..." Shamus began, only to feel Libby straighten in his arms and try to pull away. He almost laughed, knowing that without thinking, he'd said exactly the right thing. The Libby he'd come to know would respond to challenge, not comfort. He loosened but refused to relinquish his hold on her. The thought that he never wanted to let her go flickered with astonishing clarity through his mind.

"The lady knows you, then?" the policeman asked, suddenly reminding Shamus they were not alone in the alley.

"She knows me," Shamus answered, allowing Libby to shift position but retaining her in his embrace.

"And you'll be looking after her now?"

"Aye. I'll be looking after her," Shamus said.

"Are you okay, Libby?" Maisie interrupted.

Libby again pulled against his hold. This time Shamus allowed her to turn, but his arm remained lightly and possessively across her shoulders.

"I'm fine," she said. "Shamus, you know Maisie, and this is—"

"Best we be getting on our way, then," the policeman interrupted before Libby could complete her introductions.

Shamus nodded, giving the man a look of understanding. "The sooner the better, I suspect," he said. Fitting his actions to his words, he started down the alley, all but pulling Libby with him.

"Wait a minute," Libby protested. "I want to tell you—"

"You can tell me later," Shamus said, not breaking stride. "Right now, we're getting out of here."

Libby skipped to keep her feet under her as she tried to match Shamus's long strides. She pulled at Shamus's hand, still holding her securely around the waist. "For heaven's sake, slow down," she protested. "These shoes..."

Shamus swung her into his arms, barely breaking stride. Libby clutched at his shoulders, her face only inches from his. She could feel his strong steady heartbeat as he pulled her close against him and felt her breath catch in her throat.

"I can walk, Shamus. Put me down."

"Be quiet. You want to rouse the whole neighborhood?" he whispered.

"But I'm too heavy." She wiggled again. His eyes glittered dangerously. The expression on his face was one of stubborn determination. Her protest died in her throat.

He stopped at the end of the alley and, still hidden in the shadows, lowered her to her feet, turning her to face him in the same motion. Libby's pulse jerked as his eyes raked her face. She caught her breath as he pulled a handkerchief from his pocket and wiped at a spot on her cheekbone, his touch burning through the thin material. Her breath caught as his fingers tangled in her hair.

Giddy with relief, she barely managed to swallow her laugh when he plucked at her velvet headband and handed her the ostrich feather, its broken tip weaving like a tipsy barfly.

For a moment she'd almost believed Shamus was about to kiss her. For a moment she had wanted him to.

That knowledge tingled along her nerves like an electric shock. What was she thinking of? It was ridiculous. To him, she was only a duty, a responsibility. He'd made that perfectly clear on more than one occasion. Although she couldn't like the idea of being anyone's obligation, she'd have to admit that, in this time and place, he'd acted admirably. As a male of the early twentieth century, he'd even managed to sometimes accept her late twentieth century independence, at least to a degree that wouldn't have been tolerated by many of his contemporaries. Why then did she suddenly feel so bereft?

She'd realized early on that she might one day push her independence too far. Now, as she gazed up into his face, the glitter in his eyes giving the only hint of emotion in the otherwise stern mask, she wondered if that time had come.

Libby shivered and tried to move away, only to be held fast by his hand on her arm. "Shamus, I—"

"Not a word. Do you understand, Libby? Don't say a single blasted word," he told her in a tight voice. "We still have to walk down the block to where I parked, and if you start arguing now, I just might give in to this almost uncontrollable urge I have to turn you over my knee. The good saints know you deserve it for this night's caper."

"Don't you threaten me. I'm not a child," she replied.

"Libby..."

The note of barely controlled anger in his voice convinced her to abandon her protest, at least for the moment. Libby clamped her jaws together and lowered her gaze, afraid he'd see the light of battle in her eyes. And to think only a moment or so ago she'd actually tried to convince herself that he was tolerant.

He kept a firm hold on her arm as they stepped out of the alley and onto the sidewalk. Libby found herself almost running to keep up with his long strides, but was determined not to let him know of her discomfort this time. They'd covered the half block and he'd bundled her into the front seat of the car almost before she realized it.

"May I say something now?" she asked as Shamus settled himself behind the steering wheel.

"It'd be better if you didn't," he growled, keeping his eyes straight ahead. "You've already tried my temper."

"Tried your temper? Well, excuse me. I was only trying to help. And I don't care what you say, it was a good idea."

"A good idea to almost get yourself arrested? Or to get locked in a padlocked speakeasy? Of all your crazy ideas, this one was the craziest."

"It was not. If Capone had been there and I'd been able to talk to him, maybe I could have found out something about Vincent. You just don't want to admit I'm right. It was a good idea."

"But it didn't work, did it, Libby?" he said in a voice that sounded like a gentle growl. "You wouldn't have learned anything from Capone. He doesn't know where Zeke is. He's been turning Chicago upside down looking for him, and if he'd had the slightest suspicion you knew anything about the man, you would have been at his mercy. Or found yourself facedown in the river after he decided you really didn't know anything."

Shamus finally turned to look at her, his midnight blue eyes smoldering with some unfathomable expression. "Sometimes I think you're deliberately trying to drive me mad. I told you to leave it alone. But did you listen? Oh, no. You go off the minute my back's turned, dragging Eddie with you. Dammit, Libby, don't you realize what could have happened tonight?"

A feeling of near panic tinged with guilt made Libby almost gasp for breath. "Of course I do," she admitted, "but I didn't want Eddie to come. That was partly your fault."

"My fault? My fault! Saints preserve me, how do you figure that?"

"I told Eddie not to come, but he said you told him to keep an eye on me. I've tried to tell you before, I appreciate what you've done for me, but I don't need a keeper."

Shamus slammed his fist against the steering wheel. "You sure proved you don't need a keeper tonight, didn't you, Libby? What if Eddie hadn't been there, hadn't come after me when you disappeared? What then?"

"I'd have gone home with Maisie and come back to Curruther's Corners tomorrow, I guess."

"Leaving both Eddie and me sick with worry about you until you showed up."

It took a moment for Shamus's comment to register. It was more than anger that was making him so obnoxious. He was worried about her. The anguish in his voice left no other interpretation. Slowly she raised guilt-stricken eyes to meet his. The space between them shimmered with a shattering awareness. "I'm... I'm sorry," she whispered. "I really am sorry. All I wanted to do was help." She reached out to touch his arm. "Shamus, I wish—"

"Don't," he said. "Don't say anything else."

There was something in his voice Libby couldn't identify. Was it plea or warning? She could feel the tension in him, in herself, flowing between them like a river loosed from its banks. Touching him had been a mistake. It only served to magnify the strange link between them, but as she moved to extract her hand, she found it caught firmly under his.

Don't, her mind screamed. *Oh, please, don't let me do this. Don't do this to me.* The glittering intensity of his expression made her want to run and hide, but she couldn't think. She could barely breathe.

She tried to tear her gaze away from him as his head lowered. His mouth came down on hers, hard and soft, condemning, promising. She gave a tiny whimper—or did she imagine that?—and lifted her hand to push him away, only to find herself clinging tightly to his shoulder.

He kissed her as if he were starving, all hunger and frustration, an almost frantic desperation to prove he didn't really want this and found instead a need so intense it made him tremble.

She responded with a need that matched his, his nearness surrounding her, possessing her, rendering her will helpless before the onslaught on her senses. She whimpered again as his lips moved against hers.

She'd tried to deny it would be like this between them, even before she knew they could exist in the same world. That fluttering skip in the cadence of her pulse was only the harbinger of promise. The touch of his lips against hers was fire... heat that didn't consume, but fed on itself.

His mouth moved against hers again, demanding, coaxing. With a swallowed cry of surrender, Libby opened her lips beneath his, her strength to fight against her own needs weakened, then swept away as his tongue danced with hers in a ballet of desire.

"Libby. Dammit, Libby, don't..." His voice was a deep rumbling whisper of pain.

She moaned again and moved closer, shivering as Shamus's large hand caught her face firmly beneath the chin, then relaxed as his thumb begin caressing the sensitive pulse point beneath her ear, his touch telegraphing tiny signals of want through her body.

Shamus's hand tangled in her hair, the soft strains curling around his fingers like a silken net. He groaned, fighting against the tempest of wanting that touching her produced.

He'd tried to deny he'd known it would be like this between them from the first moment he pulled the leather helmet from her head and realized she was no young lad. Then later, when she'd first opened her eyes, he'd felt himself drowning in the violet-blue pools. He'd seen wild violets and white picket fences and fought against the desire, reminding himself that she was a temporary responsibility, reminding himself of the debt he owed her, reminding himself of the vow he'd made long ago to remain as untied and untethered as the winds he rode across the sky.

He tore his mouth away from hers and, closing his eyes, battled silently for control, his breathing uneven and ragged. He shouldn't want her. He shouldn't touch her. He shouldn't kiss her. He shouldn't ache every time he looked at her. But he did. And all his self-flagellation did nothing to change those facts.

Libby moaned in protest when Shamus lifted his mouth from hers. She wanted nothing more than to remain locked in his arms, mouth to mouth, breath to breath, even as warning bells rang in the fog-shrouded recesses of her mind. She couldn't let this happen, not to herself and not to Shamus. It would be so easy, too easy to fall completely under his spell, forgetting who she was and how she'd come here.

Shamus loosened his hold, and from somewhere deep within her Libby found the strength to move. She slid across the seat as far away from him as possible, her hand groping for the door handle.

"No." His hand shot across the seat, grabbing her arm, then jerking back quickly, but not before Libby felt the tingles radiating up her arm from his touch. Had he felt the same reaction? He must have. Why else had he dropped her arm as if he'd been burned?

Mentally Libby groaned. Only the fact that Shamus had seemed as determined to keep his distance as she was had kept the barriers in place between them. Now, with those barriers down, she knew she was in trouble.

"I shouldn't have kissed you," Shamus told her. "It won't happen again. You're safer with me than out on the street."

"It was a mistake," Libby agreed after a moment, "but not all your fault. We seem to...to strike sparks off each other."

"Sparks! Those aren't sparks. Beside you, Mrs. O'Leary was a fire brigade. Dammit, Libby, you're driving me crazy. Just...just promise me you won't go after Capone again."

"I still think—"

"Libby..."

"Oh, all right. I promise."

Shamus studied her silently for a moment. Libby kept her eyes averted, but she could feel his inspection. Finally, he seemed satisfied.

"All right. Let's go home."

"Is Eddie really all right? I mean, did he get away okay?"

"Except for being worried to death about you, he's fine."

Libby shifted uneasily. Her intentions had been good. She'd only been trying to help, not make things harder for either Shamus or Eddie. Guilt didn't sit easily on her shoulders. "I really didn't mean to get Eddie involved," she said quietly. "I'm sorry I upset him. I'm sorry for your worry, too."

Shamus shot her a look, but the expression in his eyes was unreadable. "Just see that you keep your promise," he growled.

AFTER THE FIASCO at the Lazy Cat, Libby abandoned all ideas of trying to help Shamus straighten out his muddle with Chicago's gangsters. Maybe he was right. He had to determine his own destiny. She had no right to interfere. She had no rights here at all.

But despite all her caution, the mere fact of her presence here caused complications.

She and Eddie were friends. He was going to miss her when she left. She'd miss him, too, and sometimes found herself wishing she could know the man he would become. As for Shamus . . . she couldn't let herself examine what she felt for Shamus Fitzgerald.

She wondered if she should tell them who she was, where she came from, before she left. They wouldn't believe her, of course, but maybe, after she was gone, they would. Otherwise Shamus, with his fierce sense of responsibility, would probably tear up Chicago trying to find her. And probably land himself right in the middle of another mess.

Libby pushed that problem to the back of her mind. She was still convinced the only way back to her own time was the way she'd come. The longer she stayed, the harder it was going to be to go. Kissing Shamus had been her greatest mistake. It made her wish for the impossible.

Her first priority, then, was getting the Jenny airworthy. For that job, Eddie proved to be both companion and knowledgeable helper. Occasionally Shamus looked in on their progress, but rarely commented. He seemed content to let Eddie spend the time away from the airfield, probably, Libby decided, because when they were working on the biplane, he knew both where they were and what they were doing.

It was a bright sunshiny morning when, at last, they rolled the Jenny outside the barn. Libby walked slowly around the biplane, inspecting the repairs in the strong sunlight. She climbed onto the wing, testing support wires and adjusting tension with the turnbuckles. Then, finally satisfied, she settled herself into the front cockpit.

She moved the control stick backward and forward, watching the tail elevators move up and down, then rocked the floor pedals to check the movements of the rudder. The ailerons along the trailing edge of the large upper wing rose and fell obediently as she shifted the control stick from side to side.

"I want to hear how the engine's running," she told Eddie, who nodded and positioned himself by the propeller at the front of the plane. Libby checked the ignition switch to see it was in the off position before beginning to hand pump air pressure into the gas tank, then opened both the air and gas intake valves. Eddie gave the propeller blades a couple of turns, allowing gas to be sucked into the engine pistons as Libby slowly closed down the air intake valves.

"That should do it," Libby said, and waited for Eddie's confirming nod.

Eddie placed both hands on the propeller. "Contact," he yelled as he gave the propeller a final heave and jumped back from the spinning blades.

"Contact," Libby answered, at the same time flipping the starting switch. The engine coughed once, twice, then fell silent.

"One more time," Libby told Eddie as the boy again took a position in front of the propeller.

This time, as the engine caught, a grin broke across Libby's face. The unmuffled roar settled into a steady drone, the propeller blades blurring as they spun faster and faster.

"All right," she yelled, still grinning as Eddie stepped to the side of the plane and gave her a thumbs-up signal. She adjusted the throttle, listening for changes in tempo and pitch until satisfied the engine was running exactly as it should.

"I'm taking her up," Libby yelled to Eddie over the sound of the engine. "Want to come?"

Eddie hesitated for a moment but, as Libby expected, the temptation proved too strong. He clambered into the rear cockpit. Libby taxied the Jenny to the side of the barn, a position that gave her more than ample room for takeoff. She motioned for Eddie to secure his seat harness. Moments later they were in the air.

The magic was still there. The wind through the cockpit sang its familiar song of joyous freedom. Libby laughed for pure pleasure. It was wonderful to be in the air again. The berries, as Eddie would say.

She flew the Jenny through a series of rolls and shallow dives, testing both her coordination and the plane's controls, before reaching for high sky. Then, with a tingle of anticipation, she threw the biplane into a spin, a final test for both herself and her plane.

As the little plane spiraled toward earth, Libby carefully counted the spins. Timing was everything.

With each complete revolution, the plane's corkscrew spirals tightened. After three complete spins, the centrifugal force would be too strong to break away. But if she did it right, she'd pull out of the spin flying in the same direction she'd started, only approximately twenty-five hundred feet closer to the ground. It was a tactic used by World War I pilots to drop quickly out of range of the machine gun mounted on the nose of an enemy airplane. It was also a necessary skill before the invention of computer controlled stabilizers when any stray gust of wind could flip a plane into a stall and spin before the pilot knew what was happening.

By the time Libby learned to fly, modern planes had become so stable, flight schools didn't allow student pilots to practice spin recovery. Howard, however, had been of the old school. He'd insisted that even with modern equipment, spins occasionally occurred and that flying antiques required not only book knowledge but practice. According to Howard, it was the ultimate test of a pilot's command of his plane.

Libby would never forget her first spin recovery, pitting herself and her plane against the forces of physics and nature—and winning. She relived that breathless excitement with each and every spin she performed. And this time was no exception. "All right!" she shouted, pleased with herself and her plane as she leveled off at exactly twenty-five hundred feet.

Still not ready to return to earth, she eased back the control stick, once again putting the Jenny into a gentle climb. As she swung to the east, she saw the deHavilland coming out of the sun.

Shamus. It had to be Shamus, she thought as she watched the larger plane approach, wings wagging. Her lips curved into a wider grin.

It was Shamus. And he wanted to play.

Libby wagged her wings at him, banked to the left and increased her rate of climb. They'd need more altitude for any aerobatics. A quick look over her shoulder told her he was following.

As the distance between the planes narrowed, Libby considered her first move. Shamus was on her tail, in the kill position. Although she'd done her share of aerobatics, she knew she was up against a master. Libby's dogfighting had all been of the reenactment kind. Shamus had flown against the real enemy. To have survived the war as a pilot told her he was very good, very careful and very lucky. Only pilots who could claim all three had made it home.

The deHavilland was a bigger plane than the Jenny, heavier, with a higher flying ceiling, and just a little faster. On the other hand, the Jenny was quicker to respond to the pilot's commands.

Libby might have an advantage of surprise, too. Shamus knew she was a pilot and a competent one, but she doubted he'd suspect she knew much about dogfighting maneuvers. There wasn't much question he'd beat her in the end, but she wanted to at least give him a good fight.

Carefully she weighed her options. At this point, they were few. She was still climbing, but nearing her flying ceiling. In a few moments Shamus would be able to overfly her. She had to get him off her tail.

She made her decision quickly, pushing her stick to the left, dropping the left wing to fall away. Shamus duplicated her maneuver, staying on her tail.

Libby grinned. She hadn't really expected to fool him with that one, but at least now she had some sky above her. She quickly threw the Jenny into a steep climb, then into a chantelle, the U-turn maneuver that would send her flying toward him. As the Jenny passed the deHavilland, she couldn't help grinning at the look of surprise on Shamus's face. He wagged his wings in acknowledgment.

As she rolled her plane onto its side, shortening her turn radius to position herself on his tail, Shamus put the deHavilland into a steep climb, chasing the sun. Grimly, Libby followed, determined to hold her position behind and out of sight, even though Shamus was aware she was there.

When the deHavilland suddenly rolled into an inside loop, pulling up and over her, Libby banked sharply, dropping altitude in an attempt to escape, but knew, even as she tried, her maneuver was doomed. Shamus's plane again dropped into position on her tail. Damn, he was good. Of course she'd expected as much.

Libby waggled her wings to acknowledge his hit, then put the Jenny into another sharp climb. Looking over her shoulder to verify Shamus's position, she kicked rudder to begin a left turn stall, pulling out after two revolutions to immediately spin to the right.

She came out of the reverse spin to find Shamus circling directly above her. When she started to climb, he moved after her, forcing her to level off. She tried again to gain altitude, and again Shamus moved to intercept.

"All right, all right. I got the message," she muttered to herself, banking the Jenny into a turn toward the field.

Holding altitude above her, the deHavilland mirrored her movement until she was well into her landing approach. Even without seeing him, she knew when he peeled away. She taxied the Jenny to a position in front of the barn doors, then spun the plane to a nose-out position before cutting the throttle.

Eddie was clambering out of the other cockpit almost before the propeller spun to a stop. "Golly, Libby, that was swell!" He patted the Jenny. "She's the berries. Soars like a bird. Think maybe I could take the stick sometime?"

Libby laughed at the eagerness in his voice and the look of excitement and anticipation on his face. "Sure," she said, remembering his many hard hours of fabric repair. "I think you've earned it."

"Here comes Shamus," he said unnecessarily as the deHavilland settled to the ground. "We sure surprised him, didn't we?"

Libby didn't answer, keeping her eyes on the deHavilland taxiing toward them. She knew she'd surprised him, but now, on the ground, she had a sudden premonition that she'd goofed. Maybe it was the way he'd set the plane down, efficiently, with no wasted movements. Maybe it was the way the plane was taxiing straight toward her, purposefully, as if stalking her.

She stole a quick look at Eddie. He didn't seem concerned. He was grinning from ear to ear. It was only her imagination, she told herself, but was unable to shake her feeling of unease. She knew the exact moment Shamus chopped throttle, watched wordlessly as the prop slowly spun to full stop, saw his tall form unfold from the cockpit, each movement of his body purposeful, controlled.

She gave Eddie another sideways glance, saw his grin start to dissolve.

She jerked her eyes to Shamus striding purposefully toward them and drew a deep, deliberate breath.

She'd often heard the term murderous rage but had never seen a facial expression she thought deserved the description, not until now.

"Oh, boy, does he look mad," Eddie said, moving a step closer to Libby.

"Get out of here, Eddie," Libby said quietly. "This is between Shamus and me."

"I think I'd better stay," the boy said. "He looks good and mad. I shouldn't have—"

"You didn't do anything. Just went along for the ride. And he has no reason to be mad. Certainly not at you. Go on now. Up to the house. No need for you to be caught in the middle."

"But I—"

Libby finally dragged her eyes from Shamus and turned to Eddie. "It'll be okay, Eddie." She gave him a small smile. "Just do as I say. Get out of here."

Eddie took a hesitant step backward, then at her reassuring nod turned away. Libby watched until he disappeared around the side of the barn. Then she took a deep breath and turned to face the man still striding relentlessly toward her, each approaching footstep a shout of temper.

CHAPTER NINE

LIBBY WASN'T SURE what she'd done this time, but there was no question about it. Shamus was furious.

And she'd thought he wanted to play!

Why, she wondered, did it seem to be her destiny to make him mad? She allowed herself a split second of self-pity, then mentally gave herself a shake and unconsciously tilted her chin.

"What in the blue blazes did you think you were doing up there?" Shamus demanded when he finally stomped to a halt only inches in front of her. His careful enunciation did more to tell her how close he was to losing control than his actual words.

"Giving the Jenny a test flight," she said, struggling to keep her voice calm and controlled.

"A test flight?" His lips thinned into a tight straight line.

"That's right," Libby told him. "Eddie and I finished the fabric repairs and I checked the engine. I wanted to make sure she was ready to go."

"Go? Go where?"

"Anywhere. Everywhere. I haven't flown in months. Not since the day I got here. It...it's been like being half alive."

Even though Shamus continued to stand rigid, for a moment she thought she saw a flicker of sympathy or understanding in the depths of his eyes. He was still mad, furious, in fact. But surely he understood. After all, he loved to fly, too.

"Look, Shamus, I didn't mean to catch you off guard like that. Up there, I mean. I thought you'd come up to play."

"Play?"

"You know, like a mock dogfight. I know I'm not as good as you. After all, you've done the real thing. But I did make a good move or two, didn't I?"

His face remained stern, but Libby was convinced that, just for a second, she saw a twinkle in his eye. "Yes," he admitted, in a voice she could only describe as reluctant, "you made a good move or two."

It was faint praise, but she couldn't restrain her sudden grin. This morning, flying after so long, she'd felt alive, complete. It was always like magic, that feeling of being untethered, one with the sky. Knowing Shamus was up there with her, sharing it with her, had made it perfect.

Libby was convinced that now the Jenny was repaired, she'd be leaving soon, but if today's clear blue skies were any indication, she might not find a storm for days. What harm would there be in enjoying herself while she waited? She wanted to share the sky with Shamus again at least once before she said goodbye.

She took a deep breath and gave Shamus a wide smile. "Well, then," she said, "maybe we could barnstorm together. You know, like partners."

Her words died at the sudden glitter in his eyes.

"Barnstorm? Dammit, Libby, you can't barnstorm."

She caught her breath at his blunt denial, her grin fading. She shrugged her shoulders, fighting to disguise her disappointment. "I don't see why not. I know you don't think much of women pilots, but now that the Jenny's ready, you wouldn't even be risking one of your planes."

"No. You'll not be barnstorming," he repeated. "Not with me or without me."

Libby managed to meet his gaze for a moment before averting her eyes. So he wouldn't fly with a woman. She was determined not to let him see how much his denial hurt. She should have expected it. The superior male doctrine was still alive and well in her own time. It dominated this time. Somehow she'd hoped for more from him.

"Too bad," she said, not quite able to keep the disappointment out of her voice. "I think we would have made a good team." She started to turn away, only to feel his fingers close around her upper arm. Although he held her firmly, his grip was not tight. Why, then, did his fingers feel like steel bands?

"Where do you think you're going?"

Where was she going? Libby didn't know. All she knew was she had to get away. Away from Shamus. She tried to convince herself that it was better if she left now anyway. Then there would be no awkward questions when she disappeared.

"To get my things. Now that the Jenny's repaired, there's no reason for me to stay."

"You can't leave," he said flatly.

She gasped, whirling on him in hurt fury. "I can't fly. I can't leave. Next thing I know you'll be telling me I can't breathe. Well, let me tell you something, Shamus Fitzgerald. You can't tell me what to do. If I want to fly, I'll fly. If I want to leave, I'll leave. And that's exactly what I'm going to do."

Shamus swallowed, unable to shift his look from her upturned face. Her violet eyes were spitting blue flame. He'd handled her all wrong. Again.

He thought she'd realized why they couldn't risk letting her distinctive red-and-white Jenny be seen. She probably would when she calmed down, but at the moment she was too furious to listen to reason. And he couldn't take a chance on what she'd do. Somehow he had to keep her and her plane out of the air.

Shamus sighed and took hold of her other arm, lifting her off her feet and setting her down out of his path. "I'm sorry, Libby. I really am," he said almost as much to himself as to her.

By the time Libby realized what was happening and went scrambling after him, Shamus had already reached his destination. He reached over the edge of the Jenny's wing, flipped open a small access panel in the lower part of the metal engine compartment and, with a few practiced movements, removed the filter sediment bowl from the fuel line, leaving the gas line from tank to engine severed.

Libby's eyes shifted from his face to his hand, her eyes widening in disbelief. "You can't do that," she sputtered in her anger. "Put it back."

"You'll not be flying." He saw her fists clench at her sides, her eyes brimming with rage and betrayal.

"You have no right. The Jenny's mine."

Shamus didn't answer. Guilt clawed at his gut. By disabling her plane, he'd violated every unwritten rule in the pilot's book, but he couldn't back down now. At the moment, she was too mad and too stubborn to listen to reason. For both her sake and his, he couldn't let her fly. Neither could he stand to see the look of accusation on her face. He started to turn away.

She hit him like a virago, all blue-eyed fury, her
hands grabbing for the fuel line filter. Shamus sidestepped to avoid her flaying fists, automatically raising an arm to protect himself. "Stop it, Libby. You'll
hurt yourself."

Libby paid his words no attention, continuing her
attack as if he didn't stand a foot taller and outweigh
her by over a hundred pounds. He sidestepped again
to avoid a flashing elbow, ducked to miss a threatening knee. He dropped the fuel line filter in the dirt and
grabbed with both hands, immobilizing her in a bear
hug.

He realized his mistake the moment he pulled her
into his arms. He'd known even before the incident at
the Lazy Cat she was dangerous to him. She was fascinating and infuriating. She made him think of wild
blue violets and white picket fences. There was no future in such thoughts. Flying was his life. It would
probably be his death. He'd decided long ago that
when the time came for his final flight he would leave
behind no regrets, no unfulfilled promises, no unfin-
ished responsibilities. Yet every time he touched
Libby, he felt his resolve wavering.

"Stop it," he told her again as she struggled to free
herself from his hold.

"You…you bully. You sorry son of a jackass! You
have no right…" She managed to free one arm.

Shamus made a grab for her arm, recapturing it a
scant inch before her hand made contact with his
cheek. "Little wildcat," he growled.

As she continued to struggle against him, he drew a
deep breath, trying to ignore the sensations of her
straining body against his. "Dammit, Libby. Stop it,
I say."

She fell against his chest, knocking them both off balance. It was enough to divert her kick from its intended target, but she caught him in the knee. As his leg collapsed beneath him, he managed to twist his body to take the impact of the fall. They hit the ground together, arms and legs in a tangle.

Even with Shamus's body cushioning hers, the fall knocked the air from Libby's body. She lay still for a moment, oblivious to her position, gasping to draw breath. When she was finally able to raise her head from his chest, his eyes captured her gaze in a trap that again threatened her breathing. She felt the heat of his body and the binding spell of his arms around her. Her eyes widened as a rush of sensation rippled through her body, leaving her weak.

"No. Don't. We can't. Let me go."

Shamus heard her words, but also recognized her sudden awareness, her involuntary response to him, and all but groaned.

She didn't mean it any more than he did. No matter what she said, the truth was in her eyes. Still cradling her in his arms, he rolled over. His hand touched her cheek, brushing her hair off her face.

Libby was so lost in the whirlwind of sensations she barely flinched as a sharp rock poked into her side.

No, no, you can't let this happen, a small voice screamed in the back of her mind. If she kissed him, she'd be lost.

Then, slowly, as if waiting for her to protest, Shamus began to lower his head.

Unable to stop herself, Libby lifted one hand to touch his face. Her other hand moved, almost unconsciously, to her side in an effort to dislodge the uncomfortable stone digging into her flesh. When her fingers closed around a piece of metal, it took her a moment to recognize what she held in her hand.

Memory of Shamus's betrayal came flooding back. The pain all but choked her. Tears blurred her eyes as she averted her head.

Even though Shamus's senses were reeling, he sensed her retreat. He levered his body away from her, searching her averted face for a reason behind her sudden rejection. His gaze traveled down her body, coming to rest on the hand clenching the fuel line filter.

Shamus muttered a curse under his breath and closed his fingers around her slender wrist. He pried the fuel filter from her fingers and stood up.

For a moment Libby lay as he left her, caught in the shadow thrown by his body, anger at his actions rendering her speechless. Then another emotion tugged at the edge of her mind, a feeling of desolation at the loss of his closeness. Deliberately, she pushed it away. Blinking against the moisture in her eyes, she pushed herself into a sitting position with her elbows.

"Shamus, give it back," she pleaded. "You don't understand. I need the Jenny."

"You're the one who doesn't understand. You can't fly the Jenny. Dammit, Libby, think! Who besides Eddie and myself have seen your plane? Who would like nothing better than to see it again? If you're so blasted determined to fly, I'll check you out in the deHavilland or even the Waco, but you can't fly the Jenny."

Libby trembled with sudden understanding. Shamus was afraid the men who'd attacked them would recognize her plane. That's why he didn't want the

Jenny flying. It had nothing to do with his feelings for her as a woman or as a pilot.

Then she sighed, her euphoria giving away to despair. He wouldn't understand her refusal to obey his orders, wouldn't understand why she had to fly the Jenny. But worse, she could think of no way to explain it to him.

"It has to be the Jenny," she told him, her voice shaking. "I don't belong here. I have to go back."

Sweet saints, he'd never met another woman so stubborn, so determined to get her own way. Did she do it just to irritate him? "Go back? Go back where?" he demanded. "Delaware? That is where you said you were from, isn't it? You haven't seemed all that anxious to go home before now. In fact, you said you didn't have a home anymore. So exactly where is it you have to go?"

Libby shut her eyes, a feeling of desolation gripping her throat. If she told him, he wouldn't believe her. She couldn't expect him to believe her. She forced open her eyes and looked at him mutely.

Shamus muttered a curse under his breath, flinching at the anguish he saw in her eyes. "All right, all right. You want to go home, I'll take you. I'll take care of your Jenny until it's safe. Then I'll fly it to you."

"You can't take me, Shamus," she said in a voice of quiet despair. "I have to go myself. You can't just... You don't understand."

"Then suppose you explain it to me." His exasperation was easy to see. "Explain why, after all this time, you suddenly have to leave. Where did you come from, anyway? Where do you have to go? Dammit, Libby, you're just being stubborn. The Jenny's going back into the barn. And it's going to stay out of sight until it's safe. And just to be sure, I'll keep the fuel filter.''

"No. Honest, Shamus, I'm not just being stubborn. I have to have the Jenny because—because . . .''

"Because why, Libby? Give me one good reason.''

"Because it's the only way I can get back to 1993,'' she blurted, then snapped her mouth shut, appalled at what she's just said.

Shamus gave her a look of utter astonishment. "What did you say?''

Libby gave a weary sigh. "I said, the Jenny's the only way I can get back to 1993,'' she repeated, her voice strained. "I shouldn't be here. Not in 1925. Shamus, I know it's hard to believe. There are times I have trouble believing it myself, but I . . . I'm from the future.''

Concern suddenly replaced the shocked look on his face. He stepped toward her. "You shouldn't have been flying, not aerobatics. Not out of practice as you are. Do you feel dizzy? Confused? Your mind kind of foggy? I've seen it before, but it'll pass. You'll be feeling more yourself in a few hours. Why don't you—''

"Stop it, Shamus,'' Libby interrupted. "I feel fine. I'm not dizzy. I'm not confused. And I'm not crazy. I know exactly what I said. I didn't mean to say it, because I know it's hard to believe. That's why I haven't told you before. But nonetheless, it's true. I don't belong here. The afternoon I saw you beside that burning plane, I'd been flying for almost an hour. But I began my flight in 1993. I am from the future.''

"Libby?''

FREE GIFT!

FREE BOOKS!

Play

CASINO JUBILEE

"Scratch'n Match" Game

PEEL OFF LABEL

PLACE LABEL INSIDE

CLAIM UP TO 4 <u>FREE</u> BOOKS AND A <u>FREE</u> HEART-SHAPED CURIO BOX

See inside ↗

NO RISK, NO OBLIGATION TO BUY...NOW OR EVER!

CASINO JUBILEE
"Scratch'n Match" Game

Here's how to play:

1. Peel off label from front cover. Place it in space provided at right. With a coin, carefully scratch off the silver box. This makes you eligible to receive two or more free books, and possibly another gift, depending upon what is revealed beneath the scratch-off area.

2. You'll receive brand-new Harlequin Superromance® novels. When you return this card, we'll rush you the books and gift you qualify for, ABSOLUTELY FREE!

3. Then, if we don't hear from you, every month we'll send you 4 additional novels to read and enjoy, before they are available in bookstores. You can return them and owe nothing, but if you decide to keep them, you'll pay only $2.71* each plus 25¢ delivery and applicable sales tax, if any*. That's the complete price, and— compared to cover prices of $3.39 each in stores—quite a bargain!

4. When you join the Harlequin Reader Service®, you'll get our subscribers-only newsletter, as well as additional free gifts from time to time, just for being a subscriber!

5. You must be completely satisfied. You may cancel at any time simply by sending us a note or a shipping statement marked ''cancel'' or by returning any shipment to us at our cost.

YOURS FREE!

This lovely heart-shaped box is richly detailed with cut-glass decorations, perfect for holding a precious memento or keepsake—and it's yours absolutely free when you accept our no-risk offer.

CASINO JUBILEE
"Scratch'n Match" Game

SCRATCH HERE

PLACE LABEL HERE

?

CHECK CLAIM CHART BELOW FOR YOUR FREE GIFTS!

YES! I have placed my label from the front cover in the space provided above and scratched off the silver box. Please send me all the gifts for which I qualify. I understand I am under no obligation to purchase any books, as explained on the opposite page.

134 CIH AH2V (U-H-SR-02/93)

Name _____

Address _____ Apt. _____

City _____ State _____ Zip _____

▼ DETACH AND MAIL CARD TODAY! ▼

CASINO JUBILEE CLAIM CHART	
🍒🍒🍒	WORTH 4 FREE BOOKS AND A FREE HEART-SHAPED CURIO BOX
🍒🔔🍒	WORTH 3 FREE BOOKS
🔔🔔🍒	WORTH 2 FREE BOOKS

CLAIM Nº 1528

▼ DETACH AND MAIL CARD TODAY! ▼

BUSINESS REPLY MAIL

FIRST CLASS MAIL   PERMIT NO. 717   BUFFALO, NY

POSTAGE WILL BE PAID BY ADDRESSEE

HARLEQUIN READER SERVICE
3010 WALDEN AVE
PO BOX 1867
BUFFALO NY 14240-9952

NO POSTAGE
NECESSARY
IF MAILED
IN THE
UNITED STATES

She shook her head, wondering how she could make him understand. Now that she'd told him, she had to make him believe.

"Have you ever heard of H.G. Wells or . . . or Mark Twain?" she asked with sudden inspiration.

"Well, sure. They're both writers. But I don't see what—"

"Wells wrote a novel called *The Time Machine* and Twain wrote one called *A Connecticut Yankee in King Arthur's Court.* Have you ever read either one of them? They're about time travel."

"That's . . . that's make-believe."

"I know the books are fiction. I thought the idea of time travel was make-believe, too, until it happened to me. But it's real. Not exactly how it happened in those books, but real all the same. I traveled through time. I'm here, alive, in 1925, and I haven't even been born yet."

She made a desperate little sound. "I know it's hard to believe, and I don't understand exactly how or why it happened. But it did. On Friday, July 23, 1993, I took off from an air show in Oshkosh, Wisconsin, and I got caught in a storm. When I landed it was July 23, 1925, and I was in Chicago."

"Dammit, Libby, do you expect me to believe that?"

Libby's shoulders slumped. "No, I guess not. It's the truth, but in your place, I probably wouldn't believe it, either. At first I thought it was all a dream, a nightmare. Then I decided it was some kind of cosmic mistake and that it would fix itself. Every night I went to sleep, expecting to wake up in the future . . . I mean, in my time. But nothing happened.

"I finally figured out it was the storm that caused it to happen. Since a storm sent me here in the Jenny, I think that's the way I'll have to go back. Can't you see, Shamus? That's why I have to have the Jenny. The biplane's my time machine. If I'm ever going to get back, I'll have to leave the way I arrived. In the Jenny. Please, give me the fuel filter."

The look of disbelief was still on Shamus's face. "You can't really believe that. It's not even logical. If you were really from the future why would you be flying a Jenny? We're discovering new and better ways to build aeroplanes every day. In another five years, there won't be any more biplanes. I'll bet future planes will be all metal craft, too. If you were really from the future, you wouldn't be flying a Jenny."

"You're right," Libby said. "In my time airplanes are built of metal, aluminum and titanium. Planes are bigger, go faster and fly higher than you can even imagine. There are only a few Jennys left. They're considered antiques. Pilots like myself keep about a dozen flying just to remind people of how it all started."

Libby saw the sudden spark of interest on Shamus's face in spite of himself.

"How big? How high? How far?"

"Big enough to carry hundreds of passengers," Libby said, without thinking. "Commercial liners usually cruise at thirty-five to fifty thousand feet and at five hundred miles an hour. Military aircraft go even higher and faster, faster than the speed of sound. Some of the military cargo planes can carry several hundred tons of men and equipment."

Shamus shook his head. "That's impossible. A pilot couldn't breathe that high up. And no engine, even dual engines, could produce the lift or power needed to fly that fast or go that high. Besides, a pilot couldn't see the ground from that high up. He wouldn't know where he was going. Oh, I know planes are going to get bigger and stronger and go faster, but not... It can't happen. Can't you see, Libby, it had to be a dream. Your whole story's impossible."

Libby sighed. "I don't suppose you'd believe me if I said that we learned how to furnish oxygen, to pressurize the cabin—that's the inside of the airplane—so it's just like being on the ground, even though the plane's several miles in the air? Or that there's a new kind of engine that's more powerful than the internal combustion engines we...you use now? That's just the beginning. An invention called radar lets a pilot know exactly where he is. Radar even lets trackers on the ground know what planes are in the air, how close they are to each other, how fast the plane's moving, its course, all kinds of things..." Her voice trailed off when she saw the look on his face. "You think I'm crazy, don't you?"

"Libby," he pleaded.

"It all happens and more. In the sixties we actually send men to the moon, and supersonic passenger jets fly from the States to Europe in less than six hours. Oh, Shamus, so many times when you were talking about the future of aviation, I've wanted to tell you things. Right now aviation's taking its first baby steps. The future's there, even bigger and brighter than you can imagine. I'm not making it up. Honest. And I'm not crazy, either."

Shamus shook his head. "I don't think you're crazy," he told her in a suddenly gentle voice. "I think you're confused. After all, you hurt your head. You were shot, Libby. I've seen head injuries before. Sometimes, well, it can make a person believe things are real when they're really not. I mean, you can have weird dreams when you get hit on the head like that. But because your head's hurt, it doesn't know they were dreams, and so when you wake up you believe it was real. That's not your fault. And it doesn't mean you're crazy.''

''I'm not confused,'' Libby said desperately. ''Please, Shamus, give me the filter. I wasn't thinking before, I mean about the possibility of the Jenny being spotted. I'll keep her in the barn out of sight. I won't take her out until it's time to go. Then I'll be gone and it won't matter anyway. I promise. I won't put you or Eddie at risk, but I have to be ready when conditions are right.''

Shamus studied her silently, wondering all the time why he was even considering doing as she asked. Heaven knew her story was crazy and impossible, but looking into her eyes, he couldn't doubt she believed it. It was all his fault, his and Zeke Vincent's. If she hadn't hurt her head, she wouldn't be believing such a crazy story. What should he do now? Pretend to believe her?

''Suppose,'' he said slowly, ''just suppose, mind you, that I replaced the filter and the Jenny was in the barn, waiting. How would you know it was time to leave?''

''I'll have to wait for a storm. And I think it's going to have to be at about midday, since that's the time I came, but I could be wrong about that. Anyway, I'll have to fly into the thunderhead and look—''

"A thunderhead! Dammit, Libby, you don't fly into thunderheads. You even see one, you take your bird to ground. Even the greenest pilot knows that."

"This is different. It's a special kind of thunderhead, one like the one that brought me here."

"A thunderhead's a thunderhead. Some might be a little bigger or a little blacker than others, but mostly they look the same. And any one of them will kill you."

"I told you, this one will be different."

"How will you know?"

"I just will. Look, Shamus we've had several storms since I got here. None of them have been right. I'm not sure how it works, but when the right one comes, I'll know. That's got to be the way it works."

Shamus frowned. Libby's story was crazy. He didn't believe it, not for a moment, but there was no doubt she did. He remembered some of the crazy stories told by pilots who'd been knocked unconscious during the war. The Air Corp doctors had said familiar routine was the best way to help them remember what had really happened. If Libby was able to fly, he'd bet she'd soon realize the foolishness of her story. But she couldn't fly the Jenny.

Damn Zeke Vincent and that blasted suitcase. It was past time for him to do something about that. He couldn't stand around any longer, asking an occasional discreet question, waiting for Zeke to show up. He was going to have to go looking. If Libby could fly, she'd soon realize...

"Shamus," Libby pleaded, her voice interrupting his thoughts. "If I promised I'd only take the Jenny out if I was sure it was time to leave, would you give me the filter? I won't go dashing after every dark cloud that rolls across the sky. I don't want to get killed. I just want to go home. I won't take the Jenny out of the barn unless I'm sure it's the right time to leave. I promise."

Saints knew she wasn't going to find any "right time" to travel to the future, Shamus reminded himself. She was a good pilot. Surely she wouldn't be daring the devil with every storm that came through. Besides, removing the fuel filter wasn't the only way to disable her plane. He could give it back to her and still, if necessary, make sure the Jenny didn't leave the ground. If she thought she could fly, would she calm down a bit? Maybe, after a time, even realize how impossible her story was?

"Shamus?"

"All right. I'll replace the filter. You were right. The Jenny's yours, but she still goes back into the barn. And you have to be careful."

"Oh, I will. I will. I promise." She hesitated a moment. "Does this mean you believe me?"

This time it was Shamus who hesitated. He didn't want to flat out tell her that her story was about as believable as a bootlegger winning sainthood.

"Let's just say I've seen some strange things happen up there," he finally told her, gesturing toward the sky.

Libby nodded. "And I guess," she said in a resigned voice, "an open mind is as good as I'm going to get."

CHAPTER TEN

SHAMUS PACED the length of the farmhouse porch, dividing his attention between the gradual graying of the sky along the eastern horizon and the closed front door. Where was Libby? Eddie already had their supplies at the airfield. Didn't she know it was time to leave? He wanted to be in the air at first light.

He hoped he wasn't making a mistake taking her to Peoria, but there'd been no help for it, not once she'd learned he and Eddie would be barnstorming this weekend. She was determined to go.

It was probably for the best, he told himself. At least he'd know where she was and what she was up to. Saints knew what trouble she'd land herself in if he wasn't around to keep an eye on her. And the Jenny would remain safely in the barn.

Shamus let out a long sigh. Libby had made no mention of flying her biplane in the past week. Neither had she repeated that crazy story about being from the future. Several times he'd been tempted to speak of it, but each time had decided not to. Maybe, he told himself, if they didn't talk about it, if he didn't remind her of it, she'd forget the whole crazy idea.

He glanced anxiously at the horizon again and fumed impatiently. Just like a woman, always keep you waiting! He couldn't imagine why he'd expected

Libby to be different. Finally, he stuck his head in the front door and yelled.

"Hold your horses. I'm here," she said, suddenly appearing in front of him.

She was, he decided, the prettiest barnstormer he'd ever seen. And, he'd admit, she looked every inch the part, from the bottom of her brightly polished knee-high boots to the new leather helmet dangling from her fingers by the chin strap. Somehow she'd even contrived a patch to cover the bullet hole in the arm of her jacket.

"It's about time," he growled. "If we don't get in the air, all the best spots will be taken before we get there."

"You can stop your grumbling. I'm here now, so let's go."

Shamus gritted his teeth and stomped off the porch after her. She was going to drive him crazy. Sometimes he wondered if she hadn't already succeeded.

Libby looked over her shoulder and grinned. He was grumpy as an old bear. Was he always such a grouch in the mornings, or was it simply because she'd talked him into letting her come this weekend? Whatever it was, she wasn't going to let him ruin her day. Only a few short hours from now she'd be a barnstormer—a *real* barnstormer. Howard had repeated the pitch he'd used in the old days so many times that she could almost hear him now.

Okay, folks, who's next? Step right up. Don't be bashful. Only five dollars for five minutes. Safe? Of course it's safe. Perfectly harmless. You, sir, want to take the little lady for a joy ride? Five minutes in the land of birds and angels. Come on now, who's next?

Shamus caught up with her halfway down the hill, and Libby had to quicken her pace to keep up with his long strides. "Do you think there'll be a good crowd?" she asked. "Or will we have to compete for riders? How many other barnstormers will be there?"

"The Peoria fair always draws a good crowd. Doubt we'll have any trouble getting customers, even with every barnstormer around the countryside there." He glanced at the sky. "If the weather holds, it should be a good weekend."

Libby grinned. She couldn't help herself. She couldn't remember being as excited since...well, since Oshkosh. And that seemed so long ago. Was long ago, she reminded herself. A different world, in fact. At the thought she grew pensive, her grin fading.

Shamus must have sensed her change of mood. "Now what's wrong?"

"Nothing. Not a single thing," Libby said, forcing a smile. "I guess I'm just excited."

Shamus frowned. "Libby, the customers...they may not want to fly with you," he warned. "I mean, well, most of them have probably never seen a woman pilot. Hell, half of them have probably never even seen an aeroplane. Up close, anyway."

Libby refused to be discouraged. "If that happens, I won't fly. I'll take care of collecting the fees, and you and Eddie can take them up. I know we...you have to make this weekend pay. But honest, Shamus, I don't think it will be a problem. All I'll have to do is hint to some big strong man that he's afraid to do something a female can do and I'll have all the customers I can handle."

Shamus gave her a rueful grin. "You're probably right," he admitted.

"The thing is, well, we're only going to have the two planes. What are you going to do if Eddie and I are flying?"

"I think you'll find having an extra pilot around useful. It gets tiring after a while, you know. Take off, once around the fairgrounds, land, then do it all again. Besides, I've got some other business to attend to," he said. "Might be a good time to see if anyone's heard anything about Zeke. I'm tired of waiting for him to show up. Peoria's far enough from Chicago that I can talk to the other barnstormers without looking over my shoulder."

"Do you think he might be there? Zeke, I mean."

"I'd like to think so, but I doubt it," Shamus admitted. "Still, if he's anywhere around, someone may have heard something. The man couldn't have just disappeared. He'll turn up eventually, either dead or alive. I don't wish him bad luck, but I sure don't owe Zeke Vincent anything, either. If he turns up dead and no one comes looking for us, I figure we're home free."

"I still couldn't fly the Jenny," Libby reminded him.

"We could change the color. It's the red-and-white that makes it so easy to identify."

Libby had considered that possibility, but discarded it, wondering how she'd explain a color change when she got back home. "I guess so," she said. "I thought about it before, but I wasn't sure how long I'd be here."

The expression on Shamus's face darkened with some unreadable emotion, and Libby muttered an unladylike expression under her breath. In the days since she'd told him she was from the future, he'd seemed content to ignore the subject. She hadn't intended to remind him, either, especially not today.

"Would you keep the money?" she couldn't help asking.

Shamus hesitated before answering. "It would be a temptation," he admitted, "but no, I don't think so. I don't want any part of it." He shrugged his shoulders. "I'd probably stick it in the church poor box. Do some good there."

Libby's mind was a sudden jumble of confused thoughts and feelings. How strange. It was almost as if she'd known he would say something like that, even though it was logical for him to keep it, or at least some of it. She knew the money would give him the means to design and build his own airplane, which was something he'd told her he'd always dreamed of doing.

For a moment her gaze locked with his. An oddly primitive warning sounded in her mind. Hastily she looked away, her eyes focusing almost without seeing on the horizon.

In the distance the sky was shading from gray to pink. It would be light enough to fly in minutes. She could make out the dim outlines of the Waco and the deHavilland now. "Time to go," she said, her voice a little breathless. "You want me in the front cockpit, I suppose."

Shamus nodded. "I'll get Eddie in the air first, then we'll be on our way."

Libby stood to the side as Shamus positioned himself in front of the Waco and signaled Eddie to prime. He gave the propeller a turn, listened as the engine let out a hoarse cough, then reached to repeat the procedure. The low rumble of the engine shattered the early morning quiet. For a moment clouds of blue smoke wreathed the nose of the plane, then were whipped away by the spinning fan of the propeller.

Eddie grinned, giving Libby a jaunty wave as he guided the plane off the grass and onto the dirt runway. "See you in Peoria," he yelled.

Shamus lifted a hand for a brief wave, then stood watching as the plane gathered speed until it floated off the runway and into the air.

Libby watched as Eddie cleared the fence at the end of the field before turning toward the deHavilland.

"Libby, wait a minute," Shamus called.

A cold knot of uncertainty formed in her stomach. "What's wrong?" she asked as casually as she could manage. If he tried to change his mind now...

"Nothing's wrong. I just thought...well, if you're going to be a barnstormer, you'll need a scarf. It's sorta like a badge. Here." He thrust a small brown package into her hands.

Libby's breath caught in her throat. "I thought—I thought..." She shook her head, swallowing her words, and tilted her head to look into his face. "Thank you" she said, unable to prevent the tiny waver in her voice.

"Well, aren't you going to open it?"

She nodded nervously and with trembling fingers tore at the paper. Her eyes grew wide at sight of the shimmering blue silk. She blinked, then looked again, letting the whisper-soft folds fall over her fingers. "It's beautiful," she said in a voice unusually husky, "but I thought a barnstormer's scarf was supposed to be white."

"I've never seen anything but white," Shamus said defensively, "but then, I've never seen anything but men barnstormers, either. Stands to reason, if a woman can barnstorm, she can wear a colored scarf. Besides..." His voice trailed off.

"Besides what?"

"Besides, the blue's the same color as your eyes," he said gruffly. "Here, let me show you how to put it on."

Libby stood stock-still as Shamus lifted the scarf from her nerveless fingers and adjusted it loosely around her neck. She drew a quick breath as his fingers brushed against her ear. He seemed to hesitate for a moment, then dropped his hands to his sides and stepped back.

"There," he said. "Now you're ready."

Libby tried to speak but for a moment couldn't seem to push the words past the lump in her throat. She ducked her head and swallowed nervously. "Thank you. I don't know what else to say...."

"You've already said it," Shamus told her a bit abruptly. "Besides, it's just a scarf. Nothing special. Now let's get this show in the air."

THE PEORIA FAIR was everything Libby had imagined and more. Crowds of people jostled each other good-naturedly along the midway. She stopped at the edge of a tent, listening to the calls of the hustlers.

"Step right up. Win a prize. Three throws for a quarter."

"You've read about him, heard about him. Now you can see him, the amazing snake boy from the deepest jungles of the Amazon."

"See the bearded lady. Watch the Amazing Alanzo walk on fire. See Zenbedo the Great swallow a three-foot sword. Right this way, folks. Rare sights and amazing phenomena gathered for your pleasure from the four corners of the world...."

Beyond the midway, livestock exhibits added their noise of quacks, moos, snorts and squeals to the general pandemonium. There were blue ribbons for best swine, chickens, goats, mules and jackasses, competitions for best jam, jelly and apple pie and contests for best yodeler, pig caller and fastest corn shucker.

Rising above it all was the hollow drum sound of droning airplane engines constantly circling the fairgrounds.

By mid-morning lines of waiting customers stood along the side of a grass runway in a nearby field, waiting a turn in the flying machines. Nearly a dozen planes were in the air. If the crowd of customers started to thin, one of the circling planes would buzz low over the midway and the pilot would yell his brief sales talk through a megaphone. Then with wings wagging, the airplane would play Pied Piper, leading a new group of riders to the edge of the grass pasture runway.

Libby was amazed at the seemingly unorganized and unenforced discipline of the barnstormers. A spirited price war between pilots competing for riders had produced complete chaos during the first hour of the morning. Then, in some kind of unspoken agreement, the barnstormers had mutually settled on a single price of five dollars a ride.

Even more amazing was another apparently unspoken agreement on where to take off, where to land and in which direction to circle the fairgrounds. With a precision that any modern control tower would have considered well ordered, the planes lifted off from a south field, circled to the east, landed in a pasture to the north, then taxied to the starting point to discharge passengers and reload.

Libby knew that without the routine, planes would have been in danger of crashing into each other, both on the ground and in the air. Still she couldn't help but be impressed at the ease with which self-discipline controlled what could have been a dangerous and chaotic situation.

But to Libby, strangest of all was the youth of the other barnstorming pilots. In her years of association with antique airplanes, she'd met only a few pilots near her own age. Most of the antiquers she knew were at least one generation older, sometimes two. "Old men and old planes," she remembered Howard teasing. None of these pilots were old. She had to keep reminding herself that in this age aviation was a young man's game. It had been less than twenty-five years since the Wright brothers' first flight at Kitty Hawk.

Never before had she understood so clearly the unique role the barnstormers had played in the history of aviation.

"Well, what would you do," she remembered Howard asking, "if there were no commercial airlines, no wars, no flight schools and no corporate jets? How would you make your living as a pilot?" Now she knew. She'd barnstorm.

These young men, with a gleam of adventure in their eyes and a love of flying in their blood, had stayed in the air the only way they could. They'd taken their flying machines across the country, stopping whenever they could find a crowd, keeping the idea of aviation alive until someone could find a peacetime role for a wartime machine. And as they waited for the future to come, they introduced hundreds of thousands of Americans to the magic and wonder of flight.

As a lady pilot, Libby was gathering more than her amount of attention from the customers and the other pilots. She found their curiosity and the notoriety uncomfortable.

"Bet I could join the show on the midway," she complained to Eddie. "You'd think they'd never seen a woman pilot before."

"That's cause they never have," Eddie teased. "I'd never seen one, either, not until Shamus brought you home. Heck, some of these people have never even seen an aeroplane. Not close enough to touch, anyway."

"Say, little lady, where'd you learn to fly, anyway?" asked Hank, one of the pilots Shamus had introduced to her earlier. She remembered his name because he flew a Jenny very similar to hers.

"An old friend back East taught me," she answered carefully. It wouldn't do to name Howard as her teacher. She knew he'd barnstormed this part of the country in the mid-twenties, and although she hadn't heard his name today, he might be around. If anyone told him a lady pilot claimed he'd taught her to fly, he would truthfully deny it. After all, he hadn't taught her... yet. And how could she explain that?

"I've picked up a few pointers from Shamus, too," she added quickly, hoping to prevent more pointed questions.

"Good man," Hank said. "Careful, but knows what he's about. That whiskey-bottle trick of his saved my bacon once, maybe more than once."

"Whiskey bottle?"

"You ain't seen that yet? No, I guess not. He don't use the bottle anymore. Besides there's no need for it on a clear day like this. But I tell you, it was a nifty idea, all right. He half-filled one of those flat pint whiskey bottles with water and taped it to the dashboard behind the stick. Claimed he could look at the way the water was rolling in the bottle and tell if his wings were level, even when he was caught in the clouds and couldn't see the ground. Thought he was crazy till I tried it."

Libby nodded, afraid to interrupt Hank's story, but she couldn't discipline her thoughts quite as easily. Hank might not know it but he was describing what had to be the very first version of a turn and bank indicator, a primitive model to be sure, but nonetheless the forerunner of a flying aid that was standard equipment in her day. And Shamus had invented it?

"Got caught in a fog once coming up the Shenandoah Valley," Hank was saying when she turned her attention back to him. "Kinda scary, it is, flying blind like that, but I *thought* I was flying nice and level even if I couldn't see. Then I took a peak at the bottle and saw that all the water was down in the bottom. Now I ain't as smart as Shamus 'bout a lot of things, but even I know something's wrong when the water's in the bottom of the bottle and that bottle's taped flat on its side. Way I figure it, I was probably flying on one wing, and that ain't no safe position to be in, not when you can't see where you are or where you're going. Yep, I reckon both the good Lord and Fitzgerald were looking after me that day."

"And it was all Shamus's idea, the whiskey bottle, I mean?" Libby asked carefully.

"Sure was. Course he don't use it anymore. Had a glassblower make up a glass tube with a colored marble in it. Says it works better and he don't have to worry 'bout the water freezing and busting the bottle. Don't work any better than the bottle, though. He gave me one of those tube things a while back. He's a good man, Shamus is."

"Yes, he is," Libby agreed. She'd noticed the tube in the cockpit of the deHavilland, but hadn't paid any attention to it. It was mind-boggling. Shamus had invented the turn and bank indicator! He hadn't tried to patent it. She knew that, for sure. It would be several years before the first patented and commercially produced TBIs were introduced. Should she suggest he apply for a patent? It would make him a millionaire.

No, she decided. She couldn't tamper with history. Besides, she could hear his opinion now. Make money from a gadget that made flying safer for everyone? He'd say, "No way," or the twenties equivalent of the phrase. Yes, Hank had the right of it. Shamus Fitzgerald was a good man.

IT WAS DUSK when the last plane discharged its last customer. The day of barnstorming was over, but activities on the fairgrounds were still in full swing.

Shamus told Libby and Eddie to wait for him at the entrance to the midway while he tied down the planes. Hank had parked his Jenny nearby and had agreed to keep a watch on all three planes while Shamus and Libby toured the fairgrounds. Then they'd return to relieve Hank of watch duty. On a clear day like today the aeroplanes were safer in the air than on the ground. Parked and unattended, they could fall prey to a long list of possible hazards—souvenir seekers, a careless sightseer with a burning cigarette, even the livestock who normally called the pasture home.

"Nothing a cow likes better than the dope and fabric on an aeroplane," Hank told her. "Why, I've seen one cow strip a whole wing, right down to the wood spars, in less than an hour."

"Sure wish Shamus would hurry," Eddie complained. "I'm right hungry. Want one of those Coney Island dogs everyone's talking about."

"He'll be along in a minute," Libby told him. "You can go ahead if you'd like. I'll wait."

"Nah. You're right. He shouldn't be much longer. In fact, I think I see him now."

Libby quickly scanned the group of people heading in their direction. Then she saw him, walking with a stranger. Her gaze moved over the second man to rest on Shamus, then swung abruptly to the other man.

There was something familiar about him. He was tall and lean, with a boyish face and light brown hair that curled over his forehead. He and Shamus were talking as they walked, and Shamus was shaking his head.

"The man with Shamus, do you know him, know who he is?" she asked Eddie a little breathlessly.

"He came to see Shamus once. They call him Slim. He's one of the airmail pilots. I heard he was trying to set up a new mail route between St. Louis and Chicago. Probably wants Shamus to sign on."

Slim. Yes, that was one of his nicknames. Libby could hardly believe it. But it was him. She was sure of it. They'd be calling him Lucky Lindy in a few years. And he was walking toward her. She might even be able to meet him.

"Do you think he'll come over here with Shamus?" Her voice must have sounded a little strange because Eddie gave her a funny look.

"I don't know," he said. "Why?"

"Because I'd like to meet him."

"Shamus said to wait here, but I guess we can walk over that way if you want," Eddie said.

Libby didn't wait for Eddie to change his mind. She wasn't going to miss a chance of meeting Charles Lindbergh. Not if she could help it.

"Why do you want to meet him?" Eddie asked, hurrying to catch up. "He's just another pilot. Don't think he even has his own aeroplane. Mostly he flies Robertson's. That's the guy he works for, the one who has the mail contract."

"I think I've heard his name somewhere," Libby said carefully. "I heard he was a pretty good pilot."

"Must have been another Slim," Eddie told her. "Shamus don't think he's all that good. Says he takes too many chances."

Libby didn't answer. There was no time, anyway. Shamus had seen them.

"Libby wants to meet Slim," Eddie said, as if to explain their sudden appearance.

Shamus frowned, but performed the introduction.

"Pleased to meet you, ma'am," Lindbergh said in a quiet, soft-spoken voice, his Midwestern drawl barely discernible.

Libby knew she probably had a stupid look on her face, but she couldn't help it. She couldn't speak, either, not face to face with the man who would soon become aviation's greatest legend. Somehow she managed to answer him with a nod and a shy smile.

Shamus's frown grew more fierce, but Libby barely noted it. Lindbergh in person looked exactly like he did in the history books. The books she'd read said he was shy. She didn't remember them saying much about him being a daredevil. Of course he'd have to be, or, at least, daring. Otherwise he would never attempt the flight that would make him famous.

Finally, she was able to find her voice. "Eddie said you fly the mails."

"Yes, ma'am. We just won the contract for the St. Louis to Chicago run. I've been checking out the route, looking for the best relay and refueling spots. And looking for good pilots. I was asking Shamus—"

"Told you, I'm not interested. Can't fly mails and run a flying service, too," Shamus interrupted him. "I like being my own boss."

"You sure? Pays five to seven cents a mile, depending on the route and the weather."

Shamus shook his head, his scowl becoming even more pronounced.

"Well, if you ever change your mind, let me or Mr. Robertson know." He turned to Libby. "It was nice to meet you, Miss Carmichael."

"Thank you. It was nice to meet you, too," Libby managed to say as Shamus took hold of her arm and urged her forward.

"You weren't very polite," she accused Shamus as soon as they were far enough away not to be heard.

Shamus shrugged his shoulders. "I just don't want to fly the mails. Why'd you want to meet him, anyway? Don't think they're looking for any lady pilots."

"She said she'd heard he was a good pilot," Eddie interjected.

"Good pilot? I don't know who you've been talking to, but believe me, Slim Lindbergh will never make old bones."

"Did you ever think you might be wrong?" Libby asked.

"About Lindbergh? Nope. He's always been a bit of an odd duck. And he'll take any dare that comes along. That's no way to grow old. Not in this business."

"He's not old. Just shy and a little reserved. He's a private person."

Shamus gritted his teeth. Why was she so interested in Lindbergh? "You sure learned a lot about the man, especially after speaking less than twenty words to him," he said bitterly.

"What in the world's wrong with you? All I said was I wanted to meet him."

Shamus knew exactly what was wrong with him. It was the look on Libby's face when he introduced her to Slim. Like he was some kind of god. She'd never looked at him that way. Why should he care, anyway? But whether he admitted it to himself or not, he did.

"Well, you met him, didn't you?" he growled.

"Yes, I met him. And one of these days you'll be proud to say you knew him, too."

"He's just another sky gypsy."

"Oh, you're impossible," Libby said, finally goaded past frustration. "Lindbergh's going to be famous. He's going to be the first man to solo nonstop from New York to Paris."

"First solo will be military," Shamus said. "Have to be. He'll have to use the new Navy carrier to refuel, and no civilian's going to get permission."

"That's right," Eddie agreed. "Have to be military."

Libby glared at them both. "Nonstop, I said. No refueling."

Oh, blast. She'd been so involved arguing with Shamus that she'd forgotten Eddie was even there. She'd let Shamus make her lose her temper again. Now what? It was too late to take it back. She wasn't going to lie about it, either.

"But, Libby, we don't have planes big enough to carry enough gas," Eddie argued.

"Not now, but soon. Say in a couple of years," Libby told him, hoping it was vague enough to stop any other questions.

"You're kidding, aren't you?" Eddie asked. "I mean, how would you know something like that?"

"She's teasing," Shamus said. He shot her a furious look.

"Are you?" Eddie asked.

"I guess you'll just have to wait and see," she said, grinning. She gave Shamus a quick glance. He had a strange look on his face, all stern and stormy, but there was something else, too. She stole a quick breath. If she didn't know better, she'd think he was jealous.

CHAPTER ELEVEN

WHEN LIBBY HAD INSISTED on coming with Shamus and Eddie for the weekend of barnstorming, she hadn't given a thought to sleeping accommodations. She'd assumed they'd stay with the airplanes, in bedrolls under a wing. That was the way Howard had always described his barnstorming days.

Neither had she taken notice when Shamus separated them from the other barnstormers, tying down the deHavilland and the Waco on a small hillside a distance away from the fairgrounds, especially when Hank chose the same hillside to secure his Jenny for the night. Then Eddie had gone off with friends and Hank announced his plans to join an all-night poker game.

As she watched Hank disappear down the hill, she suddenly realized how alone she and Shamus were on the hillside.

It was almost completely dark. Light from a harvest moon riding low in the sky failed to penetrate the shadow cast by the hill. The remains of a small campfire, reduced to a few glowing coals, gave off only a glimmer of light. A short distance away the dim outlines of the tethered airplanes stood sentry over the hillside like a trio of strange winged creatures from mythology.

Across the campfire Shamus stared off into the night, the glow from the dying coals casting his chiseled features into a bronze mask. Libby felt a sudden moment of disquiet, an ambiguous sense of anticipation and dread.

She couldn't identify the source of her discomfort. Was it caused by the look she'd seen on the faces of the other pilots when they'd asked her if she was staying in town? Or was it the result of the look on Shamus's face as she defended Lindbergh, the look she'd finally interpreted as jealousy? She supposed the origin didn't really matter, but there was no sense in denying the existence of her unease—a tingling awareness of tension and caution.

She forced a calm she didn't feel as she settled to the ground by the campfire. It was probably all her imagination, anyway. Besides, she had nothing to fear from Shamus. Weeks of living in his house had taught her that. Any danger would be of her own making. She pushed the thought to the back of her mind.

"Want coffee?" she asked, lifting the battered pot Hank had conveniently left on a flat rock by the fire.

Shamus grunted, a sound Libby accepted as assent. Gingerly holding the handle of the battered tin cup, she carefully passed it to him, then poured a second cup for herself.

"The moon's bright, but I don't see many stars," she said, hoping casual conversation would dissipate the heavy atmosphere between them.

"High clouds. Might get rain before morning, but you'll be okay in the tent."

"Tent? I didn't know you'd brought a tent. I thought barnstormers were supposed to sleep under the wings, kind of like a captain staying with his ship."

Her comment produced a slight upward curve of his mouth. "I'll play captain. You can stay dry. Besides, I thought you might like some privacy."

Libby felt the heat on her cheeks and knew it wasn't the result of being too close to the campfire. She could only hope the color wasn't distinguishable in the dim light. She should have known Shamus would consider the proprieties of the situation, even if she hadn't. He'd think it unseemly if she slept out in the open like one of the boys. She started to protest, then, remembering the knowing looks on the faces of the other pilots, decided against it. For Shamus's sake, she told herself. She'd brought him enough grief.

"It was nice of you to think of it," she said quietly. "I keep forgetting all the dos and don'ts."

Shamus shrugged. "I usually carry the tent when I'm going to be out overnight. It's saved me some uncomfortable nights."

Libby fell silent. If it rained tonight, Shamus would get wet. Sometimes the mores of the twenties were not only confusing, but downright exasperating. She knew without asking that if both of them sleeping out in the open was unseemly then sharing a tent would be thought completely decadent. All she could do at the moment was hope the weather remained clear.

"Did we have a good day?" she asked, wanting to change the subject.

"Pretty good. Enough to make the trip worthwhile. If we can fly tomorrow, we'll clear well over a thousand, even after expenses."

"Why wouldn't we fly tomorrow?"

"No need staying if it rains. No one will be wanting rides."

"Oh, I hadn't thought of that. Only crazies and pilots fly in the rain, right?"

Once again she'd managed to produce something akin to a smile from him and for a moment felt as if she'd just won the lottery.

"Some people consider them one and the same, crazies and pilots, I mean," he said. "And sometimes I think they might be right."

"You don't really believe that," she protested.

"No. No, I don't. But if I did, I sure wouldn't admit it."

"Me, either," Libby said, experiencing one of those rare moments of shared agreement. She smiled at him across the campfire, then caught her breath as something more intense replaced the look of amusement in his eyes. Hastily she looked away.

Shamus stood up abruptly. "About ready to turn in?" he asked in what seemed to Libby to be a carefully casual tone. "I want to douse the campfire."

Libby nodded, then realizing he wasn't looking at her added, "Yes, I'm ready."

She watched as he dumped a bucket of dirt over the few remaining coals and stirred the remains of the campfire with a stick, carefully extinguishing each small spark. She knew it would take only one stray spark to destroy a plane.

"That's why we're camping so far away from the others, isn't it?" she said with sudden insight. "Too much danger in a crowd."

Shamus grunted. "Get a bunch of pilots together having a good time and one might get careless. In the air, it's you and your bird. No one else to depend on. I figure it ought to be the same on the ground. Besides, that way you've got no one else to blame when things go wrong."

And that, Libby realized, was Shamus's philosophy of life. It was a matter of trust. Shamus was a generous and giving man. She certainly had proof of that. But when it came to trusting others, he'd depend only on himself.

Libby couldn't fault his reasoning when it came to taking care of his airplanes. It was a lesson Howard also preached. "It's your life on the line when you're in the air, not some mechanic's. Best depend on yourself to make sure it's done right." Generally she followed the rule, at least where her airplane was concerned. But in life? She'd trust Howard with her life. And yes, she'd trust Shamus, too. But Shamus would trust no one but himself, not with his planes and not with his life. She couldn't help wondering what had happened to him to make him so wary.

She kept her thoughts to herself as they climbed the hill toward the tethered planes. Shamus had pitched the tent next to the deHavilland. The heavy canvas was draped over a wooden frame, a far cry from the lightweight nylon and aluminum tents she was used to seeing. Of course, it wasn't quite the antique it looked, not in this time, Libby reminded herself. In fact, it could be the very latest model.

Shamus showed her how to drop the net, adjusting it for air circulation and insect control. "Of course, if it starts raining, you may have to drop the flap, too. Makes it a little musty, but it'll keep out the rain."

"I'll be fine," Libby told him. "I just hate to take the tent and leave you outside."

"I'd rather sleep outside, anyway," Shamus said. "Usually do."

"Unless it rains..."

"Then, too, except in a real storm. I'll be under a wing. That's usually protection enough. Your bedroll and spare clothes are already inside. I stuck mine over in the corner, too. I'll change in the morning after you're up and about."

Libby nodded.

He handed her the portable flashlight. "I'll just get my bedroll then and get out of the way. If you need anything..."

"I'll be fine," Libby assured him again.

"Well, if you think of anything, I'll be close by."

"I'll call," she told him, "and Shamus, thank you."

"For what?"

"For this and... and for letting me come."

Shamus ducked his head. "Ah, well, it was little enough. Besides it seemed like a good idea... at the time."

Libby couldn't repress her grin. "And now?"

"At least I know where you are," he growled. "Good night, Libby."

"Good night, Shamus," she called after his retreating back.

Libby left the net in place and the tent flap open, knowing the darkness inside would cover her movements. She hastily shed her blouse and pulled one of Shamus's soft nightshirts over her head. She suspected he only wore them in the cold of winter. The one she'd appropriated was the only one she ever saw in the wash.

Her image of a bare-chested Shamus was enough to bring heat to her cheeks. She hugged the nightshirt's soft folds to her and tried to discipline her thoughts. He wouldn't sleep without a shirt tonight. He'd be fully dressed, ready to handle any emergency. Shamus, she realized, was always ready for emergencies.

She hesitated for a moment, then, accepting the unexpected privacy of the tent, reached down and removed her riding breeches before slipping between the blankets of the bedroll. It was, she decided as she snuggled into the blankets, much more comfortable than sleeping fully clothed. It almost made up for missing the adventure of camping outside beneath a wing.

When the popping, cracking sounds of canvas being whipped by the wind startled her from sleep sometime later, it took her several moments to orient herself. Deep rolling sounds of thunder seemed to shake the hillside. Jagged bolts of blue-white light could be seen through the net-covered opening in the tent. But it was the almost continuous roaring of the wind that jolted her into full awareness.

Libby grabbed for her breeches, stuffing the oversize nightshirt inside the waistband and yanking on her boots. The airplanes would need to be double tethered in winds this strong. Shamus would need help.

She found him fighting to tie down a wing of the Waco and without instructions threw her weight over the wing.

"What are you doing out here?" he yelled. "Get back inside."

"I can help," Libby yelled back, the wind almost drowning out her words.

She followed him around to the other side of the plane and once again added her weight to the wing as Shamus tightened and double tied knots in the tether ropes. If the tethers broke loose in the storm, the winds could flip the plane, smashing the wing's delicate wooden frame.

"That's the last one," Shamus yelled as he tied off one more tether. "I'll check the cockpit covers. You get back to the tent. It's going to rain any second."

"What about the Jenny?" she yelled, gesturing toward Hank's plane.

"Already done. Dammit, Libby, go on, now. You're going to get wet."

"You come, too."

Shamus shook his head.

"There's no need for you to get wet."

He shook his head again. "I'll be fine."

Blasted hardheaded Irishman, Libby muttered to herself, but she could see no way of making him change his mind. She bent her head into the wind and, letting go of the wing she'd been holding for support, headed toward the tent.

Then she stumbled over Shamus's bedroll.

It was, she decided as she looked down at the blanket roll, as good an idea as she was going to get. Looking over her shoulder to see Shamus still working with the cockpit covers, she scooped the bedroll in her arms and, bent nearly double under the weight of her burden and the strong winds, staggered toward the tent. She heard his bellow even above the roar of the wind just as she collapsed inside.

Drops of rain drummed against the canvas tent, at first like a tattoo but quickly becoming a steady incessant din. On her knees Libby struggled to untie the tent flaps. Net was fine to keep out the insects, but no protection at all against the driving rain. The flaps had just dropped into place when they burst open again, admitting one wet and furious Shamus Fitzgerald.

"Dammit, Libby, what do you think you're doing?"

Libby scrambled to the back of the tent, not only to put a little distance between herself and Shamus, but to allow room for the flaps to close behind him.

She took a deep breath and forced herself to speak calmly. "Tie the flaps behind you. The wind's blowing in the rain."

"Why'd you take my bedroll?"

"To keep it dry, of course. If you choose to drown yourself, there's nothing I can do about it, but I saw no need to let the blankets get soaked. They're a mess to dry out."

"Libby," Shamus growled.

"Oh, for heaven's sake, Shamus. Sit down. The world's not going to come to an end because you came into the tent to keep dry. Sometimes you're impossible."

"But you... I shouldn't be here."

"Why not? If you're worried about my reputation, it's already shot to you know where. I saw those looks. You said it yourself. Ladies don't go around wearing pants and flying airplanes. Besides, who's going to be snooping around in this storm to see where you're sleeping? And even if you did stay outside, who'd believe it? Even an insane man would take cover in weather like this."

Libby took a deep breath and waited for Shamus's next argument.

He said nothing.

She flinched as a clap of thunder shattered the silence inside the tent. "Well, aren't you going to say anything?"

"You're right," he growled. "Even an insane man would take cover in weather like this."

Libby felt like a general gone to war, only to discover the opposing army had fled. "Oh. Well, I'm glad you agree."

Shamus swallowed a sigh. It *would* be crazy for him to stay outside, but sharing the tent with Libby was even crazier.

He tried, with only partial success, to ignore the strange thumping and bumping sounds coming from the direction of her bedroll.

Never had he met a woman like her, exasperating, outspoken, impulsive, incredibly brave and completely fascinating. She was a threat to his sanity and to all his plans for the future. She attracted him in ways he'd never imagined, irritated him without apparent effort and intrigued him to the point of complete frustration.

No, he told himself firmly, there was no place in his life for a woman, especially not a bossy little piece of work like Libby. She wouldn't be like the others. She wouldn't complain about the time he spent "tinkering with those dirty old aeroplane engines," or begging him not to fly. That he could handle.

Libby would be more likely to tell him how to service his planes or demand he take her with him every time he had a flight. He'd never have a moment's peace. Come to think of it, he'd had precious few of those since she first flew into his life.

Just why, he wondered, was he wasting energy arguing with himself? Libby was already too involved in his life. He didn't need more complications.

In spite of his best intentions, he couldn't resist another look in her direction. In the dim light furnished by the weakening battery of the flashlight, the strange, mystifying movements inside her bedroll continued. "What in blazes are you doing in there, the Charleston?"

The bedroll went still.

"Libby? Are you all right?"

"I'm fine" came the answer in what he could only describe as an exasperated voice.

"What's wrong? Are you tangled in your blankets?"

"No."

"Then what are you doing?"

"If you must know, I'm trying to take off my breeches."

"Your breeches! Dammit, Libby, you can't—"

"Oh, for heaven's sake. I'm adequately covered, not to mention having the blankets up to my neck. Come to think of it, you should get out of your wet clothes, too. Don't worry about my modesty. Just turn off the flashlight. I'll turn the other way and squeeze my eyes shut tight for good measure."

Shamus sighed again. The trouble was, the little minx was right. He did need dry clothing. He pulled a dry shirt and breeches from his pack then flicked off the flashlight.

Rain, still driven by the howling wind, continued its assault on the canvas tent as Shamus crawled into his bedroll a few minutes later. He heard Libby shift positions in her bedroll.

"You changed into dry clothes, didn't you?" she asked.

"Yes, I changed into dry clothes," he growled. "Go to sleep."

"Good. I wouldn't want you to catch pneumonia. I don't think they've invented penicillin yet."

"Penicillin? What the heck is that? Never mind, I don't want to know. Dammit, Libby, will you please go—"

"That's something else I've been meaning to talk to you about," she muttered.

Shamus gritted his teeth. "What now?"

"I wish you'd stop calling me Dammit, Libby. Just Libby is adequate."

"I don't call you—"

"Yes, you do. At least half the time you say my name, you preface it with dammit."

"I do not. Dammit, Libby..."

"See."

"All right, I apologize."

"I guess I do exasperate you sometimes, huh? I don't do it on purpose. Honest, Shamus. It's just things are so different here that sometimes I forget."

"Libby, will you please go to sleep?"

"Wouldn't you rather talk?"

"No, I would rather go to sleep."

"Oh. Well, I'll stop bothering you then. Good night, Shamus."

Stop bothering him? Now that was a laugh! "Good night, Libby," he managed to say.

Quiet once again descended in the tent, a quiet made all the more evident by the continuing din of the storm outside. Shamus lay on his back, staring into the darkness, listening as Libby turned in her bedroll, lay still for a moment, then turned again. If only she hadn't told him she was removing her riding breeches. He remembered the long silky length of her legs all too well. *And you should have known you were in trou-*

ble then, he thought, remembering the first night she'd spent in his bed.

Stop it and go to sleep, he ordered himself. *Forget she's there, only a few inches away.* Thankfully, she'd finally stopped threshing around in her bedroll. He rolled onto his side facing away from her and closed his eyes, willing sleep to come.

A brilliant flash of light followed almost immediately by a teeth-rattling roll of thunder lit the interior of the tent. Libby's scream was almost simultaneous.

Shamus jackknifed into a sitting position, fighting the folds of his blankets. "Libby! What's wrong?" He flicked on the flashlight.

"I'm all right. The thunder...it startled me. I'm sorry I disturbed you."

He could hear the quiver in her voice, see her eyes wide with fright. "You're scared," he said, unable to keep the surprise out of his voice. "I didn't think anything scared you. The sound of thunder won't hurt you, you know," he added in a more gentle voice.

"Not the sound. I know that. Intellectually, I know it, anyway. I won't hear the one that gets me, but I never claimed to be Wonder Woman. Lots of things scare me. I usually manage to keep them under better control, though." She made a nervous little laugh. "It's just...I don't like thunderstorms. I'll try not to bother you again."

Shamus could hear the strain in her voice. Just who the hell was Wonder Woman? he thought. Not that it mattered all that much. The important thing was to help her over her fear. Then maybe at least one of them could get some sleep. "Did it help when we were talking?"

"Yes, it gave me something else to think about. Talking . . . you know, the physical evidence that there was someone else here . . ."

"If we try to talk all night, we'll only end up fighting again."

"Maybe," she admitted, "but it's better than—"

"Than waiting in the dark for the next roll of thunder?"

"Yes," she admitted with a sigh.

Shamus answered with one of his own. He already knew he wasn't going to get any sleep, but maybe he could help her. He rolled over, moving closer to Libby and reached out to pull her to him, bedroll and all.

"I don't think I . . . Shamus! What are you doing?" she whispered, a note of panic in her voice.

"Giving you physical evidence that someone is with you. I can't talk all night, but I can hold you." He cradled her head on his shoulder. "Don't worry. You're still in your bedroll and I'm in mine. Better now?"

"I'm not afraid of you, Shamus," she said. "I don't think I've ever been afraid of you. In fact, under other circumstances, I think we . . . It's just that we're not supposed to be together."

"You don't still believe that crazy story you told me, do you?"

"I wish I didn't, but that doesn't change the facts."

"Libby, for heaven's sake . . ."

"I see what you mean, about fighting if we tried to talk," she said.

"Yeah. Well, maybe you had better just try to go to sleep. I think the storm's beginning to blow out, anyway."

She snuggled into his shoulder. "I only wish I could make you understand."

"So do I," he said. "So do I."

Shamus lay rigid, afraid to move, until he felt her begin to relax. The sound of her breathing became softer, deeper. With his free hand, he folded the blankets off his chest. Her nearness was all the heat he needed. He'd left the flashlight burning, its light now so feeble it barely penetrated the blackness inside the tent. He hoped it would give Libby some reassurance. He stared off into the near darkness, seeing nothing, but trying to conjure up images of anything that would help him ignore the woman by his side.

He'd been right about the storm, he thought idly. It was moving on. Libby shifted, rolling onto her stomach. He drew a quick breath as her head came to rest, cheek down, against his chest. The blankets of her bedroll fell away. She made an incoherent sound and threw her arms across his chest.

His breath caught in his throat. One of these days someone was going to invent a way to keep bedrolls from coming undone. He could only wish it had already happened. With no blankets between them, he could feel the heat of her skin, the softness of her body, through the two thin layers of cotton clothing that separated them. He could feel her heartbeat. Her breath caressed his neck. Her hair tickled his chin. His blood pounded in his temples. Saints help him! It was more than a mortal man should be asked to withstand.

The distant rumble of thunder was now so faint it could barely be heard above the gentle pattering of rain on the tent. Could he shift her into her bedroll without waking her? He was reluctant to try, not, he realized, for fear of awakening her, but because he didn't want to let her go.

Libby stirred, her movements pulling her from deep sleep into a nether land of not quite awareness. Her lips curved into a smile. All was right with her world. She felt comfortable, content, cherished.

The subconscious thought forced itself into her waking mind, jolting her into awareness as effectively as a physical shake. She blinked, raising her head from the pillow she'd made of Shamus's chest to lock gazes with him.

Midnight blue! His eyes, she remembered, were one of the first things she'd noticed about him...eyes soft with gentle concern. Now they were dark and unfathomable.

Other memories flooded in, sepia-tone images overlaying reality. She remembered how the old photo had intrigued her, how familiar Shamus had seemed when she first saw him, how surprised she'd been to realize his hair was black, his eyes deep blue. He moved exactly as she'd expected, with a deceptively casual loose-limbed gait that disguised the economy of his motions. And his smile...the little I've-got-a-secret quirk of his mouth widening into a full-fledged grin that exposed a dimple in his left cheek...it could steal the breath from her body.

This isn't real, a small voice warned from somewhere in the deep recesses of her mind. *You aren't supposed to be here.*

But she was here, and Shamus was real. He might not be real in her own time. He might not be real when she went back to where she belonged. But she wasn't in her own time. She was here, in his time, with him, and...she wanted him.

"Shamus, will you kiss me?" she asked in a whisper that escaped almost before she realized what was happening.

There was a sudden spark of some indefinable emotion in the depths of Shamus's eyes. "Libby, you don't know what you're saying." His voice was a hoarse whisper.

Her breath caught in her throat. "Yes, I do," she said in a faint voice. "I know exactly what I'm saying." This time her voice was stronger and contained a tone of conviction.

"If... if I kissed you now..." He shook his head. "I... It probably wouldn't end with a kiss."

"I know that, too."

"Dammit, Libby..."

Libby took a deep breath. "In my... where I come from," she amended quickly, "things are a little different. People express themselves and their feelings more openly. We don't think it's wrong to share special feelings. As long as it doesn't hurt someone else, men and women who...who like each other, who care about each other, well, they're free to express that caring without being considered...scandalous."

"You mean men and women actually sleep together without..."

"Men and woman have been doing that since the beginning of time," she chided gently.

"Not nice..." His voice trailed into silence.

Libby dropped her gaze. "You mean good girls don't. I think you know that's not true. Some good girls do. Always have. The only difference is that, in my time, the old double standard is no longer so strong. Men were never criticized or condemned as strongly as women for the same behavior. It still exists, of course, but a woman who...who expresses her feelings for a man in that way is not automatically a fallen woman."

She stole a look at his face, now set in a stern mask. "Never mind," she told him, striving for a flip tone in her voice. "You don't have to kiss me. I shouldn't have asked. It won't happen again."

She tried to roll away to her own bedroll. It didn't matter whether it was 1923 or 1993. Rejection still hurt.

Shamus's arm tightened around her.

"Let me go," she said, struggling to keep her voice calm. "You don't want to kiss me. I should never have suggested it anyway. It was a bad idea."

"Dammit, Libby," he began in a voice so tight it was a low rumble.

"And stop calling me Dammit, Libby." Again she tried to pull away.

"I want to kiss you."

"No, you don't. You made that perfectly clear. I'm a...a hussy for suggesting it. Good girls don't—"

Her last words were smothered on her lips as Shamus claimed her mouth with his own. His lips were hard and searching, sending her pulse out of control.

Libby tried to turn her head away, but his mouth pressed against hers, demanding a response. She felt herself spinning away into a world of neither fantasy nor reality, a world filled from horizon to horizon with Shamus. Unconsciously, her arms moved to clasp him more closely to her.

His kiss gentled, the tip of his tongue tracing the outline of her lips, leaving them burning with fire when he lifted his mouth from hers.

Libby drew a deep shuddering breath and forced her eyes to meet his.

"Now tell me again how it is that I don't want to kiss you," he growled.

CHAPTER TWELVE

LIBBY TREMBLED, her quickening pulse hammering in her throat. The spark of fire deep in Shamus's eyes seemed to steal her breath from her lungs. She heard the faint warning bell in the recesses of her mind and made a halfhearted attempt to regain control of her senses, but any remnant of her will to move away vanished in the reality of his arms around her.

"Shamus," she began, his name a mere whisper of sound.

Shamus groaned, a deep low roar of sound. His name on her lips sent tingles up his spine. One hand moved, traveling up the curves of her back until his fingers tangled in the mass of her unruly curls. Slowly he pulled her face down to his. "I warned you," he whispered, his voice ragged with desire. "I warned you one kiss wouldn't be enough."

A fire storm coursed through his veins as his lips brushed across hers in a feather-light caress. His chest heaved in a final futile effort to control his desire. "Damn the picket fence," he muttered as his lips took possession of hers.

She tasted sweet, so sweet. The last vestiges of restraint slipped from his mind as he deepened the kiss. Hungry, impetuous, impatient, it demanded more than it asked. With another groan, he rolled to his side, shifting Libby with him.

He raised his lips, once to trace a line of quick kisses along the edge of her stubborn little chin before returning once again to the intoxication of her mouth. With the urgency of his desperate thirst partially quenched, he softened the kiss, determined to prolong, to savor the exotic taste of her lips.

As his lips claimed hers again, Libby found herself flying in the bright blue light of an endless sky. A feeling of mindless joy curled through her body, leaving her helpless against the assault of sensations produced by his touch. He was sunshine and storm, a lightning rod to the force of desire created by his touch.

She let her hands wander across his back, reveling in the feel of heat from his body The aroma of bay rum pipe tobacco mingled with his clean, unperfumed soap scent to create an intoxicating incense. She caressed the strong tendons at the back of his neck, delighting in the feel of his warm skin and the silky texture of his hair under her fingertips. So lost was she in the whirlwind of sensations, she barely realized it when Shamus adjusted her position under him.

He nibbled at the sensitive lobe of her ear, sending electric currents of desire flickering through her body. His mouth moved down to nuzzle the side of her neck, capturing her fluttering pulse beneath his lips, then wandered lower, pushing aside the opening of her nightshirt.

Libby gasped, her breath unraveling in a soft thread of sound as her body arched closer to him. She quivered in his arms as his touch moved still lower, grazing the side of her sensitive breasts.

With trembling fingers she raised her hands, trying to work the buttons of his shirt. She wanted to see him, to feel his heartbeat, to touch his warm, solid flesh.

Shamus raised himself above her, brushing her hands aside as he divested himself of his garments. He lifted her into a sitting position, pulled her nightshirt over her head and rocked back, his eyes devouring the sleek, softly curved beauty of her body.

Libby's eyes roamed greedily over Shamus's well-muscled chest, then up to meet the heated gaze of his eyes. She reached across the space between them, aching to touch him.

Heat and need coiled deep in Shamus's loins as Libby's delicate touch brushed across his chest. Her hand came to rest on his shoulder. Then she slowly lay back, pulling him with her.

"Ah, mavourneen," he whispered, his lips once again seeking hers.

His hands slid over her breasts, cupping them gently, his long sensitive fingers caressing the rosy nipples. Libby gasped with pleasure, waves of liquid fire washing over her. His hands moved lower, stroking the indentation of her waist, the flare of her hips, sliding down her legs.

Shamus fought to control desire as his passion threatened to overwhelm him. Gently he nudged her legs apart and felt her tremble. She was small, so small, so perfect and so ready for him.

He entered cautiously, sensitive to her need for time to adjust, and felt himself tremble as she accepted him. Slowly, he began to move, calling for her to join him in the ancient rhythms of love.

They moved together, gliding on a sweet wind toward the horizon, caught a thermal of their own creation to soar faster and faster, higher and higher.

Then time fell away.

There was no now, no then, only the reality of two becoming one in an explosion of energy that mirrored the beginning of the universe.

For a time neither could move, woven together in a rapture of bright wonder. Shamus began to recover first, shifting his weight to one side, rolling Libby with him, careful to keep her secure in his hold. His ragged breathing became quieter. The mad thumping of his heartbeat slowed.

Libby lay drowsy in the warmth of Shamus's arms, reluctant to move. Never could she remember being so blissfully happy or feeling so fully alive. Outside the tent, the storm had moved on, the sound and fury of its explosive energy now diminished to a gentle rain. She couldn't help comparing it to the storm she and Shamus had just experienced.

When she heard Shamus whisper her name, the sound as quiet as the rain falling softly against the canvas, Libby found herself reluctant to answer. She wasn't ready to talk, to destroy this feeling of contentment. From the beginning, even before the beginning, and in spite of the barriers, she'd been drawn to Shamus by something far stronger than mere desire. Surely anything that felt this right couldn't be wrong. Or was she trying to kid herself?

Libby made a little sound and snuggled more closely into the curve of his body. Right or wrong, it was done. Making love had been inevitable from the beginning. She hadn't been strong enough to fight it any longer. Now that it had happened, it wasn't possible for her to regret it. But she wasn't strong enough to analyze it tonight, either. Surely tomorrow would be soon enough to think about consequences.

"Libby," Shamus called again, unsure whether to be disappointed or relieved when she failed to answer. He listened to her breathing grow soft and steady and fought the urge to shake her awake and make love to her all over again. He hadn't known how badly he wanted her until now. Or how badly he would want her again.

Shamus thought of himself as an all-or-nothing guy. The first time he'd viewed the world from the cockpit of an aeroplane, he'd known how he wanted to spend the rest of his life. He'd also known no woman would share that life. Nor would he settle for two part-time lives, one in the sky and the other tethered to the earth.

But Libby was different from any woman he'd ever known. She, too, dreamed of blue skies and white clouds, not blue shutters and white picket fences. She fit into his life as perfectly as she fit into his arms. With Libby he could have it all, the life he'd planned and the dream he hadn't dared pursue.

But would she let him fit into her life? He wished he knew more about her. She was always ready to say what she thought but didn't talk about herself or her past. Who, for example, had taught her to fly? And where? She insisted she had to go home, but he'd never been able to get her to tell him exactly where that was. As for that crazy story about being from the future, well . . .

None of that mattered anyway, Shamus decided. At the moment Libby was exactly where she was supposed to be, in his arms. And if he had anything to say about it, that's where she was going to stay.

LIBBY AWOKE ALONE in the tent. As the sound of voices outside penetrated the canvas walls, she dressed in haste, pushing her memories of last night to the back of her mind.

She made her way toward the three men standing around a small campfire a short distance from the tent. Morning had arrived reluctantly, an overcast gray day with the smell of rain in the air.

Eddie greeted her with his usual enthusiasm. Hank nodded, mumbling, "Good morning, ma'am." Shamus turned and stood watching her silently as she approached. She could feel his eyes searching her face and struggled to keep her expression calm.

"You've got time for a quick cup of coffee," Shamus told her without preamble. "There's a line of thunderstorms moving this way. We've got to get into the air if we're going to beat them home."

So much for worrying about the morning-after confrontation, Libby thought. Shamus seemed to be ignoring the entire situation, as if nothing unusual had happened at all. But even as she tried to convince herself that their night together had meant nothing to him, she knew it wasn't so. That blue gleam deep in his eyes, the one she'd come to recognize as grim determination, glittered dangerously. He might be ignoring the situation for the moment. After all, they could hardly discuss it with Eddie underfoot, but the promise that the time would come was implicit in his look.

Almost before she realized it, Libby was strapped in the front cockpit of the deHavilland. Shamus was anxious to get underway. Even with the steady tail wind blowing from the southwest, the trip from Peoria to Curruther's Corners would take a couple of hours and at least one stop for fuel.

Eddie took off first, into the wind, then circled the fairgrounds to alter his course toward home. He wagged his wings over the pasture before heading north. Shamus piloted the deHavilland into the sky after him.

A few moments in the air told Libby today's flight would be no pleasure run. The air was so heavy with moisture that the deHavilland's engine had to strain to stay in the air. Capricious winds buffeted the small craft constantly. Only Shamus's iron control on the stick and rudders kept the wings level.

The line of storm clouds seemed to hang in the air behind them. Libby knew they only appeared to be holding still, but were in fact rolling north at at least the same speed as the plane. She couldn't repress a shiver at the memories they provoked. She peered into the distance ahead, catching a glimpse of Eddie in the Waco. Like Shamus, he was pushing his plane to the limit. She, Shamus and Eddie were in a race with the storm front, but unlike them, the storm wouldn't care who won or lost.

Eddie had already refueled and was in the air when Shamus and Libby landed for gas. The threatening clouds were still following, some distance behind, but closer.

Shamus crawled across the wing to the front cockpit as soon as they were on the ground. "Are you all right?" he asked.

"I'm fine," she assured him. "A little cold, of course, but nothing we can do about that. Besides, you're the one doing all the work. Do you want me to take the stick for a while?"

Shamus shook his head. "Just sit back and enjoy the ride."

"Think we'll beat the storm?" She was trying to keep her voice nonchalant, but her nervous glance over her shoulder must have given her away.

"I think we'll outrun it," Shamus told her, his voice suddenly low and reassuring, "but I won't take any chances. If it becomes a threat, we'll land and wait it out. I'm not going to let anything happen to you."

"Shamus, I..."

"Libby, I know we have to talk about things... about us," he said, "but for now, I think we'd better get home." Behind his goggles, his eyes were gentle and reassuring.

Libby nodded. "Yes. We have to get... home."

He reached over and rearranged the blue scarf around her neck, his gaze searching her face. Then he gave her a reassuring smile and jumped lightly to the ground.

They took off into the wind, directly into the face of the storm. Libby forced herself to look into that dark swirling mass and felt her stomach clench into knots, fighting the memories of the last time she'd faced such a destructive force. She didn't realize she was holding her breath until Shamus banked the plane into a turn that would adjust their course to the north, running ahead of the storm.

The knots in her stomach gradually unraveled as she realized the storm seemed to be keeping pace but was not gaining ground on them. Besides, Shamus knew what he was doing. He'd go to ground if the storm drew too close.

She allowed herself a small sigh. Worrying about the storm was only a diversion, she admitted to herself. What she really didn't want to face was thinking about Shamus and what had happened between them last night. It was too late for regrets. Besides, she didn't regret it. The love she and Shamus shared last night had been beautiful, perfect. Still, she couldn't ignore or forget her belief that she was here temporarily, that she had no real place in Shamus's life, or he in hers.

Shamus would not agree. He'd already warned her that they had to talk, and she could guess what he'd have to say. She'd seen the warm, protecting, possessive look in his eye. She didn't try to delude herself into believing that last night had been nothing but a pleasant diversion for him. Oh, he'd undoubtedly entertained himself in the past with the twenties version of a one-night stand, but he wouldn't consider last night in that light. By now, she knew how he thought. They'd grown to know each other too well to pretend either a casual acquaintanceship or a casual encounter. And because of the way they'd met, he'd always considered her his responsibility. How much stronger would that instinct be now?

She'd been wrong when she'd convinced herself she had no regrets. She did have one, not for herself, but for Shamus. She knew, had known at the time, that any relationship between them would be temporary. She'd accepted the memory of his love as payment against the pain of parting, but she had not given him that choice. He didn't believe her story of being from the future. He didn't know that the relationship between them was doomed by forces neither one of them could challenge or control.

She had to leave. Now. Before she did more damage. Even if she couldn't get back to her own time, she had to leave Shamus and Curruther's Corners.

Maybe it was finally time, she thought, remembering the feeling of déjà vu she'd experienced when she saw the storm chasing them. She looked over her shoulder one more time. The churning clouds were closer and looked as threatening and as familiar as they had earlier this morning.

Libby shivered. Did she really have the courage to fly her Jenny into that caldron? Did she have a choice? Had she ever had one?

They were nearly home. Libby recognized the landmarks, the water tower on the edge of town, the railroad tracks that skirted the southern boundary. The bright green Shamrock Flying Service painted on the side of the white shed acted as a beacon. Shamus circled the field, positioning the deHavilland into the wind for landing. She could see Eddie and the Waco already on the ground.

Shamus landed the plane lightly, floating in as if there were no blustering winds trying to upend the craft. He taxied off the runway and spun the plane around into position to be pulled backward into the shed before cutting the engine.

Libby knew she had little time. The storm was nearly on top of them. As soon as the plane had come to a stop, she unclenched the seat harness and climbed from the cockpit. Somehow she had to slip away from Shamus and Eddie, get the Jenny out of the barn and into the air before either of them realized what she was about.

Shamus made it easy.

"Told you we'd make it," he yelled at her, his voice carrying over the sound of the rising wind. "You can go on up to the house. Eddie and I will get everything tied down and be up in a minute."

Libby nodded, afraid to trust her voice. Her eyes drank in the sight of him hungrily, trying to record this final impression. He stood, feet spread, the white scarf he wore around his neck floating in the breeze. His head was tipped back, the wind blowing through his hair. He was smiling his wide, heart-stopping smile, the one that exposed that now-you-see-it, now-you-don't dimple in his left cheek, and she could see the twinkle in his eyes even behind the goggles.

This is it, then. Goodbye. And I can't even tell you. Libby swallowed against the lump in her throat and started up the path toward the house. But she couldn't do it, not without a last touch, a last farewell, even if he didn't recognize it as such. She turned back, running to him, throwing her arms around his neck. "Thank you, Shamus, for... for keeping me safe."

Not sure if he'd heard her, not giving him time to restrain her, she slipped her arms from around his neck and whirled away.

Bemused, Shamus watched her run lightly up the path toward the house until a particularly strong gust of wind reminded him of what he should be doing.

He turned to Eddie, caught the knowing grin on the boy's face and glowered. "Come on, boy. Give me a hand with this. We haven't got all day."

"I'm ready when you are, if you are," Eddie teased.

With the practiced movements of men who had done the same job many times before, they quickly pulled the two planes under cover. Eddie unloaded their camping supplies from the Waco and began fastening down cockpit covers. Shamus tethered the planes, then checked tie downs on the two other planes that rented space at the field. By the time they finished, the storm was almost on top of them.

"Let's get to the house before this breaks," Shamus shouted, urging Eddie to hurry.

"I'm ahead of you," Eddie yelled back. He was already on the path.

Shamus bent his head into the wind. The path was so familiar he could walk it almost without looking. He was halfway up the hill when he heard Eddie yell. His head jerked up to see Eddie pointing at something in the sky.

Disbelief, then fear clutched Shamus's stomach when he caught the flash of something red-and-white against the dark clouds. *Dear God...*

"It's Libby," Eddie screamed. "What's she doing?"

Shamus shook his head helplessly. He didn't know what she was doing, but she was going to kill herself if he didn't stop her. He started running toward the airfield, heard Eddie following him even above the noise of the fast approaching storm.

"You can't go up," Eddie yelled, clutching at his arm. "You'll never get off the ground. Besides, what could you do?"

Eddie was right. There was nothing he could do, not from the ground, not in the air. There was nothing to do, nothing but watch and pray. Shamus clenched his fists so tightly his nails cut into his flesh.

She was trying to go home. She'd warned him she would. He should have paid more attention. He didn't believe for a minute that she was really from the future, but he knew that she did. He should have tried harder to convince her, to prove to her that it was impossible. He hadn't because she'd seemed content enough the last week, and after last night, he thought she'd realize her home was with him.

The tiny red-and-white Jenny was little more than a dot against the mountain of black clouds. If her plane was any other color, he probably wouldn't be able to see it at all. He almost wished he couldn't. Surely his imagination wouldn't be as bad as this. If she tried to enter those clouds, she wouldn't have a chance. And if she got much closer, she wouldn't have a choice. The churning caldron would pull her in like water being sucked through a straw, then spit her out like so many matchsticks.

Please, God. Please, mavourneen, turn back now. Before it's too late. That's not the way home.

"What's she trying to do, Shamus? She's going to kill herself."

Shamus could hear the sound of tears in Eddie's voice, but he had no comfort to give. And he didn't dare take his eyes off the Jenny. The tower of clouds seemed to grow even taller, forming into strange shapes and fantasy figures. A bolt of lightning zig-zagged toward earth from the bottom of the dark mass.

She's afraid of thunder. How can she fly into that?

The small speck flew closer and closer to the black cloud. From the ground it looked like a large open hand, ready to grasp. Then the tiny plane disappeared into the giant fist.

"No!" The hoarse scream erupted from Shamus's throat, but even before the sound died on his lips, the small red-and-white dot seemed to fall backward, almost as if the fist had flung it out of the way.

"Did you see that?" Eddie gasped.

Shamus was afraid to answer, unable to accept what he thought he'd seen. But there was no question that the distance between the tiny speck and the dark cloud was growing. Libby wasn't out of trouble yet. Although from this distance the plane looked intact, she was in a spin. He held his breath, tears clouding his vision until he could barely make out the Jenny plummeting toward earth.

Pull out. Pull out, he screamed silently. *Dammit, Libby, kick that rudder and pull out. Now!*

CHAPTER THIRTEEN

LIBBY APPROACHED the black churning mass of clouds, her eyes tearing behind her goggles. She blinked frantically, trying to keep her vision clear. She had to be able to see. Once inside that cloud, she needed to find the tunnel that would lead her to where she belonged.

She could never remember feeling so frightened. She was deliberately flying into the storm to test a theory that was, at best, only guesswork. If her theory was wrong, she'd pay for the mistake with her life. Did she have the courage to do it?

She tightened her grip on the stick. She had no choice. She couldn't stay here any longer. She had to go home.

No, you don't, a small voice chastised. *You could stay here with Shamus. You could be careful to avoid storms. You could even give up flying, then you'd be in no danger of being zapped back.*

For a moment Libby hesitated. She still had time to return to the ground, but what kind of life awaited her there? And what kind of imbalance in the universe would such a decision create? She wasn't supposed to be here. She didn't belong. No, she was doing the only thing she could do, the only way she knew how. If she had the courage to follow through.

She was approaching the storm mass now. She
could see the separate churning clouds that made up
the weather cell. Gusting winds rocked the Jenny from
side to side despite her efforts to hold the wings steady.
Deliberately she aimed the nose of the Jenny straight
into the nearest cloud bank.

Libby tried to remember what had happened the last
time. She'd been trying to drop away, to escape the
storm, but the clouds had swept up and over her anyway, enveloping her in their grasp before she could
escape. Now, for some strange reason, and even
though she was flying straight for it, the storm continued to dance just out of reach.

She could feel the cold. The howling wind muffled
even the sound of the engine. Frantically, she juggled
stick and rudder pedals, trying to hold a steady course.
Her altimeter spun wildly, and fear boiled into her
throat like raw acid. The Jenny shuddered, then, as if
caught by some unseen force, seemed to fall away.

Libby didn't know what had happened, what was
happening. Her head was spinning dizzily. No, not her
head, her plane. She blinked, trying to clear her vision, but all she could see through the windscreen was
a blur of green and brown.

Her mind seemed unable to function, but her subconscious must have recognized the situation.
"Now!" came the silent command, and her body re-
acted automatically. She kicked the rudder, jammed
the stick forward, then pulled up the nose. The Jenny
shuddered again and leveled off.

Where was she? Had she made it back to her own
time? With hands still shaking, Libby banked her
plane into a turn, looking out the side of the cockpit
at the ground below. She saw the green Shamrock

Flying Service sign. She looked to the storm clouds still hanging in the southern sky, just out of reach. Should she try again?

She knew the answer even before she finished asking the question. There was no way she could make herself face that again. With a sigh of resignation, she circled the field to position the Jenny for landing.

Shamus watched Libby line up with the runway, almost afraid to believe his eyes. How had she escaped?

"Did you see that?" Eddie asked, his voice shaking. "I thought she was a goner for sure. I ain't never heard of anything like that. It was like... like that storm just tossed her away. I mean, that's what it looked like. Did you see it, too?"

Shamus couldn't find his voice. His eyes were glued to the Jenny coming in for landing. As the plane touched down, he began heading toward the runway. The plane was still rolling when he grabbed hold of a strut and pulled himself onto the wing.

With hands visibly shaking, Libby automatically compensated for the additional weight on her wing. She kept her eyes forward, knowing Shamus was riding her wing down the runway, but she was afraid to acknowledge him. Finally, as the Jenny rolled to a stop, she dropped her hands to her lap and turned to look at him.

Shamus reached into the cockpit, his hands fumbling with her harness release. "What did you—" he began in a shaking voice that still sounded like a bellow. He swallowed, then tried again. "Dammit, Libby, you could have—"

Once again he bit back his words. He was no good with words, he decided. No good at all. Finally he gave her one long look, then reached into the cockpit and plucked her from the seat.

"Shamus?" Like his, Libby's voice was shaking, and for the first time since he'd known her, she seemed unsure.

"Dammit, Libby. Don't you say a word. Not a word. You can have your chance to yell at me later. Right now, I need to hold you... just hold you, understand? I still can't believe you're alive."

He eased the goggles over her head and looked down into her eyes, large, violet-blue and swirling with emotions he couldn't read. She continued to tremble in his arms, whether from exhaustion or fear, he couldn't tell. He wanted to yell, to scream. Didn't she know, didn't she understand what she'd done to him, leaving him to watch helplessly from the ground while she flew into the face of certain death?

He felt a tug on his arm. "Is she all right?" Eddie's voice contained a note of awe, as well as barely controlled panic.

"I'm... I'm fine," Libby answered before Shamus could say a word.

"I want to take her up to the house," Shamus told Eddie. "Can you get the Jenny to the barn by yourself?"

"Sure," Eddie said. "It looks like the storm's decided to give us a miss, after all."

Shamus and Libby jerked their eyes skyward. The storm did seem to be swinging northeast, moving away.

Shamus didn't understand, but then the day had been full of things he didn't understand. He wouldn't question. Not now. It was enough he had Libby back, and safe. "And if you ever try a crazy stunt like that again and live to tell about it, I'll throttle you myself," he said. "Understand?"

"I won't, I promise," Libby told him, her voice sounding almost normal. "I would never be able to make myself do that again."

IN THE DAYS THAT FOLLOWED, Libby briefly discussed the reasons for her aborted attempt to return home with Shamus. She'd heard Eddie's version of seeing the storm throw her out of the way, as well Shamus's reluctant confirmation of the tale. She'd reached the same conclusion. The storm hadn't wanted her, hadn't wanted her to find the gateway to the future. And although she knew Shamus still couldn't accept her story of being from the future, he seemed to believe her when she told him she now believed she was here to stay.

Life seemed to fall into a routine. Libby returned to work at Marshall Field's, and although she often shared lunch hours with Maisie, her friend had stopped inviting her to join excursions to Chicago's varied night spots. In fact, Maisie seemed quieter and more content with her life since their adventure at the Lazy Cat. There was a new sparkle in her eyes, one that Libby found in her own eyes when she looked into a mirror. But if Maisie had fallen in love, she wasn't discussing it with Libby, and Libby wouldn't ask.

Although Libby was sure Eddie knew at least something of the relationship between her and Shamus, they behaved circumspectly when Eddie was in the house. And by mutual and unspoken consent, the Jenny stayed hidden in the barn. But sometimes, when Shamus had a weekend delivery, Libby would join him in the deHavilland. It was her favorite part of her new life, sharing the bright blue sky with Shamus by day as they watched the earth slip by under the wings of the airplane. That and sharing stolen nights, under the stars, locked in each others' arms.

When Eddie began rebuilding a Jenny he'd acquired from another pilot, Libby volunteered to help him with the restoration. She passed on the tips and secrets Howard had taught her and couldn't help thinking how ironic it was that the skills she'd learned in the nineties were more pertinent now than when she'd learned them. Often the movements of Eddie's hands, the way he worked the wood to shape a new wing framework, reminded her of the times she'd watched Howard perform the same tasks. When the poignant memories caught her unaware, she'd turn away to regain her composure, knowing she couldn't explain.

Shamus had learned nothing about Zeke Vincent or his possible whereabouts on their trip to Peoria. Now he stepped up his search and his inquiries. He was, he told Libby, determined to get rid of the suitcase so they could get on with their lives. Although she couldn't help being afraid for him, Libby couldn't protest. She, too, felt the unresolved threat of the suitcase hanging over them.

She knew Shamus was frequenting the more unsavory haunts of underworld Chicago, looking for clues. Each time he disappeared, she fretted until she heard him arrive safely home, then pretended to be asleep when he quietly opened her door, as if to confirm she was still there.

She was down at the airfield working with Eddie on his plane late one afternoon when Shamus arrived at the airfield looking tense and worried.

"Zeke's turned up dead," he said bluntly. "Eddie, I want you and Libby on a train for Denver tonight. I've already contacted a friend. You can stay with him until we find out what's going on."

"No," Libby and Eddie protested in unison.

"This is no time for arguments. He didn't die of old age. Someone found him and probably forced him to talk before he was killed," Shamus said. "And that means he told them he hired you for the flight," he added, looking at Eddie.

Libby felt the color drain from her face. "Shamus is right, Eddie, you've got to get out of town."

"You're going, too," Shamus insisted.

Libby braced herself for the argument she knew was coming. It was one she couldn't afford to lose. "No, I'm not. No one's looking for me. The more things seem normal around here, the better off we'll be."

"Dammit, Libby..."

"Dammit, yourself. I'm not going."

"What about the Jenny?"

"What about it? It's safely hidden in the barn. Besides, you're the one who's always said no one would connect it with me." She tried to keep the exasperation out of her voice. Staying with Shamus was all that was important now. "How many times have I heard you say it? Ladies don't fly aeroplanes."

"Let her stay," Eddie interrupted. "She can help at the field. Besides, you won't go off half-cocked if you've got her to look after."

Shamus threw up his hands. "I suppose I'll have to," he grumbled. "If she doesn't want to go, she'd probably jump train at the first stop."

"You're right, I would," Libby told him, smiling sweetly. Then she winked at Eddie.

With Shamus urging haste, the three of them were at the train depot in less than an hour. "Telegraph us when you get there," he told the boy.

"Send it to the Shamrock Flying Service from Denver Aviation and just say 'Cargo received,'" suggested Libby.

"How'd you think of that?" Shamus asked. "It's a good idea."

Libby shrugged her shoulders. "I read it somewhere."

Libby and Eddie hugged each other. Shamus offered his hand, then pulled the boy into his arms for a hug, too. "Be careful and take care of yourself," he said gruffly.

Eddie nodded, his eyes looking suspiciously misty. "I will," he promised. "You two take care, too."

Shamus nodded, then, with his arm around Libby's shoulder, watched the train disappear into the night.

"Isn't there anything we can do besides wait for them to come looking for Eddie?" Libby asked after she and Shamus returned to the farmhouse.

"I wish I knew what." Frustration deepened Shamus's voice. "I'm still sure it was either Capone or Moran. If I only knew which one owned the suitcase, I'd turn it over and let the two of them fight it out. I'm tempted to pick one and try it anyway. Maybe they'd get so busy fighting each other, they'd forget about Eddie."

Libby knew there should be some way she could help. Maybe there was, if Shamus meant what he'd just said. But first she'd have to convince him. "Would it matter if you knew which one eventually wins?"

"Sure it would, if we knew," Shamus said. "Even if the suitcase doesn't belong to him, he might be strong enough and grateful enough to protect Eddie."

Libby took a deep breath. She knew Shamus dismissed the idea that she'd come from another time, but she was going to have to discuss it if she was going to help. "I don't know who owns the suitcase," she said carefully, "but I do know who eventually wins the war between Moran and Capone. I told you once before, it's history."

Shamus gave her a sharp look. "I thought you'd decided all that business was nonsense."

"No," Libby told him, shifting uncomfortably under his gaze. "I only said that I no longer believed I was supposed to go back to my own time."

"Just the same..."

"Listen to me," Libby pleaded. "I know what I'm talking about. If you mention the word gangster fifty years from now, the name that pops into most people's minds is Al Capone. And I don't mean just people who live in Chicago, either. Capone wins the gangster wars here and becomes notorious all over the country. He outlives most of today's other gangsters. He finally goes to jail on charges of federal income tax evasion and lives until sometime in the late forties. And he dies in bed of some kind of illness, not bullet wounds."

"Libby, don't," Shamus said gruffly. "We can't make a decision like this on what...what has to be some kind of dream."

"I know you think I'm imagining all this, but I do know what I'm talking about. I wouldn't say so unless I was. Do you think I'd put Eddie's life at stake if

I wasn't sure?'' Libby twisted her hands in frustration. "Please, Shamus, believe me. Capone comes out on top.''

"Well, I'll admit he looks stronger than Moran at the moment," he said reluctantly. "If I was going to approach either one of them, I guess it would be Capone."

"We can't just sit around and wait for something to happen," Libby protested.

"We'll wait until we're sure Eddie's safe. Then we'll decide."

Libby knew that waiting for Eddie's telegram would make the next three days seem like forever, but she also knew Shamus was right. They had to wait until they were sure Eddie was safe before making a move. Besides, the decision to make contact with Capone was only the first step. Next, they would have to find him.

"I wish you'd gone with Eddie," Shamus said. "Dammit, Libby, I want you safe."

Libby shook her head. "I had to stay. I'm not going to say I'm not afraid—for all of us, but I feel safer here with you than I would somewhere else."

"Ah, Libby, I hope you didn't make a mistake."

"I didn't. This is where I want to be. Except...I mean, I know we have to be careful around Eddie, but tonight I...I don't want to be alone."

"You won't be, mavourneen," he said, pulling her into his arms. His lips grazed her forehead then settled on her lips in a kiss as tender and light as a butterfly's wing. "I'm not going to let you out of my sight."

Libby quivered at the sweet tenderness of his kiss. "Shamus," she sighed against his lips, "let's go to bed."

They made love with a passionate tenderness that brought tears to Libby's eyes. Danger was forgotten as her body melted into his and the haven of his love. Never had she felt so safe, so cherished, so complete.

Shamus saw the tears on her cheeks, glimmering like diamonds in the moonlight filtering through the curtained windows, and trembled. "Are you all right? Did I hurt you?" His voice was tense with concern.

"I'm fine. More than fine. Perfect," Libby assured him, her voice husky with passion. She reached up to touch his face.

Shamus turned to bury his lips in the palm of her hand, then dipped his head to sip the silver tears from her cheeks. "Like nectar," he whispered. He shifted his weight to the side and curled her into the contours of his body.

Libby snuggled into him, conscious of how perfectly they seemed to fit together, even in repose.

"Go to sleep, mavourneen," Shamus whispered. "Tomorrow's going to be a long day."

Although he urged Libby to sleep, Shamus found himself unable to do so. It was, he decided, time to make plans to leave Chicago. Libby was right. They couldn't wait around and do nothing. But it wouldn't be over even after he returned the suitcase. The Chicago underworld had a long memory.

The only solution was to shut down the flying service and move. Tomorrow he'd start making plans. After he dumped the suitcase, he and Libby would disappear, join Eddie in Denver. He'd have to build the business again, and it would take time. But he'd done it once, he could do it again. And this time he'd have Libby to help. Finally, satisfied with his decisions, he, too, slipped into sleep.

Shamus wasn't sure what woke him up, the roar of a car engine or the sound of glass breaking somewhere near the front of the house, but one or both jerked him abruptly awake. Libby, too, must also have heard the noise. She sat up abruptly.

"What was that?" she whispered, clutching at his arm.

"I don't know. Stay here."

"Shamus..."

"Keep the lights off and stay quiet. Watch the windows, but stay out of sight. From here you can see the back of the house. If you see anything, anything at all, yell. Can you do that? I'm going to slip out and see what's going on."

Libby nodded, her heart in her throat. "Please, be careful."

Shamus gave her shoulders a squeeze, then dropped a quick kiss on her lips. "I will," he promised.

It was ten minutes, although to Libby it seemed much longer, before Shamus returned to the bedroom, his face grim.

"They're gone," he said. "Just drove up, chucked a brick through the front window and took off."

"But who was it—and why? What did they want?"

"I don't know who it was." Shamus's voice was strained and anguished. "They want the suitcase. They... they say they've got Eddie. They've got Eddie, and damn it all, I still don't know who it is."

"They've got Eddie?" Libby managed to choke out the words, praying she'd heard him incorrectly, knowing she hadn't.

"That's what the note wrapped around the brick says." The bleak desperation was clear in Shamus's voice. "I've got no reason not to believe them."

"But when . . . how?"

Shamus crushed the paper in his fist. "They must have taken him off the train. They must have been watching the airfield and followed us."

Libby blinked back threatening tears. Shamus had enough to deal with. Besides, weeping would accomplish nothing. She swallowed, determined to keep her threatening hysteria at bay. "What do they want us to do?"

Shamus drew an audible breath. "The note says they'll contact me with directions on where to bring the suitcase in a couple of days. Then they'll release Eddie."

Libby caught the doubt in his voice. "Why wait two days? What are they planning to do?"

"I think they want to keep us off balance. Make us worry. Intimidation. It's an old mob trick."

"But Eddie... They won't hurt him, will they? He's just a boy."

Shamus held her close. "I don't think they'll hurt him, not until they've got the suitcase in their hands, anyway."

"And . . . and then?" Libby couldn't help it. Her voice broke. "You don't believe they'll release him, do you?"

"No," Shamus said, his voice bleak. "They've already killed Zeke. I think they'll kill Eddie, and us, too, if they get a chance, as a lesson if for no other reason."

For a moment Libby clung to Shamus, unable to control her trembling. It wasn't fair. She'd been through too much, come too far for it to end this way. She had to think of something. She wasn't going to lose Shamus or Eddie, not without a fight. She pulled herself from his arms and pulled a bracing breath deep into her lungs. "Then we haven't got much time," she said deliberately. "We have to find Capone."

"I know we discussed it, but I'm still not sure that's our best plan." Shamus's voice was ragged.

"Do we have another? Other than just waiting around for it all to happen?"

"But what if Capone's the one who has Eddie?" Shamus countered.

"What if he is? We'll only be doing exactly what he wants, giving him back his damn money, right? Maybe we can convince him we would have returned it if we'd known who it belonged to. The fact that you haven't disturbed it should help convince him we're telling the truth. Besides, we can't be any worse off than we are now, can we?"

Shamus dragged his fingers through his hair. "No," he admitted, "we can't be any worse off. Okay. You win. As soon as I get you somewhere safe, I'll start looking for Capone."

Libby had no intention of being left behind. Even after they found Capone, she still thought she was the best one to approach him. But she wasn't prepared to fight that battle at the moment. First, they have to locate Capone. She'd let Shamus think he'd put her safely out of harm's way, then get on with what she had to do. With both of them looking, they were likely to discover his whereabouts that much quicker.

"All right, Shamus, I'll let you stash me away while you look for Capone," Libby finally agreed. "I can stay with Maisie. I'll be safe enough there. But you have to promise you'll come tell me what's going on. Otherwise it's no deal."

Shamus had expected an argument. He was so relieved Libby hadn't insisted on coming with him, he would, he realized, agree to anything she suggested. "I promise," he told her. "I know you're as worried as I am. I just want you safe."

Libby knew that and she loved him for it, even though she couldn't agree.

Maisie agreed to help Libby as soon as she heard her friend's abridged version of Eddie's kidnapping. She sent out the message that she had a friend who needed to contact Capone to every old neighborhood contact she could think of, and by late afternoon the activity paid off. One of Maisie's acquaintances reported that Capone was planning a private party at his Cicero mansion the following evening.

Shamus greeted Libby's news with relief until he realized she was going to insist on going with him. He groaned when he recognized the challenging tilt to her chin.

"No. Absolutely not. I go alone. Dammit, Libby, you can't go. It's too dangerous."

"I can approach him easier than you can," Libby insisted. "From what I understand, he has an eye for the ladies."

"That's exactly why you aren't going. Bootlegging isn't Capone's only illegal business. He likes the ladies, all right. But with him, it's business, not personal."

"Stop fighting, you two," Maisie interrupted. "It's supposed to be a swanky affair. Written invites and all. The guards'll never let a man alone inside if they don't know him. They won't pay so much attention to a man with a pretty lady on his arm. As you said, Capone's got an eye for pretty ladies."

Libby gave Shamus a triumphant smile. "That settles it. I go."

"I don't like it," Shamus told her. "Eddie's already in trouble. I don't want anything to happen to you."

"I don't think Capone will allow trouble at the party," Maisie said, attempting to calm Shamus. "Going to have a bunch of big shots from City Hall there, even the mayor, I hear. I bet it's going to be a fancy do."

Libby could see Shamus was still reluctant. "You have to take me. You don't have any choice. It's the only way to get in, the only way we can help Eddie."

"I guess you're right," Shamus admitted. "I still don't like it, but if I don't find any other way by tomorrow night, I guess we'll have to go to the party."

CHAPTER FOURTEEN

"DO YOU REALLY THINK the party will be safe?"
Libby asked Maisie after Shamus left.

"Oh, sure. Capone won't want anything ugly to
happen, not with all those society people there. It
oughta be a swell party. Afterwards... well, that's
something different."

"You want to come with us, Maisie?" Libby asked.
"Just to the party, I mean. Once we got inside, no one
would have to know you came with us."

Maisie looked a little wistful for a moment, then
shook her head. "Joe wouldn't like it if I went without him, and he sure wouldn't go."

"Joe?" Libby couldn't help asking. "Who's Joe?
Your new beau?"

Maisie nodded. "You remember. Joe McGillicutty.
We've kinda been seeing each other."

Yes, Libby thought, she remembered the young
policeman who'd helped them the night of their Lazy
Cat adventure. She'd thought at the time that Joseph
Francis McGillicutty was more than an old neighbor-
hood pal or, at least, that he'd like to be. "I'm glad,
Maisie," she told her friend. "He seemed awful nice."

"Anyway, Joe's on duty tomorrow night. Besides,
it wouldn't be any fun without him. Now what we
gotta do is figure out something for you to wear. As I
said, it's going to be a fancy do..."

As Libby inspected her dress in the mirror the next evening, she couldn't help thinking that she had been born in the wrong period. She wore the twenties' silhouette much better than many of the clothes from her own era.

The light blue silk georgette crepe dress hung in an unbroken line from the shoulders to hips, then flared gently to the knees. A crystal beaded belt encircled her hips, giving a flash of sparkle every time she moved. The same beaded design decorated the rounded neckline. Black silk round-toed pumps with an inlaid design of rhinestones on the mother-of-pearl heels and two long strands of faux pearls completed her outfit.

"Now for the headband," Maisie said, gesturing for Libby to sit down on the vanity stool. She tied the jeweled band around Libby's head, adjusting several strands of hair until they fell in soft curls onto Libby's forehead, then stood back to admire her handiwork. "Oh, Libby, you look fantastic."

Libby knew the dress looked good on her, but it wasn't as flashy as what she'd always imagined a gangster's moll would wear. "Is it fancy enough to get into Capone's party?"

"You're going to knock 'em dead," her friend assured her. "Are you ready now? Shamus is waiting."

Shamus felt his breath catch in his throat as he watched Libby enter the room. He tugged at the knot of his white tie. Oh, Lord, she was beautiful. Her dress was a blue swirl of color that teased the eyes by clinging softly to the curves of her body every time she moved. How in the name of Hades was he supposed to keep his mind on business and at the same time keep Libby out of trouble? Every Lothario at tonight's shindig would be trying to get her behind the bandstand.

As his gaze locked with hers, he saw her start, as if she was as unprepared for him as he was for her. "Is everything all right?" she asked, hastily dropping her eyes.

Shamus cleared his throat. "As right as it's going to get, I guess. I still think it would be better if you stayed here. It's not too late to change your mind."

"Don't start that again. I'm going. You know it's our only chance to get inside."

He'd also known he wasn't going to be able to convince her to stay behind, but he'd had to try. Now, with a groan of frustration, he gave in. "We'd better go, then. We want to arrive with the rest of the crowd. We'll have a better chance of slipping in unnoticed."

Maisie had told her it would be a "swell party," but nothing had prepared Libby for the sight that awaited them at Capone's Cicero estate. The large house stood well back from the road, behind high rock walls and guarded by a strong wrought-iron gate. As their car approached the entrance, the gate swung slowly open. Libby counted over half a dozen men, looking completely uncomfortable in their ill-fitting evening clothes, loitering in and around the gate. It took only a little imagination to see them dressed as the bodyguards they probably were. Two other men, dressed in dark blue uniforms, approached the car as Shamus braked to a stop.

"Smile and bat those pretty long eyelashes," Shamus muttered under his breath as one of the uniforms leaned in the car window and demanded to see an invitation.

Libby held her breath but managed to smile at the guard as Shamus extended the envelope one of Maisie's friends had provided. The guard examined the envelope, then handed it back, motioning Shamus to continue up the drive.

"So far so good," Shamus said quietly, proceeding up the driveway as Libby slowly let out her breath.

Shamus turned his car over to a muscle-bound valet, and he and Libby joined the stream of partygoers moving toward the front entrance. More guards, as ill-disguised as those at the gate, were stationed at various points along the portico that stretched across the front of the three-story stone mansion, but it was a very proper butler who bowed politely and checked invitations at the front door.

Libby hadn't been sure what kind of party a bootlegger would host, but she couldn't help but gasp at the obvious opulence as she and Shamus entered the ballroom. A series of sparkling chandeliers stretched down the middle of the long room. Gilt chairs and small intimate tables for two were scattered along one wall. A bandstand, banked with hothouse flowers, its occupants dressed in full evening attire, filled one corner at the far end of the room. Linen-covered tables lavishly spread with silvery trays and crystal bowls occupied another wall.

A small army of white-coated waiters moved discreetly among the milling crowd of richly dressed men and women. It didn't take Libby but a moment to realize that the sparkle and glitter of jewelry worn by many of the women in the room was not produced from glass beads such as those she wore, but from real gems.

A large marble fountain graced the center of the room directly beneath the largest chandelier. Libby's mouth formed an astonished O as she watched a cluster of partygoers fill stemmed glasses with the pale golden liquid that splashed from an urn held in the marble arms of a scantily clad water nymph.

"Is that what I think it is? A fountain of champagne?" she asked Shamus in amazement.

"Probably. You'll have to admit Capone shouldn't have a problem with supply."

The man's name drew Libby's thoughts to the reason they were there. She looked anxiously around the room. "Do you see him anywhere?"

"No, but he'll be around."

"Why don't I go around the room this way and you go the other. We can meet at the bandstand."

Libby almost gasped as Shamus tightened his hand around her waist, pulling her close against him. "You stay with me," he said gruffly. "Do you understand, Libby? I'll not have you harrying off on your own."

"But we could cover more territory if we looked separately for—"

"Enough, woman. You talked me into letting you come, but I'm not about to let you out of my sight."

Libby started to protest again, then, taking note of his stern, set features, let her argument die. It was obvious Shamus wasn't going to change his mind.

"Let's dance," he said abruptly. "I'll move us closer to the bandstand. Keep your eyes open. Word is Capone doesn't dance, but he likes to be near the music."

They danced for the next hour, stopping only occasionally to sit for a moment at one of the small tables, sip a glass of champagne and let Libby rest her feet. In other circumstances, it would have been a fairy-tale evening, dancing in Shamus's arms to the music of one of the best bands she'd ever heard, and Libby found herself having to concentrate to keep her mind on the task at hand.

So far neither she nor Shamus had spotted anyone who looked remotely like Capone. She was beginning to find it difficult to retain her optimism. She'd been so sure that this was the way to approach the mobster. Still, common sense told her he had to be somewhere near. Why would he be hosting a party like this if not to curry political favor? To do that he would have to make his presence felt, and so far, he hadn't.

"It's his party. Why isn't he here?" Libby asked Shamus, fighting to keep the desperation out of her voice. "This may be our only chance. It'll be two days tomorrow."

Shamus took her hand in his. "It's early hours yet, especially for this kind of shindig. I saw the mayor and his wife and one of our congressmen arrive a few minutes ago. Capone's probably waiting until all his important guests are here before making an appearance. Wants them all to be waiting on him. It's a form of intimidation and a reminder of who's the power here."

Libby nodded. Shamus's analysis made sense, and she recognized the power play. It was one still used in her own time, the boss making the underlings wait.

Despite Shamus's insistence she not move from his side, Libby finally convinced him he could not follow her into the ladies' room. She was struggling to control a fierce urge to giggle as she followed instructions from a maid down the hallway to the rest room. A quick look over her shoulder told her Shamus had taken up station near the hallway door.

She was halfway down the hall when she heard a door open and automatically turned to look. A man, another one of those who looked completely out of place in formal black-and-white evening dress, exited from a room, shutting the door behind him, but not before Libby caught a glimpse into the room of the man sitting behind a desk.

Libby stopped abruptly. She couldn't make her legs move. Her heart thumped frantically in her chest. It was him, Capone. She was sure of it—round face, bulbous nose, dark bushy eyebrows and a scar down the left side of his face.

She waited until the other man disappeared down the hallway, then her hand moved automatically to the doorknob. Without stopping to think of the consequences, she turned the knob and slipped silently into the room.

She felt rather than saw the presence of a second person and turned, eyes wide with fright, as the second man, with gun drawn, moved toward her. He hesitated, looking toward Capone for instructions, then stepped back.

Libby whipped her head toward Capone and felt her stomach muscles clench when she found herself staring straight into the gangster's hard eyes.

"What're you doing here, girlie? What do you want?"

Libby shivered, her gaze captured by Capone's merciless eyes.

"Speak up, girlie. What're you looking for? A job?" His eyes raked her body. "You got guts, I'll say that. A little on the thin side, but you're a classy-looking dame. I might find something for you."

The idea that Capone thought she wanted to work for him, would even think about working for him, galvanized Libby into action. She took a step toward the desk, a move she didn't realize was mirrored by the man behind her.

"My name's Eliz—Libby Carmichael, and no, I don't want to work for you," she told him, her words tumbling over her tongue in her haste to get them out. "But I do need to talk to you. I've been looking for you all evening. At the party, I mean. When I accidently saw you in here, I took a chance you'd talk to me."

Capone leaned back in his chair. "So you wanted to talk with me. What about? Well, go ahead, talk. I ain't got all night."

Libby clenched her hands in front of her in an effort to stop their trembling. "I have a friend," she began, "a young friend, really just a boy, and...and he's disappeared. I thought...I thought..." Libby hesitated, trying to figure out just how to phrase it. Capone took her words out of her mouth.

"Disappeared, huh? You thought I might know where he is?"

Careful, now, Libby, she admonished herself. "I thought you might help me find him," she said.

"And why did you think I'd do that? I don't have time to go around looking for lost kids. I got businesses to run."

"I understand that, Mr. Capone," Libby said, surprised to hear how steady her voice sounded. "But in this case, my friend's in trouble because he once did a favor for a man who I think used to work for you. I thought under the circumstance you might want to help.''

"Lots of people work for me," Capone said, his voice expressionless. "What's the man's name? Why come to me instead of going to him?"

"I can't go to him because he's dead. Please understand, Mr. Capone, I'm not sure that the man did work for you. I only heard that he might have. You were—are—the only one I could ask for help. My friend, Eddie, he's just a kid, not even shaving full time yet, and he's in an awful lot of trouble. I...I have to try and help him."

"What's the friend's, the dead one's, name?"

"He was no friend of mine. I never met him," Libby explained. "But his name was Zeke. Zeke Vincent."

"Vincent! That damned son of a—" Capone's fist slammed into the desk.

At the same moment, the door behind her opened, crashing into the wall. Libby whirled, knowing even as she did that Shamus had found her.

"Excuse the interruption," Shamus announced, his voice cool, although the look he shot Libby was one of barely restrained fury. "I was looking for my girl. Looks like I found her." He turned toward Libby. "I knew you'd get lost the minute I let you out of my sight."

Libby was afraid to say a word. All she could do was glare at him.

Capone nodded as the guard stepped quickly behind Libby. "Damn office's like Grand Central Station," he growled. "Shut the door, then frisk him."

Shamus stood immobile as the guard patted him down. Libby held her breath.

"He's clean, boss," the guard said.

"Now, let me get this straight," Capone said, after a moment. He turned to Shamus, who was still standing just inside the door. "You're looking for your girl. And your girl's looking for a friend. How many other players we got in this game? Anyone else likely to come busting in here?"

Libby moved to Shamus's side, clutching at his hand like a lifeline. "Mr. Capone," she began, a little breathless, "this is Shamus Fitzgerald. He's Eddie's...well, like an unofficial brother, I guess. We came together to try to talk to you, and no, there's no one else with us. I would have told you about Shamus but I haven't had time. And I guess he got worried about me because I told him I was going...I mean, I was going to the...the powder room, but when I saw you, I was afraid I wouldn't get another chance to talk to you and—and..."

"She always this much trouble?" Capone asked.

Shamus grunted.

Libby glared first at one man, then the other.

"Okay, enough," Capone said, his voice suddenly like ice. "You people got guts, I'll say that. As for your young friend, if he was working with that traitor Vincent, I sure got no reason to help him. Or you, either. It's no secret I was looking for Vincent. But I didn't find him. That much I'll tell you. And I don't know nothing about your young friend."

"Eddie wasn't working for Vincent," Shamus announced in a quiet voice. "He's a pilot and he works for me. Zeke hired him to make a certain flight from Canada into Chicago last year, but the boy didn't take the flight." He deliberately looked at Capone. "I did."

Capone's face went still. "What kind of flight? What was the cargo?"

"Two cases of bonded Scotch," Shamus said quietly. "At least that was what Vincent told Eddie. Actually there turned out to be a little more to the cargo than that."

"What happened to it?"

"Someone attempted to hijack it. I got away, but crashed the plane in the effort. The fragile part of the cargo broke up and burned. The rest..." Shamus hesitated, then met Capone's eyes. "The rest I have safe," he said deliberately. "It isn't mine. I don't know who it belongs to. I never found out who Vincent was working for. I figure anyone who can help me find Eddie probably owns it."

Libby held her breath, looking first at Shamus, then at Capone. Would it work? Did Capone have Eddie? If he didn't, would he be willing to help?

"Any idea where the boy is?" Capone asked, his voice bland. "What's he know about the missing cargo?"

"He knows it exists. He doesn't know where it is. Zeke must have told someone about hiring Eddie. Which is why I got a note suggesting I trade a certain suitcase for the boy. Now, I got no quarrel in doing just that, Mr. Capone, but the trouble is the note wasn't signed. I don't think much of business arrangements when I don't know who my partners are. It's a matter of trust, you see."

Capone held Shamus's gaze for a moment, then nodded. "Blind partners do have a way of disappearing without living up to their part of the bargain, don't they? You two might as well sit down. This is going to take a few minutes."

He looked over to the guard. "Joey, see if the boys have heard anything about any of our business acquaintances entertaining a secret guest."

Still clinging to Shamus's hand, Libby slumped thankfully into the chair in front of the desk. Shamus slid into an adjacent chair.

Capone turned his attention to Shamus. "I'm a businessman, Mr. Fitzgerald. Oh, I know, some people call it different names but I'm like any other businessman. All I do is supply a demand. It's a legitimate demand. They call it bootlegging when it's on my trucks. They call it hospitality when your host serves it to you on a silver tray. Don't matter what they call it. It's the same business."

Capone paused to pick up his cigar. "Now any business, even one like mine," he continued, "needs loyal employees, employees with some brains and with guts. I think you got what I need—loyalty, brains and guts. The organization needs men like you. Once we get your other little problem worked out, how'd you like to come to work for me? I need a pilot I can trust."

Oh, Lord, Libby thought. What would Shamus do now? She knew he'd never consider working for the man, but did he dare turn Capone down, especially since they needed his help?"

"Thank you for the offer, Mr. Capone," Shamus answered carefully, "but the truth is, I'm getting out of the air freight business. Plan to build aeroplanes of my own design. I only stayed in the business long enough to build a little nest egg, enough to carry me until I got my own plane in the air. All men have dreams. Mine has always been to build better aeroplanes. You're a man with vision yourself. I'm sure you understand.''

Capone frowned. ''A nest egg, huh? You ever open that suitcase you claim you've got?''

Shamus didn't flinch. ''Yes, I opened it, and you're partly right in what you're thinking. Beside it my little nest egg looks like pocket change. But the nest egg's mine. The suitcase isn't. That's the difference. As I said, you help me find Eddie and the suitcase is yours. All I want to do is build planes.''

Libby saw Capone start to protest and again held her breath. Then the gangster seemed to change his mind.

''Maybe we can discuss it again,'' he said mildly, ''when you're not so worried about your young friend.''

A quiet knock sounded at the door and the man named Joey slipped inside. ''Word is that Bugs might be entertaining down at his river warehouse. His guest arrived a couple of nights ago.''

Capone looked at Shamus, who nodded.

''Don't look so surprised, Miss Carmichael,'' Capone told her. ''A good business organization always knows what the competition is up to, but as boss, I don't care to know all the details unless there's reason to. I didn't have reason until now.''

Libby nodded, afraid to trust herself to speak.

''Joey, take Mr. Fitzgerald to Georgio. Explain the situation and tell Georgio to take enough boys with him to handle the situation. Tell him to send the kid back here. Then he can accompany Mr. Fitzgerald to retrieve the other package.''

''What about Miss Carmichael?'' Shamus asked quietly.

"I'm sure Miss Carmichael will be more comfortable waiting for you here," Capone said smoothly.

Shamus started to protest. Libby squeezed his arm. "Yes, thank you, Mr. Capone. I appreciate the hospitality."

"I'm going to join the party, Miss Carmichael. Would you like to come with me? Or I can provide you with a private room where you can wait."

"I think I'd rather rest, if you don't mind," Libby said slowly. "It's been a very busy day."

Capone nodded. "After you find Georgio, come back and show Miss Carmichael to the blue room," he told Joey. "I'll send up a bottle of champagne. Anything else I can get you?"

"A cup of coffee would be nice," Libby said quietly.

"Sure, no problem. Anything else you want, you just ask Joey here. He won't bother you, but he'll be right outside your door in case you need anything."

"I understand," Libby said. "Thank you for your consideration."

She turned to face Shamus, knowing he would be glowering, silently begging him not to make a scene. "I'll be fine waiting here for you," she said. "Go find Eddie, and please be careful."

He pulled her against him. "You, too," he whispered as his lips grazed her cheek. Then he turned to Joey. "I'm ready. Let's go."

Libby twisted her hands together, the words she was afraid to speak stuck in her throat. Would she ever see either Shamus or Eddie again?

CHAPTER FIFTEEN

ONCE AGAIN Libby paced the length of the room on the third floor of Capone's mansion. The man hadn't needed to go to so much trouble to make sure she remained here, she thought grimly. Didn't he realize she wasn't about to go anywhere until Shamus returned? But what was taking so long? It had been hours.

She pulled the curtain back from the window to look at the few cars remaining in the parking area. Most of the partygoers had gone home.

She didn't dare think about the possibility that Shamus and Capone's men wouldn't find Eddie or that they might find him too late. But where was he? Why didn't he come? She swallowed a sob and once more stared out the window.

When a quiet knock sounded at the door, Libby jumped. With her heart in her throat, she pulled the door open, almost afraid of what she'd find.

"The boss said for you to come back to the office now," the man called Joey told her.

Libby nodded, afraid to trust her voice, and stepped into the hallway.

"He said for you to go on in," Joey told her when they stopped in front of the room where she'd last seen Shamus.

Libby stepped cautiously into the room that at first glance looked empty. Then she saw him, a slight figure almost hidden by the high back of the overstuffed chair where he was sitting.

"Eddie?' she asked tentatively.

The figure stirred at the sound of her voice.

"Eddie! Oh, thank God, it is you."

"Who... Is that you, Libby?" He struggled to stand up.

"It's me. Oh, Eddie, am I ever glad to see you." She hugged him tightly. "Are you all right? Are you hurt?"

"I'm ... I'll be fine. I'm just a little tired."

Libby knew that wasn't exactly the truth. His face was bruised and scratched, but she could see that for the most part he spoke the truth.

"Where am I? And where's Shamus? Is he all right?"

"Didn't you see him?"

"I thought I did, but then some big guy threw me over his shoulder. I couldn't see a thing. The next thing I knew, I'm here. Where am I, Libby? And what are you doing here?"

Libby let out a breath of relief. "It's a long story, but if you're here, then Shamus is fine. He'll be along in a few minutes. He...had an errand to run first. Oh, Eddie, I'm so glad to see you. I was so afraid."

"Me, too," the boy said. "I tried to get away. Honest, Libby. But it was no good. I still don't know where I was. Or who had me."

"I think Bugs Moran had you. It was Mr. Capone's men who rescued you. Shamus and I came to him for help."

"I don't understand."

"It doesn't matter now. All that matters is that you're here and safe." Libby couldn't help it. She had to hug him one more time. "Shamus will be back soon," she assured him, "then we can leave."

"Leave? Just like that? What about the . . . the suitcase?"

Libby refused to think about the possibility that Capone wouldn't let them go. After all, they had a deal, didn't they?

"Shamus has gone to get the suitcase," she told Eddie. "We made a deal with Capone. He agreed to help get you back and Shamus said he'd turn over the suitcase. That's all he ever wanted to do with it, you know. Get rid of it. Give it back."

Libby wasn't sure how much longer they waited, but with Eddie there, knowing he was safe, the time passed more quickly. Still, it was a welcome relief when she finally heard a noise in the hall.

Eddie's eyes opened wide when Capone, followed by two of his bodyguards, entered the room.

"This your young friend?" he asked Libby. "He all right?"

"Yes, it's Eddie. And he's going to be just fine."

Capone turned his head to look at the boy. "You got good friends, kid. Hope you know it."

"I know it, Mr. Capone," Eddie managed to stammer.

"Good. Respect for his elders. That's good, too."

"I don't know how we can thank you for your help, Mr. Capone," Libby began.

"No thanks needed. It was a business deal. Right? One of my boys called from the gate. Georgio and Fitzgerald are on the way up."

Libby clasped her hands in her lap, her eyes glued to the door. Shamus entered first, carrying the suitcase. The man she guessed was Georgio followed.

Shamus's eyes went immediately to Libby's face, then, as if satisfied with what he saw, moved on to Eddie. "You all right, son?" he asked, his voice gruff with emotion.

Eddie nodded. "I'm sure glad to see you."

Shamus swung the suitcase onto the desk. "As I told you, Mr. Capone, I opened it. But it's all there. Just like I found it."

The gangster opened the case, looked for a moment, then closed the lid and motioned for Joey to take it off the desk.

"Looks good," he said. "I like it when a deal goes down right. You're an honest man, Mr. Fitzgerald. Sure you won't come to work for me? I'd make it worth your while."

Libby struggled to keep a straight face. She felt an almost uncontrollable urge to giggle. Just the thought of a man like Capone wanting to hire someone like Shamus because he was honest was laughable.

"I appreciate the offer, Mr. Capone," Shamus said easily, "but as I explained earlier, I have other plans."

"Then I guess we've got a done deal. We're square. Agreed?"

"Agreed," Shamus said.

As the wrought-iron gates clanged shut behind them, Libby let out a heartfelt sigh of relief. "Am I ever glad to get out of there," she said in a shaky voice.

"And boy, will I be glad to get home," Eddie added.

"I'm sorry, Eddie, but you're not going home," Shamus told him. "We're going straight to the train station. I want you in a Pullman and headed west as soon as we get there. And I don't want you to even stick your head outside the door until you're well out of Chicago. Understand?"

"But...but why? You returned the suitcase and—"

"And Moran's going to be mad as hell. I don't know how long it'll take him to figure out what happened, but it won't be long. He won't go after Capone, not immediately. But he'll come looking for us. I want you out of the way now."

"What about you and Libby?"

"We'll be following you as soon as it's light enough to fly. That's only a few hours from now. I'll have to leave the Waco, but we can get out with the de-Havilland and Libby's Jenny. If all goes well, we'll meet you in Denver."

"I could fly the Waco," Eddie protested.

Shamus shook his head. "We can't take a chance, Eddie. Of the three of us, you're the one they'll recognize the easiest."

"I thought it was all over," Libby said, not surprised to hear the wobble in her voice. "Won't Capone—"

"He won't lift a finger, Libby. He has what he wants. A done deal, he called it. We're on our own with Moran. I'm sorry, but I can't think of anything to do but run."

Libby squeezed his arm and made herself smile. "I'm ready to see some more of the country anyway. I've never been to Denver."

Shamus lifted one hand from the steering wheel and laid it over Libby's. "We'll be fine," he told her. "I think you'll like Denver. Eddie, as soon as you get there, transfer our bank funds. I'm not going to have time to do it, but we'll need them to start up again.

And you can start looking around for a hangar to rent. You know what to look for. Libby and I may not make it until sometime next week. Once we're out of the area, I don't want to push the planes. We've got the weather to worry about, too.''

"Okay," Eddie said in a subdued voice. "I'll do it. I'll try to do it right."

"You'll do it just fine," Shamus assured him. "If I didn't think you would, I'd let it wait until we got there."

It was still a couple of hours before dawn when Libby and Shamus arrived at the airfield. Shamus asked Libby to pack for both of them while he prepped the aeroplanes for flight.

"I want to be off the ground as soon as we can," he told her. "Weather looks a little chancy, but all we need is to get out of the immediate area, even if it's only a few miles. If we're gone before Moran shows up, he won't know where to start looking. I'll check the Jenny first, then go down to the airfield. I'll be back as soon as everything's ready."

Libby slipped out of her blue dress and put on her flying clothes. She gave the dress a lingering look then laid it aside. She'd have to leave it behind. They didn't have much room for luggage. She had to be practical.

Thunder rumbling in the distance warned her that the storm was moving closer. She could only hope Shamus was right, that they'd have enough time to get away from Curruther's Corners before the storm arrived in earnest. Maybe they wouldn't have to wait until dawn. Shamus knew the countryside. If they could get in the air, she could follow him until it was light enough to see where they were.

She tried to shake off her feelings of urgency. Eddie was safe and heading west, she told herself. Soon she and Shamus would be on their way.

She finished packing Shamus's clothes, at least all she could fit into the saddlebags, then went to the kitchen. She might as well pack up what food they could carry. On their cross-country trip, they'd be spending a lot of nights in fields far away from any restaurant.

Once finished with that task, she wandered aimlessly through the farmhouse. Everything had seemed so strange when she'd first arrived. It was here she'd first seen Shamus. Here she'd first realized she was a long way from home. Here she'd finally admitted she'd fallen in love with a hardheaded, stubborn Irishman she should never have met. Simply put, it felt like home, and she was going to miss it.

Outside, the rumbling of thunder was closer, louder. If they were going to beat the storm, they were going to have to hurry. She flinched at the sound of another crack of thunder that seemed to last forever and suddenly realized it wasn't thunder at all.

Gunfire! Had Moran's men found them already? Libby's knees grew weak. It was gunfire, and it sounded as if it was coming from the airfield.

Shamus! She had to find him. She ran for the front door, hesitating only after her hand was on the knob. In the recesses of her mind she heard a tiny voice urging caution. She'd do neither Shamus or herself any good if she raced outside without thinking. She had to find out what was happening.

Libby retreated through the house, then slipped out the back door. If she could get to the barn, she'd have a view of the airfield.

The wind was blowing harder as Libby slipped inside the barn. She heard the first drops of rain hit the tin roof. Not wanting to use a light, she felt her way around the Jenny to the back of the barn. She'd be able to see the airfield from the loft.

The sound of gunfire was louder now, almost a steady ack-ack sound, just like a movie. Fitting, she thought. It all seemed unreal, anyway.

But it was real enough. Shamus was real. The airfield was being attacked, and Shamus was out there somewhere. If they'd found him, they wouldn't still be shooting, would they? She had to see, to know what was going on.

Libby climbed the ladder, felt her way to the front of the loft, then pushed against the swinging doors of the hay drop. Moran's men had set fire to the hangar. She could see the rosy glow from the flames. Where was Shamus? Had he been able to get away? Frantic, she scanned the hillside.

There, halfway up the hill, a movement in the shadows. No, it wasn't Shamus. She saw the silver flash of metal, a reflection from the fire off a gun barrel. One of Moran's men waiting? But for what? Her eyes began to search the hillside, moving slowly, inch by inch, over the terrain.

At the sudden sound of an explosion she knew the maintenance shed was gone. Despite the driving rain, the flames leaped high into the night, fed by the mixture of volatile fuels and high winds.

There he was, moving up the side of the hill toward the house. It was Shamus, she was sure of it. He was hugging the ground, moving from shadow to shadow. The watcher, the man with the gun, wouldn't see him. He was going to be all right.

Libby's relief lasted only a moment. Shamus was heading for the house, expecting to find her there. But she was in the barn. She'd have to intercept him.

Quickly climbing down the ladder, she left the barn and began running for the house.

She heard the roar of the engine before she saw the car. It careened up the drive, swung in front of the farmhouse, seemed to hesitate for a moment, then roared down the drive. Seconds later the front of the house burst into flame.

Libby saw Shamus stand, exposing his position and start running toward the house. He didn't see the man with the gun, but the man saw him. He, too, stood, gun cradled, waiting for Shamus to come closer.

Libby knew Shamus wouldn't be able to hear her, not above the fury of the storm, even if she dared yell a warning. She began running full tilt down the hill. As the gunman raised his gun, she launched herself at his back and hung on.

Her attack caught the gunman by surprise. His tommy gun jerked upward, waving wildly, spewing a spray of bullets into the air. The man dropped the gun and reached backward, clawing to dislodge her from his back.

Shamus heard the gunshots and crouched, spinning toward the sound. In the dim light he could make out the struggling figures, and with a curse that would have curled his mother's hair, he began running, fear and adrenaline all but blinding him. In a rage he swung at the man with all his strength. The man crumpled to the ground, Libby beneath him.

With another oath, Shamus grabbed for the gun, and threw it down the hill. Then he reached for Libby, jerking her from the ground. "I thought you were in the house," he said shakily. "Are you hurt?"

"I'm fine. Dear Lord, I was so afraid for you."

"Afraid for me? Dammit, Libby, you were supposed to stay at the house." He shook her in frustration, then pulled her against him.

"We don't have time to argue now," Libby reminded him. "We've got to get out of here and hide somewhere."

"We'll take the Jenny."

"The storm?"

"We have to try. It's our only chance." Shamus bent to make sure the gunman was still out cold, then, grabbing Libby's hand, began running for the barn.

He swung the large double doors open. "We'll fire the engine inside and come out rolling. With the engine warmed up, it shouldn't take us but minutes to get in the air. Even if they realize what's going on, we should be able to get away before they make it up the hill."

Libby nodded, then stood on her tiptoe and pressed a quick kiss to his lips. She was scrambling into the front cockpit before he had time to react. Not that they had time, anyway, Shamus thought. Later, once he had them safe, they'd have all the time in the world. Then he'd tell her just how much she meant to him.

He took position in front of the propeller and debated with himself whether to ask if he could take the stick. The Jenny was Libby's plane, and she was a good pilot. But he had more experience in conditions such as these.

"Shamus," Libby called from the cockpit, "once the engine fires, you take the stick." It was almost as if she'd read his mind.

As the Jenny roared across the barnyard, Libby was thankful she'd asked Shamus to take the controls. She didn't think she would have had the strength to hold the plane in the face of the whirling winds. Dawn had arrived a few minutes before, but with the storm blocking the sun, the difference between daylight and dark was only one of degree.

Shamus threw the biplane skyward, ignoring the low-hanging storm clouds. Libby knew without being told that they'd need the height to get away. Moran's men realized they were trying to escape almost as soon as they rolled the Jenny out of the barn, but Shamus had been right. The distance between the airfield and the barn had given them enough time to fly clear. Now, if they could only stay airborne long enough to put some distance between them, to disappear into the sky, they would make it.

She shivered, the cold of the altitude and the gusting winds chilling her wet clothing. She knew Shamus would be freezing. He hadn't even had time to grab his aviator's jacket. Thankfully, she always kept goggles in the cockpits. At least their eyes were protected. She'd heard stories of eyelashes being frozen together in conditions like these.

The air was heavy, almost as if the storm was determined to push them into the ground. Only a little farther, she thought, then Shamus could descend. She'd be glad to get closer to the ground, to put more distance between them and the clouds.

She laid her hand lightly against the stick. Through the vibrations she could feel the effort it was taking Shamus to keep the small plane in the air. She could also feel the fatigue threatening his control. It was almost as if he was willing the plane to keep flying.

The sudden updraft took them both by surprise. One moment the small biplane was laboring to stay aloft. The next, it was being sucked upward, as if being pulled by a string. Libby grabbed the stick, lending her strength to Shamus's, trying to pull the nose down. Their efforts made no difference. The little plane was pulled into the churning mass of cloud.

Hail battered the plane and its occupants. Libby watched helplessly as first one, then a second tear appeared in the wing fabric. The plane shuddered, caught by forces too powerful for its delicate framework to withstand. She knew they had only minutes before the aircraft began to break apart. She looked at the rear cockpit, saw Shamus's features set in grim lines as he battled the bucking, vibrating plane.

Then she saw it, a pool of calm in the turbulent churning clouds and without thinking kicked the rudder, sending the biplane spinning into the placid sea of gray.

Reality seemed to slip away as the eerie quiet enveloped the tiny plane, and Libby shivered.

Then, as suddenly as they'd entered the sea of gray, they were free. Above them, a bright sun burned hot in a clear blue sky.

Libby looked to the left of the cockpit, caught sight of the long, winding ribbon of concrete and gasped. She knew where she was. She knew what she'd done.

The engine coughed, then sputtered. Despite the calm skies, the Jenny continued to shimmy and shudder. Shamus took control of the stick and pointed the Jenny toward a rolling field to the west. If he had any idea of what had happened, he gave no indication of it, concentrating instead on taking the wounded plane to ground.

The engine gave one final cough, then fell silent. Seconds later, Libby felt the jolt of the wheels as they touched earth. Without power, Shamus continued to fight the controls, trying to keep the wings level until the plane rolled to a stop, but it was an impossible task in the rough field. The wheels hit a bump, tipping the plane's precarious balance. One wing dug into the earth, spinning it like a top. The splintered wing acted as an anchor, forcing the plane to a sudden jerking halt.

Libby slumped in her seat, mentally and physically exhausted, trying to find the energy to unfasten her seat harness. She could hear Shamus in the cockpit behind her, already in the process of climbing down.

How was she going to tell him what she'd done? How would he react? Would he believe she'd acted instinctively, only wanting to save their lives?

She was still trying to sort out her thoughts when Shamus appeared at the side of her cockpit. "That was a rough landing," he said unnecessarily. "Are you all right?"

"I'm fine," she managed to stammer. "Shamus, I don't—"

"I don't know where we are," he interrupted, "but I don't think we have to worry about Moran finding us for a while. Did you see that road? Must be one of those new turnpikes they're talking about building. I tell you Libby, if they ever get roads like that one built all over the country, aviation's going to be in trouble. Why, on a road like that a man could drive anywhere he wanted to, even all the way across the country."

"I don't think aviation's in any trouble," she said, then took a deep breath. "Shamus, I have to tell you..."

Her explanation was unnecessary after all. Shamus's gaze jerked skyward as the roar of a low-flying military formation shook the ground. His eyes widened as they followed the sleek silver aircraft streaking across the heavens, leaving only four white vapor trails to mark their passage.

"Blessed saints, what was that?"

"A military formation, jet-powered aircraft. That's what I've been trying to tell you." She took a deep breath for courage. "We're not in the twenties anymore, Shamus. Welcome to the 1990s."

CHAPTER SIXTEEN

SHAMUS WAS hardly conscious of Libby scrambling out of the cockpit or of her taking his arm and pulling him away from the wrecked Jenny. He squinted into the bright sun, trying to follow the silver dots streaking across the sky. Even as he watched, the glittering dots blinked out in the distance. Their white smoke trails seemed to waver, blurring into indistinguishable shapes.

What had Libby said? That they were in the 1990s? Impossible! She was talking about that crazy dream of hers again. Only...only this time, it was *his* crazy dream.

Shamus shook his head in an unsuccessful effort to clear his thoughts and turned to stare at Libby. Why was she looking at him with that strange, sorrowful expression in her eyes?

"Shamus, I'm sorry," she said. "I didn't mean to bring us here. The Jenny was breaking apart, and when I saw that void...I didn't even think about consequences."

Shamus shook his head again. If this was his dream... Well, it had to be, didn't it? But nothing about this made any sense. He remembered telling Libby she had probably dreamed up her crazy time-travel story when she'd hurt her head. Something similar must be happening to him. He must have crashed the plane, must have a head injury, too. He was dreaming, hallucinating. There was no other way to explain it.

At least he'd survived the crash. He was alive, had to be or he couldn't be dreaming. But what about Libby? She was in his dream and she was still looking at him with that strange expression in her eyes.

"Shamus, are you all right? You're white as a sheet," Libby said, her voice holding a hint of fear. "Are you hurt? Did you hit your head?"

"I must have hit my head," he agreed after a moment.

Libby's eyes widened. "Why didn't you say something? Does it ache? Are you dizzy? Maybe you should sit in the shade for a few minutes. We can sit under the wing. If the Jenny was going to burn, it would already be cinders." She clutched at his arm, pulling him in the direction of the biplane.

"I'm all right," he protested. "My head doesn't hurt. I'm not dizzy."

"Then why...?"

He turned to take another look at the unfamiliar ribbon of road in the distance, then turned his eyes to the sky where only a few wisps of white remained of that wonder. "I must have hit my head," he muttered, more to himself than to Libby. "That's the only explanation."

"I know it's hard to believe," Libby said in a quiet voice. "At first it all seems strange and impossible. But it will make sense later, some of it, anyway. At least we're together. Everything will be all right, Shamus. You'll see."

Nothing about this was ever going to make sense. Shamus knew that much, but why argue? He never won arguments with Libby, anyway. Besides, none of this was real. It was all a dream, one in which he seemed to have no control. If he was in control, Libby would be smiling, happy, not looking as worried and concerned as she did right now.

"You're right," he said, knowing it was an attempt to convince himself as well as reassure her. "Everything's going to be fine. If we survived Capone and Moran and that storm, we can beat anything."

When his efforts were rewarded by a smile, Shamus was almost able to believe his own words. Unable to resist, he pulled Libby to his side. "I wonder how far we are from help. It's for sure the Jenny's not going to be flying for a while."

"She's been in worse shape," Libby told him. "She'll fly again. Besides, I have to leave her where she is until the FAA investigates. I guess we should start walking toward the highway. We'll probably be able to hitch a ride into Oshkosh."

"The FAA? What's that? And how do you know we're near Oshkosh?" he demanded. "Do you know where we are?"

"The FAA is the Federal Aviation Administration. They investigate all airplane crashes," she explained. "I'm sorry. I forgot you didn't have such regulations in your... in the twenties. And yes, I do think I know where we are. I just don't know when."

Shamus took a deep breath. She was talking about that time-travel thing again, he thought, unable to control his frown.

Libby must have seen the question on his face. "Shamus," she said quietly, "when I told you we were in the 1990s, that we had returned to my time, did you understand what I said?"

"I heard you," he said, refusing to tell her he understood or believed.

Libby realized he was avoiding her question. She was expecting too much too soon. She remembered how long it had taken her to believe she was in the past, even when the evidence was all around her. It would take him a while to accept that he was now in the future. But he'd helped her, even when he didn't know the trauma she was experiencing. Surely, understanding his confusion, she could help him.

"I know this is going to be hard to understand," she began patiently. "I don't understand it all myself. But when I told you we were in the 1990s it was because I recognized certain things, things like the highway over there and jets in the sky. I also recognized enough of the landscape to think we're near Oshkosh, but as I said, I just don't know when."

"None of this is real," Shamus said slowly. "It's all a dream. It can't be happening. I don't understand."

"It is real," Libby told him, trying to explain. "I don't understand it all, either, but I was in your time for nearly a year. I don't know how much time passed here. Was it the same amount of time or different? I was flying in an air show at Oshkosh when I . . . I traveled to your time. From the number of planes in the air, I think there's an air show underway now, too. The trouble is, I don't know if it's the same show I was flying in or maybe the next year's show."

"You mean you might have come back at the same time you left?" he asked, an incredulous note in his voice.

"It's possible, I guess. Or I might have been gone so long, every one thinks I'm dead."

"I wonder if they'll think I'm dead. I mean, if I'm really in 1993, am I dead in my time? Will I ever be able to go back to 1926?"

Libby gulped. If there was one question she didn't want to face, it was this one. Would Shamus go back? It seemed likely. After all, she'd returned to her own time. She didn't want to think about it. Not now.

"I don't guess it really matters what anyone else believes," she told him. "You're not dead and neither am I. We're here. As to whether you go back to the twenties or not, I don't know that, either. I guess we'll just have to wait and see."

"So, what do we do first? Dammit, Libby, I feel so helpless. All I can do is ask questions."

Libby couldn't help smiling at the sound of the familiar expression. Shamus was beginning to sound more like himself. "That's all either of us can do right now," she reassured him. "I guess the first thing we need to find out is the date. Then we can decide the next step."

They left the Jenny in the field and began the long walk to the highway. Shamus asked if they'd be able to find the crash site again, and Libby assured him they would. Then she tried to explain about the emergency locator transmitter hidden in the tail of the old biplane. The ELT was one regulation the Federal Aviation Administration had refused to waive in deference to the demands for authentic restoration of antique planes.

The transmitter hadn't worked when she was in the twenties because there had been no receiving station to pick up the radio transmissions, but she had no doubt the crash site would soon be swarming with the curious, as well as with FAA investigators.

It was also one reason she wanted to get Shamus away from the site quickly. If she'd returned before she'd been missed, how was she going to explain picking up a passenger in midair? If, on the other hand, she'd been missing for a year, how was she supposed to account for the sudden appearance of the crashed plane?

For a moment Shamus seemed to forget he didn't believe he was in the future. He was more excited about the idea of using radio beams to locate aeroplanes than the implications that discovery of the crash site might mean.

"I knew there had to be a way," he said. "I just couldn't figure it out. How does it work?"

Libby tried to explain and found herself helplessly out of her depth. "I don't know how it works," she finally told him. "All I know is that it does."

"But don't you understand how important it can be to aviation?" Shamus exclaimed. "I bet you could use the same principles to guide a plane from one airport to another. Don't you see what that could mean? You could fly at night. You wouldn't have to depend on watching for landmarks on the ground. It would revolutionize aviation!"

"Shamus," Libby said gently, "it did just that. If you remember, I tried to tell you all this once before. I can't explain it any better now than I could then. But I'll help you find out how it works. If we can't find it in books, then I have a friend who can explain it all. I promise."

Shamus fell silent as they continued walking. Libby tried to remember the things that had shocked her the most about life in the twenties. Shamus needed a quick course in daily living in the nineties, even if he didn't

know it. She told him about supermarkets and shopping malls, the cost of living, the average hourly wage,
movie theaters, television, the cost of food and clothing and credit cards.

"The credit card is really the result of the buy-now-
pay-later philosophy that started in your time," she
explained. "In fact, once I looked around, I could see
the roots of most of our way of life came from the
twenties. This is the age of mass communications.
Radio was just a baby in your time, but it was the beginning. We listened to the president speak, as he
spoke, on the radio in the parlor. Now, with television, we can listen and see the president as he speaks
and it doesn't matter if he's at the White House or
visiting somewhere in France.

"Today we advertise everything from soap flakes to
presidential candidates. That started in the twenties,
too. Then there's the automobile. In your time every
family had to have one. Today they're bigger, faster,
and most families have two. Of course, today both the
husband and the wife usually work, but that started in
your time, too. Once you get used to it," she said,
trying again to reassure him, "you'll find there's not
that much difference. Not really. It's mostly a matter
of degree."

A quick look at the expression on his face told her
he still wasn't ready to believe. Well, seeing's believing, she reminded herself as they neared the highway.
Shamus was about to get another shock, and there
wasn't anything else she could think to do to help him.

They caught a ride with a truck driver almost as
soon as they made the highway. The double trailer rig
rolled to a stop at the side of the road with a whoosh-
ing sound of air brakes.

"You folks from the air show?" the driver called down from the cab high above them. Until now, Libby had forgotten just how large and intimidating these giants of the road were. This shiny chrome monster was certainly a far cry from a Model-T. She threw Shamus a reassuring glance.

"That's right," she told the trucker. "We had a little trouble."

"Thought as much when I saw you standing there. Don't usually pick up passengers. Too dangerous, if you know what I mean. But, well, I'm based in Oshkosh and even though we natives grumble every year when you folks are swarming around, we know the air show means lots of money in the community. Climb on up. I'll get you back to town."

"Thanks," Libby told him, as she climbed into the high cab. "We appreciate it." She saw the newspaper lying on the seat and grabbed it, ostensibly to make room for Shamus to follow. But her relief at seeing "July 23, 1993" on the front page was almost audible.

"This today's paper?" she asked innocently as she slipped it into Shamus's lap.

"All day, if it doesn't rain," the truck driver answered cheerfully. "I'm not going by the airfield, but I can take you as far as the highway junction if you want."

"That'll be perfect," Libby told him. "Our motel's near there."

After the truck driver dropped them off Shamus remained quietly at her side as Libby collected a spare key from the motel office. "Motels haven't completely replaced hotels," she explained, as she led

Shamus to her room, "but most people find them more convenient to use."

Shamus followed Libby into the room, a dazed look in his eyes. "It was true," he said in a hushed voice. "That story you told me. Even if I was dreaming, I couldn't imagine all this. The size of that truck, all those colored motorcars... We were going down that highway as fast as an aeroplane." He swallowed. "Even if I was dreaming, I couldn't have imagined all this. You really were from the future and... and now I'm here. It was all true."

"Yes. It was true, but I don't blame you for not believing me," Libby said. "I'm sorry, Shamus. I know what a shock it is."

Shamus raked his fingers through his hair, his eyes moving around the room, examining the shaggy-looking carpet that completely covered the floor and the extra large bed that dominated the space, finally resting on the strange-looking box with a frosted window on the table. "At least I was warned," he said. "Sweet saints, you must have thought you were going crazy. Or that I was."

Libby smiled in spite of herself. "The thought crossed my mind," she admitted.

"I'm sorry I didn't believe you, Libby. I could have made things easier. I was a fool."

"Don't you say that. If it hadn't been for you—"

"If it hadn't been for me, you wouldn't have been shot or caught in the middle of a bootleggers' war. You'd have been able to fly your Jenny. You'd probably have found your way home sooner."

Libby shook her head. "That's not true. If it hadn't been for you, I would probably have ended up in a crazy house somewhere. You helped me, took care of me..." *Loved me,* she added silently. *And I wouldn't have missed a minute of it, even if it meant never coming home.*

"Yeah, well, that doesn't count. I owed you." He hesitated. "Anyway, you're here, and I'm here, so what happens now?"

"I haven't the slightest. Go with the flow, I guess."

When she saw the look of confusion on his face, Libby felt guilty for being so flip. "I'm sorry," she apologized again. "That was slang. I've had to be so careful not to say anything outrageous for so long, I guess I'm giddy. The truth is, I don't know what happens next. I guess we'll just have to wait and see. What I have to do right now is report the crash. You can wash up if you like. As soon as I report in, I'll clean up, too. Then I think we'd better hit one of the shopping centers to find you some clothes. Between the fire and the storm, we look like a couple of refugees."

Libby didn't realize Shamus was listening as she contacted the FAA through the tower at the airfield to report the crash and the approximate location of the downed biplane. Then, afraid Howard would hear about the crash, she placed a second call to Chicago to assure her friend she wasn't hurt. She purposely kept the call brief, not mentioning either her trip into the past or Shamus.

"Who's Howard?" Shamus asked as soon as she'd hung up the phone. "A beau?"

Libby shook her head. She couldn't help smiling. "Howard Winters is his name. And no, he's not a boyfriend, more of an adopted grandfather, I guess. He taught me everything I know about antique planes. He was a barnstormer in the twenties. That's why I was afraid to mention him. If you knew him, or if we happened to run into him, how could I explain that I was supposed to know him when we wouldn't meet for another seventy years?''

"I guess that would have been a little hard," Shamus admitted.

"Did you . . . I mean do you know him? Have you ever heard of him? He always said he barnstormed in the Chicago area.''

"Howard Winters. No, I don't think so. Why?''

"Because I think he knew you," Libby told him. "He never said so, but he has a picture, an old photograph of you. I saw it once.''

"A photo of me? You saw a picture of me, here, in your time, before you came back to my time? Did you recognize me?''

Libby nodded. "Almost at once, even though I wouldn't admit it for a long time. I really did think I was going crazy for a while.''

The scowl on Shamus's face had disappeared, replaced by a look of tenderness that made Libby's heart turn over. "I didn't know how difficult everything was for you," he said quietly. "I'm only beginning to realize how hard it must have been, trying to fit in without giving yourself away. It's going to be easier for me, because I have you. I just hope you'll be able to keep me from making too big a fool of myself.''

"I slipped up occasionally," Libby told him. "It would have been much worse if I hadn't had you to depend on and to take care of me. I'm not worried about you making a fool of yourself. Even when I made mistakes, no one suspected that I was from the future. How could they? No one will ever suspect you're from the past, either. An idea like time travel is unbelievable...unless, like us, you've experienced it."

She leaned over to give him a quick hug, but Shamus had other ideas. His kiss left her head spinning.

"Shamus, we don't have time for this. Not now. We've got to get you some new clothes and invent a cover story to explain you. I've got friends that may be stopping by to make sure I'm okay."

"Why can't I just tell them I'm from Chicago and that I fly antique airplanes? I sure can't claim to know anything else and I'd never be able to fake it."

"You can't claim to be from Chicago because it's too close to Oshkosh. Antique airplane enthusiasts are almost a closed community. Everyone knows everyone else. Most of those from around Chicago will be here, and they won't know you. We'll have to think of something else. Maybe you can be from California. There're so many people there, no one would expect to know everyone."

"This isn't going to work."

"It'll work. Remember, no one would believe the truth. Have a little faith. But clothes first, okay?"

"Wait a minute. From what you told me, things are a lot more expensive now, but I want to pay my own way. Much as I can, anyway."

"It doesn't matter, Shamus. You took care of me for almost a year, if you remember."

He gave her an ironic smile. "We've had this conversation before," he said. "The last time, I was on the other side of the fence. You always won. Now it's my turn."

He pulled a handful of coins out of his pocket. "This is all I brought with me. I cleaned out the safe at the hangar. Will it be enough?"

Libby's eyes widened at the collection of gold coins in his hand. "We don't use gold coins anymore," she told him, a little breathlessly. "They're all collector's items now, worth at least a hundred times the face value. In most cases more. At a guess, I'd say you have several thousand dollars there. We'll get them valued by an expert when we get back to Chicago."

"Enough to buy my own clothes then?"

"More than enough," she told him. "Just don't try to spend them today. You'll cause a riot. I'll advance you, and you can pay me back later, okay?"

Libby wasn't sure who enjoyed their shopping trip more, she or Shamus. Although he seemed quite happy to leave the selection of his wardrobe to her, he wanted to stop in every store and examine every gadget he saw. He was fascinated with zippers, the lightweight man-made fabrics and modern running shoes. As they walked through the mall, something on display would suddenly catch his eye and he'd grab her hand, almost dragging her with him for a closer inspection.

She nearly died of mortification when he stopped in front of a lingerie shop and insisted she buy an ice blue lace teddy displayed in the window for herself.

"So much for any basic difference between the male of a half a century ago and his modern counterpart," she muttered under her breath.

But it was the bookstore that gave Libby the most pleasure. She selected contemporary histories, books on modern society and aviation history with great abandonment, then added several modern novels, a techno-thriller, even a contemporary romance. "To give you an idea how the modern woman thinks," she told him sweetly. A selection of magazines, ranging in subject matter from news to aviation to baseball, completed her selections.

Her choices at the video store included several "chronicles of" selections, more material on aviation and several classic movies. Almost as an afterthought she grabbed a collection of animated cartoons from the shelf. For some reason she was sure Shamus would find the antics of the desert bird and his coyote adversary funny.

"Libby, have pity," Shamus finally protested. "Can't we save something to buy tomorrow? I'll either have time to learn all this, or it won't matter anyway."

"There's nothing old-fashioned about you," Libby complained. "You're just like every other man I know. You hate to shop."

"I can't see that women have changed that much, either," he countered. "Every woman I've ever known would rather shop than eat."

Libby found her rental car parked in the motel parking lot, as well as a message from Helen when they returned to their room.

"I warned you to watch those clouds," Helen complained when Libby called. "Are you all right? I left the keys to your car at the motel office. What about the Jenny?"

"I'm fine. The Jenny's a wreck, and yes, I got the keys. Thank you for thinking of it," Libby told her.

"Well, I was in the tower when you called. I thought you might need it."

"I appreciate it, really," Libby assured her. "I'm going to have an early night of it, but I'll see you tomorrow. And Helen, thank you for worrying."

"Worrying? You scared me out of about ten good years. When I saw that thunderhead suck you up, I thought you were a goner for sure."

"So did I," Libby admitted. "So did I."

"Do we plan for company tonight?" Shamus asked as she replaced the phone.

"Not tonight, I think. Helen will spread the word that I'm fine, but tired."

"So what shall we study first? Economic history? Politics?"

Libby smiled. "I've got a better idea for your first lesson," she said. "I think it's time to introduce you to a truly wonderful modern invention."

"Something more important than understanding economic factors leading to inflation?" Shamus asked, reading from a table of contents. The twinkle in his eye told her he'd recognized her teasing mood. "What could be more important than that?"

"This is much more important." Her smile grew even wider. "It's called a water bed."

Libby lay awake long after Shamus had fallen asleep, his body curled around hers, an arm holding her lightly at the waist, as if he wanted to assure himself she was with him.

What was going to happen to them now? she wondered as she turned her head to look at his face. How much longer did they have to be together?

After her futile attempt to return to the present, Libby had convinced herself she would stay in the past. She'd been content, even happy with Shamus, and yes, thankful that through some cosmic accident, they'd found each other. She hadn't intended to try returning to her own time again, certainly hadn't intended to drag Shamus into the present with her. Sliding the Jenny into that void had been an act of desperation. Only that. And now, the promise of sharing a life with Shamus was in jeopardy again.

He was bewildered, confused and feeling as out of place here as she had when she first arrived in his time. When she'd found herself in the past, she had, at least, possessed some knowledge of history. Shamus had none, only the knowledge that his dreams for the future had already been achieved and that he'd had no part in those accomplishments.

Would he be content to stay here in the present with her, as she would have been staying in the past with him? And even if he was, would it make a difference? In the end she'd been given no choice about returning to her own time. She was afraid Shamus wouldn't be given a choice, either.

How much more time would they have together? A day? A week? A year? What happiness could they find together now, waiting for the cosmic clock to correct itself once again?

CHAPTER SEVENTEEN

LIBBY AWOKE ALONE in the bed and for a moment panic all but paralyzed her. Then she saw Shamus sitting in a chair facing the window, engrossed in one of the books they'd purchased the day before. He'd pulled on a pair of his new jeans but hadn't bothered with either shirt or shoes. She watched him silently for a minute, trying to capture the image in her mind, afraid memories would soon be her only consolation.

She slipped from the bed, pulling her robe around her as Shamus looked up, the expression on his face telling her that for the moment, at least, he was content.

The book on his lap slid to the floor as he stood, the look in his eyes making her catch her breath. She crossed the space between them, slipping into his arms as if she belonged there.

"Liked the water bed, huh?" she asked teasingly.

"I liked the water bed." His voice was husky. "I liked being in the water bed with you even more."

Libby knew the heat curling through her body had nothing to do with the temperature in the room. "Maybe we can try it again."

"I intend to," he whispered wickedly. "Soon."

"Good." Libby grinned, feeling warm and wanton and wanted. She slipped from his embrace and leaned down to pick up the book. "So, what are we studying this morning?"

"Trying to catch up on the last fifty or sixty years," Shamus told her, his mood sobering. "Saints, Libby, it's impossible. So many things we didn't, couldn't even dream of in my time—planes that travel faster than the speed of sound, men actually walking on the moon..."

"It was like erecting a building, one block at a time," Libby reminded him gently. "One dream becoming reality, one discovery opening up a whole new world for new dreams. Don't forget how far we'd come from Kitty Hawk to the twenties. Two years before the Wright brothers flew, only a handful of people believed man would ever get into the air. In your time a few people believed we'd be able to fly across the oceans. Before the first moon landing, only a handful of people believed in space travel. Now a few people believe man may someday be able to travel out of our solar system."

"I saw a picture of him," Shamus said abruptly. "I should have believed you." He shook his head. "When I think..."

"A picture of who? What are you talking about?"

"Slim. There's a picture of him in the book. Hell, there's pictures of him in most of these books." He raked his fingers through his hair.

"Oh," Libby said. "You mean Lindbergh."

"Yeah, Lindbergh. The guy I said was just another sky gypsy."

Libby gave him a soft smile. "You were right, you know. That's what he was, a sky gypsy."

"Are you kidding? Even if the books are only half right, he's a legend."

"That's right. A legend. A symbol. Shamus, that day when I said Lindbergh would be the first man to solo the Atlantic, did you think I was crazy because I said man would fly the ocean or because I said Lindbergh would fly the ocean?"

"Because you said it would be Lindbergh. It was only a matter of time before someone did it. Alcock and Brown had already done it as a team in 1919."

"Exactly. And there were probably a half a dozen pilots at Peoria that day who could have done it as well as Lindbergh. He just happened to be the first. I think you were right about him, you know. He couldn't resist a dare. He set out to fly the ocean and didn't dare back down. He said as much in the journal he kept on the flight."

"You were so excited about meeting him. I was jealous, although I'm not sure I knew what was wrong at the time," Shamus said bluntly.

"Of course I was excited about meeting him," Libby explained. "After all, he was a legend. And I knew you were jealous. At least, I figured out what was bothering you after a while. That was as exciting as meeting Lindbergh. It helped me believe that you might think about me as something more than just a nuisance."

"You were never a nuisance, Libby."

"Ha! Now that's a bald-faced lie and you know it, Shamus Fitzgerald. You spent half your time cussing at me, afraid of what I'd do if you let me out of your sight, and the other half ruing the day you first set eyes on me."

"Yeah, well, maybe," he told her with a guilty look. "But I still figured you were *my* nuisance."

"Sort of your cross to bear," she teased.

"Sort of," he admitted. "Now, I'm yours."

"Never," she protested adamantly.

As they ate breakfast in the motel coffee shop, Libby told him she had to go to the airfield to file a written report of the crash. "Want to come?" she asked. "You could tour the air museum or wander through the exhibits or watch the demonstrations. The books will be there when we get back."

"And the water bed?" he asked, a bright twinkle in his eyes that softened, then erased the worry lines on his face.

"And the water bed," she said, horrified to feel the sudden heat in her face.

She knew they were marking time, that soon they were going to have to face the question of the future. But Oshkosh happened only once a year, and it laid the world of aviation, past, present and future, at Shamus's feet in a way that couldn't be duplicated. Whatever would happen next, seeing the Oshkosh air show was a chance she couldn't deny him.

When they were ready to leave for the airfield Libby offered him the keys to the car, but Shamus shook his head. "I'm still running on a Model-T four cylinder," he told her. "Besides, I don't know where we're going. Are you sure I won't make a fool of myself, won't embarrass you?"

Libby felt a stab of sympathy. She remembered too well that feeling of being out of step with the world.

"I'm sure," she told him, her voice husky. "You'd never embarrass me. There'll be hundreds, thousands of people there who know less about airplanes than you do, if that's what you're worried about."

She dropped Shamus off in front of the Air Adventure Museum, promising to meet him as soon as she filed her report. When she returned she found him in the Eagle Hangar, inspecting the museum's World War II B-25 Mitchell bomber. Together they walked through the exhibits dedicated to displaying other World War II aircraft.

"I couldn't believe it when I first saw the sign," he said bitterly. "We all thought we'd done the job right in the Great War. That was supposed to be the war to end all wars. Now they call it World War I and this was World War II. Has there been a World War III?"

"There have been wars, but not a World War III," she told him. "Hopefully, there never will be."

"I've got a lot to catch up on, haven't I? Aeroplanes are just part of it."

"One step at a time, remember. You can't learn everything at once. We'll have time later to—"

"Will we? Will we have time later? Dammit, Libby, I feel like a fish out of water. I'm a dinosaur," he added after a moment. "When I go back...if I go back..." His voice trailed into silence. "If I can't go back, how will I ever fit in here? There's so much to learn. I'll never catch up."

Libby heard the despair in his voice and blinked her tears away. "Everything will be all right. You'll see," she told him. "After all, you just got here. In a little while things will be more familiar, make more sense. I know it's frustrating. Believe me, I know."

Shamus shook his head and fell silent. Libby clutched at his hand, trying to think of something to snap him out of his depression. "Come on, Shamus, I want to show you the very newest thing, the home-built kits."

"Kits? To build aeroplanes?"

"Yep, just like the old days. You buy a kit and build your own personal airplane in your garage. See, things haven't changed that much after all."

Shamus's mood slowly lightened as they toured the show, moving from exhibit to exhibit. Later in the afternoon, when they ran into Helen at the refreshment tent, Libby introduced Shamus as a friend of hers from California.

"You fly? Antiques?" Helen asked in her usual blunt fashion.

"Some," Shamus admitted, "but I spend about as much time keeping the old birds together, making sure they can fly."

"From California, huh? Don't think I've ever seen you before."

"I guess we just haven't been in the same place at the same time," he said easily, shooting Libby a teasing look. Libby had to bite her tongue to keep from laughing out loud.

It was nearly dark when they arrived at the motel. Despite Libby's complaining feet, she was relieved to see Shamus looking happier, more relaxed.

"Can we go back to the show tomorrow?" he asked. "There're dozens, hundreds of things I haven't seen yet."

Why not, she thought. She'd considered taking Shamus to her apartment in Chicago, but they might as well stay here for a few days. Besides, she wanted to avoid seeing Howard as long as possible. When they returned to Chicago, she'd have to introduce him to Shamus.

Would Howard recognize him as the man in the photo? And if he did, how could she explain, short of the truth? Howard was an old man with a bad heart.

Even if he believed her, shocks weren't good for him. Yes, she decided, it was better they stay here. Given a little time, maybe she could think of something. Besides, Shamus would be happier here than anywhere else. It would make his adjustment easier.

"Sure, we'll go back," she promised him. "The show lasts all week. This is only the second day."

When Libby answered a knock on the door a short time later, the last person she expected to see was Howard. It was almost as if her thoughts had called him.

A smile spread across the old man's face. "I had to come, had to see for myself that you were okay," he told her.

Libby's eyes misted. "I'm fine. Honest, Howard. I told you I was. What about you? Are you feeling all right now?"

"Better. Better every minute," he said gruffly. "Aren't you going to invite me in?"

"Of course I am," Libby stammered. There was no help for it. Howard and Shamus, the two most important men in her life, were about to meet. She stepped back from the door. "I'm glad you're here," she told him. "I...I've got a friend I want you to meet."

Shamus heard the voices as he came out of the bathroom. He stopped, his eyes moving from Libby to the old man who'd just entered the room.

"Shamus, come here." She stretched out her hand to him, and when he took it, he could feel her trembling, even though her voice was light. The look she gave him was almost pleading.

"I want you to meet my oldest friend," she told him, a little breathlessly. "Howard, this is Shamus...Shamus Fitzgerald. Shamus, this is Howard Winters. I told you about him."

So this was the old pilot, the one she considered a grandfather. That explained why Libby was so nervous. "I'm glad to meet you, sir," he said, politely offering his hand.

Howard's handshake was firm and surprisingly strong for such an old man. He'd once been a tall man, almost as tall as himself, Shamus judged. He still had a full head of hair, now almost snow white. "I understand you live in Chicago."

The old man smiled, a smile that Shamus couldn't help thinking looked familiar. "That's right. But I had to come, see for myself that Libby was all right. It sounded like a nasty crash."

Libby laughed, a nervous little sound that told Shamus she wasn't completely relaxed. "The crash was the easy part," she said. "It was riding out the storm that was rough. But I'm fine. Not a scratch. I told you that. Still, I'm glad to see you."

She gave the old man a hug. "Well, come on, sit down." Shamus watched her perch on the edge of the bed, leaving the motel room's two chairs for him and Howard.

"Did you get a motel room? Are you staying for the rest of the show?"

"'Course I'm staying. Told that doctor there wasn't a thing wrong with me other than old age and he couldn't do anything about that. Should have come with you in the first place, just like we planned."

"There wasn't anything you could have done," she told him gently. "I should have watched the clouds a little closer. The storm was on top of me before I knew what was happening. We... I really smashed up the Jenny, Howard."

"So? We'll put her back together again. Wasn't her first crash. Not her first storm, either, I'll wager. She'll be in the air again. You wait and see." He gave a little chuckle. "Can't keep a pretty little bird like that out of the clouds."

Shamus straightened in his chair, his gaze moving from Howard to Libby, then back to Howard again. For a moment the old man's voice had sounded so exactly like... No, that was crazy. Still, there was something he didn't understand. Howard hadn't asked him one question. Not where he was from. Not where he'd met Libby. Not even if he was a flyer. Surely those were all normal questions for a first conversation, especially if you'd just found a strange man in the room of a woman you loved like a granddaughter. And Shamus was sure Howard did love Libby. He saw the old man's eyes soften every time he looked at her.

It was almost as if Howard was ignoring his existence—or, he thought suddenly, was accepting his presence in Libby's life because he already knew the answers.

Shamus swallowed and turned to look at the old man more closely. Howard's eyes were blue, a clear light blue that hadn't dulled with age. His hair waved carelessly off his forehead, still thick, still a little undisciplined. As a young man, it must have been an unruly mop. Then Howard turned his head slightly, exposing a cowlick that looked exactly like...

Shamus's eyes fell to Howard's hands, resting lightly on his knees. Long tapering fingers, a little knotted and gnarled now, but he could almost see them as a young man's, carefully sanding down a piece of hickory to replace a broken propeller. There! There it was, an old, old scar barely visible, a thin white line around the base of the left thumb, a reminder of an almost tragic accident as a very young boy.

"Eddie?" he breathed so quietly he wasn't even sure he'd spoken, but the old man must have heard him. He turned in his chair, his gaze resting on Shamus's face.

"Eddie?" Shamus asked again, his voice firmer this time and he saw the old man's eyes mist with tears.

"I wasn't sure you'd remember me," Howard said, his voice gruff with emotion.

Shamus heard Libby gasp, but his eyes were glued to the boy, now an old man, he'd loved as a son. "I didn't have any trouble remembering you. I saw you day before yesterday," he said, discovering his own voice husky with tears. "It was the recognizing that took a little time. What...what are you doing here?"

The old man chuckled. "I've been here all along. Now there's a question I could more logically be asking you. Here you are, not looking a day older than the last time I saw you, while I..." He raised his hands in a helpless gesture.

"Two days older," Shamus said. "I saw you two days ago when Libby and I put you on that train."

"What...what's going on here?" Libby's voice was strained, questioning, with a tint of rising hysteria. "You can't be Eddie. You're Howard." Her eyes searched his face, then she let out a little sigh. "You are Eddie, aren't you? Why...why didn't you tell me?"

"I've been Howard for a lot of years, honey," Howard said softly. "There was no reason to tell you my real name was Eddie. That was another life, one dead and buried long before I met you."

"But why didn't I recognize you?" Libby asked, her voice shaking with shock. "Not before, I don't mean that. But tonight, when you arrived. I saw Eddie two days ago, too."

"Because you've known me much longer as Howard," he said gently. "Remember, you knew Eddie for less than a year." He chuckled again. "And most of that time, you had your mind on other things."

Libby knew she was blushing. She couldn't help it. She darted a glance at Shamus, saw him looking at her, a silly grin on his face.

"And you weren't any better," Howard chided Shamus. "There were days when I don't think you knew where you were."

"There were days when I didn't even know my own name," Shamus admitted. "Libby Carmichael nearly drove me crazy."

Howard chuckled.

"You knew, you knew who I was. You knew what was going to happen," she accused him. "You should have told me I was going to go traveling around in time. Or at least hinted at it. At first I thought I was going crazy."

Howard shook his head, denying her accusation. "I didn't know, at least, not for sure," Howard told her gently. "It seemed like such a crazy idea. I had no reason to suspect that the Elizabeth I loved now and the Libby I knew as a young boy were the same person. At least not until..."

"Not until when?"

"I begin to wonder when you found that picture," he admitted. "It started me thinking. There were so many coincidences. But time travel? It was impossible..."

Howard shrugged his shoulders in a helpless gesture. "The first time I saw you, I couldn't help noticing the resemblance between you and the Libby I knew back when I was a kid. Since you both had the same name, I figured it was either coincidence or some kind of family resemblance. Remember when I kept asking you about your family?"

Libby nodded.

"You said there was just you and your mom, that your dad had died when you were just a little tyke and you never knew any of his family. It was possible you were Libby's granddaughter. In fact, much as you loved to fly, I figured it was more than possible, but there wasn't any way to know for sure. Besides, it didn't matter. When you first came to me about learning to fly antique planes, you were a lot younger than the Libby I remembered. Sure there was a resemblance, but my memories of the first Libby were shadowed by a lot of time. Besides, I loved the first Libby like a big sister. You...you could have been my granddaughter. In my heart you are."

Libby felt her eyes mist.

"There were times, like when you insisted that your Jenny was going to be red-and-white, that I really wondered if I was going crazy." He turned to Shamus. "Craziest color scheme for a Jenny I've ever seen. Except it was the same color as Libby's, the first Libby's, I mean."

Shamus nodded sympathetically. "It was a strange color for a Jenny, all right. I always said so. 'Course that was back then."

"Well, I'll tell you, it's still a crazy color. Most antiquers restore to original colors. When Libby, the 1990s Libby I mean, said her plane was going to be red-and-white, it gave me quite a turn. But I couldn't make no sense out of it. Had to be another coincidence, I told myself. You'll have to admit, it's a crazy idea . . . time travel. Told myself I was just an old man growing senile. I didn't . . . didn't really believe it until I walked into this room tonight. But with Shamus and you together . . . soon as I saw you . . . I knew it had to be true. Can't say I understand it, though. And nobody else is going to believe it."

It took another half hour for Howard to explain what had happened to him after he left Chicago that night so long ago when his name had still been Eddie.

"I made it to Denver without any trouble. Then I waited. I waited and waited, but I never heard from you. Finally after about two months, I decided I had to go back, find out what had happened.

"I was real worried when I found the airfield burned to the ground and no one could tell me anything about either of you," Howard admitted. "But Doc Baker said no one had been hurt. At least they hadn't found any bodies. I had to think that you had escaped, were maybe hiding somewhere, not wanting to contact me because you were afraid someone would follow you. So I decided to go back to Denver. I figured you'd get in touch with me when you could."

"Do I go back, Eddie?" Shamus asked, his voice tense. "Did you ever see me or hear of me again?"

Howard shook his head. "I never heard of you again," he said. "I always thought I would, but I never did. Once, I thought I saw you, that time I went back to Chicago after you disappeared. I was never sure it was you, though. That's why I returned to Denver to wait. Then, about a year later, I changed my name and disappeared myself for a while. So if you were looking for me, you might not have found me. You might have changed your name, too."

"I heard a story that you'd bet Lindbergh would be the first man to solo the Atlantic and that when you won, you decided to change your name," Libby said suddenly. "I wasn't sure I believed it. I was going to ask you when I got back to Chicago."

Howard grinned. "It's true," he admitted. "I was poking around, trying to find out if anyone had heard anything about you two. I was in one of the pool halls in Capone's territory. Figured I'd be safer from Moran there. Anyway, a couple of bookies were taking paper on the Orteig prize. He'd just offered twenty-five thousand dollars for a New York to Paris flight. The bookies, they were talking all the big names like Curtiss and Byrd and Fonck."

He looked at Libby. "Suddenly I remembered what you said that day at Peoria. I didn't even stop to think. 'It'll be Charlie Lindbergh,' I told them."

This time Howard laughed. "You should have seen their faces. They all thought I was crazy. 'Course, if I'd stopped to think about it, I probably would have thought I was crazy, too. But I'd said it. I couldn't back down. Before I knew it, I'd made bets with every one of them. Looking back now, I think I was so worried about you two that remembering what Libby said and betting on it was a way to feel closer, to make you more real. I was afraid to admit I might not ever find you. Anyway, the rest is history."

He looked over at Libby. "After Lindbergh landed in Paris and I collected my winnings, I went West again and changed my name. Figured that if any of those bookies were looking for me, I'd make it as hard as possible. I kept an ear open for news of you two, but I never heard a thing. But for some reason I always expected to see you two again. Funny how things work out, isn't it?''

Libby blinked away the tears. ''Yeah. Funny...''

''Do you remember when you thought you saw me?'' Shamus interrupted suddenly, his voice tense. ''Do you really think it was me?''

''I always thought it was you,'' Howard answered him. ''And yeah, I remember. It was the same day I made the bets. August 1, 1926, it was, at exactly eleven o'clock. I was walking down State Street. Planned to see Maisie at work, ask her if she'd heard anything from you. About a block away from Marshall Field's I looked up and could have sworn I saw you standing there. You know, under the clock. You were just standing there, looking at something across the street. I called your name, and I thought you heard me, because you looked around. Then someone walked in front of me and for a moment I couldn't see you.''

Howard shook his head, as though reliving the time. ''I never did understand it. It was a moment, only a couple of seconds, but when I looked again you were gone. Just like that. You'd disappeared. There wasn't anybody else there, either. I mean, there wasn't anybody I could see that I might have thought was you. You, or whoever it was, had just...disappeared.''

A SHORT TIME LATER Howard made arrangements to meet them for breakfast and said good-night. ''Now don't you go disappearing on me again,'' he said, ''we've still got a lot of catching up to do.''

"We don't plan to go anywhere," Libby promised. Shamus said nothing.

To Libby it seemed Shamus was especially quiet, almost brooding, after Howard left. She felt chilled and rubbed at the goose bumps on her arms, knowing her discomfort had nothing to do with the room temperature.

"How did you know you'd come back to your own time?" Shamus asked suddenly. "What made you so sure?"

"I didn't know, not all the time," Libby told him, fighting to keep her voice steady. This was the discussion she hadn't wanted to face, the one she'd known was waiting for them. It was time to talk about the future . . . and the past.

"At first I *was* sure. I mean, it was the only thing that made sense. I didn't know exactly how I'd traveled to your time, but I knew I didn't belong. I thought it had to be a mistake, a mistake that would correct itself," she finally told him.

"But later I changed my mind. After I tried to fly into that storm and it didn't work, I decided maybe I'd been wrong, that maybe I was supposed to stay there. After all, everything seemed perfect for coming back. My Jenny, the storm . . . Everything matched what happened the first time. Except it didn't work."

"It did work," Shamus said. "You were right all along. You came back to your time, in your plane, in a storm, just like you believed you would, only . . . only—"

"Only I brought you along with me. I'm sorry, Shamus. I didn't mean to."

Shamus heard the tears in her voice. "It wasn't your fault," he said, feeling guilty because he'd hurt her.

"If you hadn't done what you did when you did it, we'd probably both be dead. The Jenny couldn't have held together more than another couple of minutes. You did what you had to do, what you were supposed to do. I don't blame you, but...but how am I supposed to get back?"

"Maybe you're supposed to stay here."

"No." Shamus was vehement. His voice softened when he saw the look of pain cross her face. "I don't belong here any more than you belonged in my time." His voice strained as he tried to get her to understand. "I told you. I'm a dinosaur. I'll never fit in. What can I do here? How can I live? I'm as much an antique in this time, as...as your Jenny."

"There's a place in this world for Jennys. Maybe you could find your place, too," Libby pleaded. Didn't he know how much she needed him?

She knew instinctively that she could never go back. If she was going to be allowed to stay in Shamus's time, she wouldn't have been pulled back. But there had to be a reason for it all, for traveling into the past to meet Shamus, for bringing him to the present with her. There had to be a reason. She clung desperately to the thought.

Shamus shook his head. "Find a place? Here? As what? The Jenny's a flying museum. Is that what I'm supposed to be, too, a living example of the past? I can't think of anything I could do. I bet I couldn't even sell shoes. I'll bet they don't even make them out of leather anymore."

"Only the very best," Libby said with an attempt at humor. Shamus obviously didn't think her joke was funny. His eyes held a look of pain.

If anyone could know what Shamus was feeling, how strange and bewildering everything seemed to him, it was Libby. When she'd landed her plane in Shamus's time she had at least known something of the past. She'd had that thread of reality to cling to and could look toward a future she knew existed. For Shamus, the disorientation of finding himself in the future must be terrifying. It was even more strange and frightening than the past had been to her. She had known, at least in a general way, what was to come. For Shamus, the future was a complete unknown, but even worse, in his catapult into his future, he had lost his dreams.

In his own time Shamus had been a man of vision, predicting the potential of aviation and confident of his place in the realization of that potential. Now he found himself in a time that had leapfrogged over even his wildest imaginings. His visions had already been fulfilled and were now regarded as history. He'd had no part in their achievement, not even the satisfaction of watching them come to fruition. She couldn't blame him for wanting to go back. She'd have to help, if she could.

"We'll rebuild the Jenny," she told him. "That's how you got here. If you're supposed to go back, that's probably how it will happen. At least we know it can happen that way. That we're here is proof enough of that."

Shamus shook his head. "I don't think so. Not this time. The Jenny's yours. It carried you into the past, then brought you back where you belong. I don't think that's going to happen to me."

"Then maybe you're supposed to stay here," Libby began, unable to keep the note of hope from her voice.

"No." The harshness of his voice exploded in the room like a clap of thunder. "No, I can't," he repeated, his voice no longer as strident, but still strained. "I can't stay. Dammit, Libby, can't you see? I don't belong. I'm useless here. But the Jenny's not the way back. Not for me."

Libby stared into his face for a moment. She wasn't sure whether the ache in her heart was from hurt or helplessness. "But the Jenny's the only way I can think of."

Shamus shook his head again. "Eddie thought he saw me on August first. That's less than a week from now. We couldn't have the Jenny in the air by then. If he was right, if I'm back in my own time on August first, then there's got to be another way."

The look on his face was pensive. "August first," he said quietly, almost to himself. "That's the key. If I'm there, in 1926, then I can't be here. If it was me Eddie saw that day, I have to already be back by then. Or maybe that's the day I go back."

There was a sudden look of hope in his eyes. "Maybe Eddie did see me. Bugs will still be looking for me. I probably do change my name and go into hiding, and by the time I surface, Eddie's changed his name, too. That's why we missed each other. It all makes sense. But this time I'll be able to find him. I know his new name, where to look. Maybe that's why I was brought here, so I could discover how to find Eddie when I went back. If I'm in Chicago, under the clock, on August first . . ."

Libby saw the look of anticipation on his face even through the veil of tears in her eyes. She was afraid, so afraid he was right. It all made sense or at least as much sense as anything else did in this crazy mess. She

had been strong enough to say goodbye to him once—
for his own sake. And that time fate, or whatever was
manipulating the cosmic clock, had been kind enough
to give her a reprieve. For a time. She shouldn't expect more. If she'd been able to do it once, she could
say goodbye again...for Shamus's sake.

Shamus placed his fingers under Libby's chin and
slowly, gently tilted her face toward him. Her eyes
were bright with tears. He felt the moisture in his own
eyes. "I have to try," he pleaded with her and with
himself. "Don't you see, I'm not supposed to be here.
I have to go back if I can."

"I know," she said, her voice hoarse. "I know you
have to go back. I...I'll help all I can."

CHAPTER EIGHTEEN

HOWARD CONVINCED LIBBY and Shamus to stay at Oshkosh a few more days. "After all," he said, "there's nothing you can do in Chicago until the first. Might as well look around here. Maybe you'll learn something helpful to take back with you."

"A big dose of frustration," Shamus commented dryly. "It's going to be frustrating as Hades to know what's coming and have to sit around waiting for it to happen. I almost wish . . . No, I have to go back."

If Libby thought it would do any good, she would have tried arguing with him. But deep in her heart she was afraid he was right. But even if he didn't want to go back, he probably wouldn't have any choice about it. She hadn't.

During moments of optimism she allowed herself to hope that he wouldn't go back, at least not on the first. It seemed so impossible, to stand on a sidewalk in broad daylight and be suddenly whisked away. But if there was anywhere in Chicago where past met present, it was under the old Marshall Field's clock. It had been a favorite meeting place for Chicagoans for nearly a hundred years.

Only occasionally did she let herself feel the hurt of his desertion. Even if she did believe he would be forced to return to his own time, did he have to be so enthusiastic about it?

She was happy to delay their return to Chicago for as long as possible. As long as she and Shamus were at Oshkosh together, she could at least try to pretend everything was all right.

The days passed swiftly, the nights even faster. Suddenly it was the morning of the thirty-first, the day they had to leave.

Howard refused to go with them.

"I'm not sure that's the right thing for me to do," he told them. "Way I figure it, I was there, that morning I thought I saw him. Now Shamus, he was either here or there but not in the same place in both times. Don't think I'm supposed to be, either, so I guess I'll stay here at Oshkosh. Don't want to meet myself going and coming. Besides, I can use the time to finish making arrangements to get the Jenny shipped back home."

Libby wasn't sure she understood what Howard was trying to say, but she guessed it made sense, at least as much sense as any of this made. She hugged the old man goodbye. "I'll see you soon," she told him.

"Soon as I get back to town," he said.

"I'll see you soon, too," Shamus said, holding onto the old man's hand. "One place or the other. I'll find you. You just stay put."

"Can't change what's already done," Howard growled. "Told you I always believed I'd see you again. Just didn't expect it to take sixty-five years. Now you take care of yourself, you hear? If you go back, you be real careful. Capone doesn't manage to take care of Moran until February 14, 1929."

"How do you know that?" Shamus asked.

"Because it's history," Howard told him.

"The Valentine's Day massacre!" Libby exclaimed. "Now why didn't I remember that?"

"That doesn't matter now," Howard said, turning to Shamus. "You just remember, if you find yourself back in 1926, watch out for Moran. He'll be around for another couple of years."

When they arrived in Chicago, Libby took Shamus on a quick tour of the modern city. She drove him past the one-hundred-story John Hancock building and the one-hundred-and-ten-story Sears Tower, the tallest office building in the world. They traveled along Lake Shore Drive, hugging the shoreline of Lake Michigan, then down the Miracle Mile of North Michigan Avenue, but she avoided State Street, knowing she would see it soon enough tomorrow.

Finally, they arrived at her apartment, a modern complex with a view of Chicago's famous skyline. Libby found it strange to realize she'd left less than a week ago, especially since she'd been gone for almost a year.

"No water bed, I'm afraid," she told him.

"Any bed's fine, as long as you're there. You know that."

Tears blurred Libby's vision. She wiped at them, savagely. "I've turned into a regular watering pot in the last few days," she complained.

"Libby...mavourneen. Don't..."

"I'm sorry, Shamus. Really, I am, but I'm going to miss you so much."

Shamus pulled her into his arms, holding her gently. "And I'm going to miss you. More than I ever thought possible." He pushed her hair away from her face, his eyes holding hers captive.

"Maybe you won't go tomorrow. Maybe Howard was wrong."

"Maybe," Shamus said, but Libby knew he didn't really mean it. He was convinced that tomorrow he'd be returned to his own time. It hurt that he hadn't asked her to go with him, hadn't even considered trying to stay with her in the present.

"I don't want you to go," she said, her voice shaking. "And yet, I know you have to. I don't think you'll have any choice."

"I don't know what will happen tomorrow. I guess whatever happens, happens. But we still have tonight."

They made love with a desperation that reflected their shared fear of no tomorrows, then made love again, a slow, sweet fire that Libby was sure would burn all the way to her soul.

Morning came all too quickly, a dull gray day that seemed completely right for her mood. Shamus told Libby she didn't have to come with him, but she wasn't going to say goodbye until she had to. They arrived on the corner across the street from the clock a few minutes before the hour.

"Goodbye, Shamus," she said, her voice almost a whisper. "I'm going to miss you."

Shamus pulled her into his arms, paying no attention to the stares of the other people on the street, not even caring who saw them. "I'll never forget you," he told her. "Never. I wish...I wish things could have been different."

Libby nodded. "I know," she said softly. "I do, too." She glanced up at the clock. "You'd better go. Howard said eleven o'clock." She stepped back, out of his arms, and gave him a weak little smile.

Shamus's eyes searched her face one last time. He wasn't trying to memorize her face. He didn't have to. He knew he'd never forget the freckles marching across her small straight nose or her stubborn little chin and violet-blue eyes that were so bright and deep a man could drown in them.

"Go on, now," she said, giving him a little push. "If you don't, you'll be too late."

He couldn't say goodbye. He couldn't. Without a word, he turned and started across the street.

She'd said goodbye. He'd wanted her to come with him, but she hadn't asked. Why hadn't he asked her? She'd been happy enough with him before. Why had she changed her mind? She hadn't asked him to stay, either. He wasn't sure he *could* stay, but if she had asked, he would have tried. She was back where she belonged, in her own time. In minutes he might be back where he belonged, too. That was the way it should be, but it didn't feel right. In fact, it felt all wrong.

Shamus reached the sidewalk and stepped under the clock. Slowly he turned around. At least he could see her one more time....

Libby watched Shamus walk away, his image blurring because of the tears in her eyes. She saw him step up onto the curb, then turn to look at her. Their gazes locked and for a moment she thought she read a plea in his eyes.

Then the air around him seemed to shimmer. She blinked, trying to clear her vision, but it didn't change. He was there, but he wasn't. A Model-T chugged down the street, passing between them. The displays in the window flickered, modern sports clothes giving way to the fashions of the jazz age—sleek straight-line dresses that stopped at the knees, soft cloche hats, feather boas. He was back where he belonged, in the twenties.

He was leaving. Why hadn't he asked her to go with him? What would he say if she came anyway?

In that split second Libby knew she wanted to go with him. She didn't care if he'd asked or not. She belonged with Shamus, and if he didn't know that, she'd just have to convince him. She moved to the curb, started to step into the street and found she couldn't move.

Tears blurred her eyes again. It was too late. She'd waited too long. Choking back a sob, she looked up for one last look at the man she'd always love.

Shamus saw Libby start toward him and his breath caught in his throat. Then she stopped, as if frozen in place. The look of pain on her face made his heart turn over. He pulled his eyes from her face, dazed, uncertain, and turned to look around him.

It had worked! He was back in the past. The cars on the street, the fashions in the windows, they were familiar, comfortable. He heard someone calling his name, looked down the street and saw Eddie hurrying toward him.

He didn't want to be here, not without Libby.

He turned to face the street and, without thinking, took a step toward her. The air around him began to shimmer. It took him a moment to realize what was happening.

She couldn't come to him, but he could go to her. The decision was his. If he stepped back, turned around, he would walk into his old world. If he stepped forward, he would remain with Libby in her time.

He hesitated only a moment, looking over his shoulder into the past one last time. Then he darted across the street.

Libby was crying as he pulled her into his arms. "Don't cry, mavourneen. Don't cry. I love you."

"You came back," she whispered. "You came back to me. I tried . . . I was going to come to you, whether you wanted me or not. I tried, Shamus. But I couldn't."

"Shh. I know. I saw. You weren't supposed to go back. I'm supposed to stay here—with you. I should have known it sooner."

"Are you sure? All your friends. Eddie. Your old life . . ."

"We'll build a new life. Together. Eddie doesn't need me. He does fine on his own. Besides, we haven't lost him. I'll bet we see him tonight."

"Oh, Shamus. I love you. I can't believe . . ."

"Believe, mavourneen. I don't know how or why, but we're supposed to be together."

"Forever," she whispered. "Even across the barriers of time."

EPILOGUE

THERE IT WAS. Dead ahead. The bold green Shamrock Flying Service sign painted on the side of the white hangar beckoned from below. Elizabeth Carmichael Fitzgerald was almost home!

Libby gently banked her Jenny into a wide lazy turn, her eyes seeking the green-and-white wind sock flying atop the tall flagpole to verify wind direction. Her eyes sparkled behind the aviation goggles protecting her from the wind that whipped through the open cockpit. The deep-throated drone of the engine played bass beat to the whistling melody of her biplane's vibrating wing wires. Her blue aviator's scarf floated behind her, a fluttering trademark as identifiable as the flashing red wings of her biplane.

Below, sunlight reflected off the wings of more than a dozen 1920s-era airplanes, each now restored to original flying condition. The new Shamrock Flying Service's collection of airworthy antique aircraft was in constant demand for use in movie and television productions. Libby's mouth curved into a rueful smile. So much for Shamus's worries of being able to find a place in this world. He'd simply pulled his old world forward. Hopscotching across the country for location shoots was the 1990s version of an original barnstormer's practice of following the county fair circuit from town to town, state to state.

In the beginning Libby and Shamus had been able to fly together to location sites. But as their collection of antique planes grew and their fame spread, the demand for their services outstripped available pilots, often forcing them to follow separate schedules. This week had been one of those situations. Shamus had spent the week in Texas. Libby was returning home after three days in Kansas.

With hope, Libby reminded herself, two newly hired pilots would allow enough flexibility in scheduling that she and Shamus would no longer have to separate to meet contract commitments.

Libby checked her altimeter as she positioned the Jenny into the wind for her landing approach. She was anxious to be home. As she took the Jenny to ground, her eyes scanned the row of planes, hoping Shamus had already arrived. She swallowed a knot of disappointment when she failed to find what she was looking for and maneuvered the Jenny into position in the line.

It was then she saw it, the deHavilland DH-4, pulled into the shelter of the open door hangar. She felt a fluttering skip in the cadence of her pulse, that same strange skipping pulse she'd first felt so long ago when she'd looked at a particular old photograph, the same strange physical reminder she still experienced each time she and Shamus were separated, then found each other again.

As the Jenny rolled to a stop, Libby saw his tall familiar form emerge from the shadows inside the hangar and move toward her. His mouth curved upward in a soul-stealing smile that exposed the peekaboo dimple in his left cheek. By his side, a smaller figure danced in anticipation, the three-year-old boy's exuberance restrained only by the firm hold of his father's hand.

Libby's gaze rested lovingly on her young son, and she smiled as she noticed the devilish twinkle in his midnight blue eyes. Not even the soft chubby curves of his baby face could completely disguise the tilt of his stubborn little chin. Eddie Fitzgerald was a miracle child, Libby thought, physical proof of a love that couldn't happen, but had.

She pulled her goggles and helmet from her head, tossing them into the seat, then climbed from the cockpit and walked toward the two most important people in her life. Libby knelt in front of her son and hugged him close, blinking back tears of happiness as she felt his chubby baby arms encircle her neck. Gathering her child in her arms, she stood to face her husband. His gaze captured hers, the devilish twinkle in his eyes softening, tender emotion swirling in their depths.

He dipped his head to capture her lips, a gentle beguiling touch holding all the promises of love—yesterday, today and tomorrow. He placed his arm around her shoulder, pulling both her and their child close to him.

''Welcome home, mavourneen,'' he said softly.

Libby smiled, love shining in her eyes. This was her place, regardless of when or where. In Shamus's arms, she was always home.

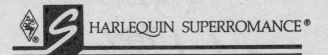

HARLEQUIN SUPERROMANCE®

COMING NEXT MONTH

#538 HALFWAY HOME • Marie Beaumont
Mickey Mulvaney and Cameron Scott were locked in battle over
possession of a house. On his side, Cameron had money,
influence and the good will of all the neighbors. On her side,
Mickey had only her determination . . . and her hidden
vulnerability. But against that, Cameron didn't stand a chance.

#539 REMEMBER WHEN • Anne Laurence
Nate Fields had returned to the Missouri town where he'd been
raised to avenge himself on Amber Reinhart, daughter of the
area's wealthiest family. When he purchased her failing family
business, he expected to feel triumphant. But how could he,
when Amber was so warm and kind, and when she'd adopted a
young girl, who, he'd just learned, was his own daughter. . . .

#540 FOR THE LOVE OF IVY • Barbara Kaye
Ivy Loving had come to Texas at her grandmother's request.
But nothing in her background had prepared her for the fast-
paced life-style of Fort Worth. Ivy was an island woman and
was looking forward to returning to her Indonesian home.
However, she had underestimated her Texas grandmother's
determination to keep her in Texas—and the tall dark stranger
who featured strongly in her grandmother's plan.

#541 CRADLE OF DREAMS • Janice Kaiser
Women Who Dare, Book 3
Caroline Charles knew she had a lot of nerve. Tyler Bradshaw
had no reason to love her. No reason to even want to
see her. And certainly no reason to agree to make her
pregnant . . . again.

AVAILABLE NOW:

#534 UNCOMMON STOCK
Terri Lynn

#535 DREAM BUILDER
Julie Meyers

**#536 REFLECTIONS OF
BECCA**
Lynda Trent

#537 WINGS OF TIME
Carol Duncan Perry

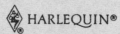

The most romantic day of the year is here! Escape into the exquisite world of love with MY VALENTINE 1993. What better way to celebrate Valentine's Day than with this very romantic, sensuous collection of four original short stories, written by some of Harlequin's most popular authors.

ANNE STUART
JUDITH ARNOLD
ANNE McALLISTER
LINDA RANDALL WISDOM

THIS VALENTINE'S DAY, DISCOVER ROMANCE
WITH MY VALENTINE 1993

Take 4 bestselling love stories FREE

Plus get a FREE surprise gift!

Where do you find hot Texas nights, smooth Texas charm and dangerously sexy cowboys?

Crystal Creek

DEEP IN THE HEART

Wedding Bells—Texas Style!

Even a Boston blue blood needs a Texas education. Ranch owner J. T. McKinney is handsome, strong, opinionated and totally charming. And he is determined to marry beautiful Bostonian Cynthia Page. However, the couple soon discovers a Texas cattleman's idea of marriage differs greatly from a New England career woman's!

CRYSTAL CREEK reverberates with the exciting rhythm of Texas. Each story features the rugged individuals who live and love in the Lone Star State. And each one ends with the same invitation...

Y'ALL COME BACK...REAL SOON!

Don't miss **DEEP IN THE HEART** by Barbara Kaye. Available in March wherever Harlequin books are sold.

HARLEQUIN SUPERROMANCE®

WOMEN WHO DARE DRIVE RACE CARS?!

During 1993, each Harlequin Superromance **WOMEN WHO DARE** title will have a single italicized letter on the Women Who Dare back-page ads. Collect the letters, spell D A R E and you can receive a free copy of **RACE FOR TOMORROW**, written by popular author Elaine Barbieri. This is an exciting novel about a female race-car driver, **WHO DARES ANYTHING ... FOR LOVE!**

OFFER CERTIFICATE   O85-KAT

To receive your free gift, send us the 4 letters that spell DARE from any Harlequin Superromance Women Who Dare title with the offer certificate properly completed, along with a check or money order of $2.50 for postage and handling (do not send cash) payable to Harlequin Superromance Women Who Dare Offer.

Name: _____

Address: _____

_____

City: _____   State/Prov.: _____

Zip/Postal Code: _____

Mail this certificate, designated letters spelling DARE, and check or money order for postage and handling to: In the U.S.—WOMEN WHO DARE, P.O. Box 9057, Buffalo, NY 14269-9057; In Canada—WOMEN WHO DARE, P.O. Box 622, Fort Erie, Ontario L2A 5X3.

Requests must be received by January 31, 1994.
Allow 4-6 weeks after receipt of order for delivery.   R-O85-KAT